PEACH TEA SMASH

PEACH TEA SMASH

Tea Shop Mystery #28

LAURA CHILDS

BERKLEY PRIME CRIME
New York

M

BERKLEY PRIME CRIME
Published by Berkley
An imprint of Penguin Random House LLC
penguinrandomhouse.com

Copyright © 2024 by Gerry Schmitt & Associates, Inc.
Excerpt from *High Tea and Misdemeanors* by Laura Childs copyright © 2024
by Gerry Schmitt & Associates, Inc.

BERKLEY and the BERKLEY & B colophon are registered trademarks and
BERKLEY PRIME CRIME is a trademark of Penguin Random House LLC.

Library of Congress Cataloging-in-Publication Data

Names: Childs, Laura, author.
Title: Peach tea smash / Laura Childs.
Description: New York: Berkley Prime Crime, 2024. |
Series: Tea shop mystery; #28 |
Identifiers: LCCN 2023059761 (print) | LCCN 2023059762 (ebook) |
ISBN 9780593201015 (hardcover) | ISBN 9780593201022 (ebook)
Subjects: LCGFT: Cozy mysteries. | Novels.
Classification: LCC PS3603.H56 P43 2024 (print) |
LCC PS3603.H56 (ebook) | DDC 813/.6—dc23/eng/20240105
LC record available at https://lccn.loc.gov/2023059761
LC ebook record available at https://lccn.loc.gov/2023059762

Printed in the United States of America
1st Printing

This is a work of fiction. Names, characters, places, and incidents either are the product of
the author's imagination or are used fictitiously, and any resemblance to actual persons,
living or dead, business establishments, events, or locales is entirely coincidental.

PUBLISHER'S NOTE: The recipes contained in this book are to be followed exactly
as written. The publisher is not responsible for your specific health or allergy
needs that may require medical supervision. The publisher is not responsible
for any adverse reactions to the recipes contained in this book.

PEACH TEA
SMASH

1

Masked figures slipped down twisty paths as a neon orange Cheshire cat peered down from its perch high atop a crumbling stone wall. The Red Queen cackled as she held court on a candlelit patio overflowing with guests dressed in tuxedos and cocktail dresses. Over on a patch of manicured lawn, excited shrieks rose up as bets were placed on a do-or-die croquet match.

It was the Mad Hatter Masquerade, an autumn fundraiser for the Charleston Opera Society, and what Theodosia Browning decided was a voyage into crazy town. As the owner of the Indigo Tea Shop on Charleston's famed Church Street, Theodosia was used to staging exciting events. A Firefly Tea at an old plantation, a Murder Mystery Tea in a haunted house . . . even a Honeybee Tea in Petigru Park. But the Opera Society's masquerade party at the old Pendleton Grist Mill near the City Marina was the most unconventional venue she'd ever seen. The grist mill's twisty walkways, jagged walls, and flaming torches brought to mind the ancient battlements of a ruined Scottish castle. Sprinkle in strolling musicians, fire-eaters, dancing fairies, a dozen or so *Alice in Wonderland* characters, two bars, and three hors d'oeuvres stations and you had yourself a first-class high society soiree.

Gathering up her ankle-skimming black silk skirt, Theodosia turned to Drayton Conneley, her tea sommelier, peered through the eye slits of her peacock-feathered mask, and said, "Can you believe this party?" She was practically agog at the revelers and entertainers streaming past them.

Drayton, who was decked out in a tuxedo and white half mask reminiscent of *The Phantom of the Opera,* said, "It's really quite magnificent. The Friends of the Opera have truly outdone themselves this time." He took a sip of his peach tea smash and nodded to himself as if to punctuate his words.

"Aren't you glad we helped with the appetizers?"

"I'm just tickled we got invited."

Theodosia laughed a rich, tinkling laugh that crinkled her startling blue eyes and caused her mass of auburn hair to shimmer in the candlelight. She'd never consider herself Charleston high society, but that didn't mean she couldn't party her head off. After all, she was still mid-thirties, unmarried . . . well, okay, she *was* in a relationship . . . but did love a big-time gala. A girl had to slip into her dancing shoes once in a while, right?

Drayton, on the other hand, was sixty-something, well-heeled, and accustomed to rubbing elbows with Charleston money. He served on the board of directors at the Heritage Society, did stints on the boards of the Dock Theatre and Carstead Folk Museum, and, at last count, owned three tuxedos. While Theodosia came from a hustle-bustle marketing background, Drayton had cut his teeth at the tea auctions in Amsterdam and taught culinary classes at the prestigious Johnson & Wales University. Theodosia may be the clever entrepreneur bubbling with new ideas, but Drayton has been *around.*

A White Rabbit dressed in tie and tails skittered past them followed by a fairy dancer in a long, diaphanous gown. As the fairy ran by, she thrust a crown of flowers with trailing pink ribbons into Theodosia's hands.

"Tea roses and freesia," Drayton said as Theodosia placed the floral crown atop her head and scrunched it down over curly locks that were suddenly reacting adversely to the evening's high-test humidity. "With all those flowers in your hair and your long dress, you look as if you just stepped out of a Renaissance tapestry."

He'd barely uttered his words when a short fellow wearing a floppy blue suit and an enormous mouse head ran up to them.

"It's the Dormouse," Theodosia exclaimed. "Which means Alice must be dancing around this wonderland as well."

The Dormouse shoved a silver scepter into Drayton's hands and then scampered away.

"I'll say this," Drayton said, giving the scepter a playful twirl. "This certainly is an immersive experience. I mean look at this place. Who'd have thought you could turn a historic old grist mill into such a magical, slightly secretive setting?"

"I know," Theodosia said. "The twisty paths, the crumbling walls with curls of ivy, the fact that every time you step around an old stone pillar or column, another weird tableau presents itself."

"Speaking of which, shall we help ourselves to another peach tea smash?"

"I'm so glad you allowed them to use your signature drink recipe," Theodosia said.

"White tea, peach slices, and fine old bourbon," Drayton said. "You can never go wrong with that."

They walked down a cobblestone path and entered one of the grist mill's open sheds where a crowd of masked partygoers danced to a jazz trio playing an up-tempo rendition of Dave Brubeck's "Take Five."

"It's hard to recognize your friends when everyone's wearing masks," Theodosia said. "But I think I see Delaine. The one in the black lace dress dancing with the fellow in a Chinese mask?" Theodosia turned to study another group of guests. "And maybe, over there, the man behind the silver bird mask is Timothy Neville?"

"I'm sure they're both here tonight, along with half the inhabitants of Charleston's Historic District," Drayton said. "After all, this is one of the major events of the fall season."

"On second thought, I think *that* might be Delaine," Theodosia said as she eyed a woman in a red sequin dress with strappy black leather stilettos. "You see when she kicks up her heels there's a hint of red on the soles of her shoes?"

Drayton touched a hand to his bow tie. "What's that mean?"

"Louboutins," Theodosia said in a knowing tone.

"Ah, shoes. Expensive are they?"

"You have no idea."

But the woman in the spendy party shoes saw them watching, and suddenly spun away from her partner and danced over to Theodosia and Drayton. She lifted her red-and-gold Venetian mask and gave a knowing wink. "Right shoes, wrong name."

"Cricket!" Theodosia exclaimed. Cricket Sadler was the executive chairperson in charge of the Mad Hatter Masquerade. She'd single-handedly come up with the theme and roped in Theodosia and Drayton to help with hors d'oeuvres.

"Dear lady," Drayton said, taking Cricket's hand. "Your party is exquisite. There's so much merriment and exotic entertainment going on around us. It's dizzying."

"Believe me when I say I had *beaucoup* help," Cricket said, fairly bubbling with excitement. "Entire committees, if you must know, tasked with decorations, performers, costumes, entertainment, and even lighting." She rolled her eyes expressively. "Then there was the food and liquor—well, *you* know about all that because you catered it. And I have to say, our guests are love-love-loving it!"

Theodosia was pleased by Cricket's words. She, Drayton, and Haley, their young chef at the Indigo Tea Shop, had kicked around lots of ideas, but finally settled on steak bites, miniature shrimp kabobs, duck pâté on crostini, and a selection of local cheeses. They'd spent the entire afternoon prepping, cooking, assembling, and then, finally, schlepping everything over here. But that had been earlier in the day, before all the candles and twinkle lights were lit, and before the musicians and performers arrived to spin their magic.

"We were just on our way to grab another drink," Drayton said to Cricket. "May I get you one as well?"

"A tasty offer," Cricket said. She was petite, had short brown hair with chunks of honey blond, and was draped in real-deal gold earrings and necklaces. She hitched up her shoulders, leaned forward, and said, "But right now I need to make the rounds and see if I can hustle up a few more donations from our invitees. Then, I for sure have to find my husband. Last I saw of Harlan, he'd wandered off with the Red Queen."

"And probably having a merry time of it," Drayton said. He turned back to Theodosia and said, "The bar is which way?"

"I think maybe over here," Theodosia said. They crunched their way down a dimly lit gravel path past a giant papier-mâché mushroom, turned a corner, and—whoops, this wasn't the right way to the bar at all. They suddenly found themselves smack-dab in the heart of the grist mill.

"Looks like we took a wrong turn," Theodosia said, then stopped dead in her tracks to gaze at the hulking pieces of machinery that stood in the center of the room. There were interconnecting wheels and some kind of old motor attached to pulleys, chains, and leather paddles. Overhead was a honeycomb of low wooden beams and a ragged hole in the ancient roof that let in a small spill of moonlight. A faint rustle of wings filled the air as birds flitted from beam to beam.

"Amazing," Drayton said as he walked a few steps closer to the apparatus. "This old grist mill is really something."

"It's also a little scary," Theodosia said. In the semidarkness the wood beams and stone walls seemed to press in on them as well as tamp down the sounds of outside revelry. In fact, she could barely hear any music at all.

But Drayton remained fascinated. "Early grist mills were water-run, powered by sluiceways. But this particular mill was automated in the late eighteenth century. You see that large wheel?"

Theodosia nodded. From her perspective it looked like something from a torture chamber.

"Throw the bevel gears and that wheel drives the whole she-bang. See, there's the giant millstone where grain was ground then carried up by those leather paddles."

Theodosia walked a little closer and peered at the central workings of the old grist mill. "This is some place. And I'm amazed at how well-versed you are about its operation."

"Because it's interesting, a piece of Charleston's history. And you know how much I like history."

"Oh, I do," Theodosia said. Drayton was known to go on for hours about Charleston's old churches, mansions, single houses, plantations, hidden lanes, and narrow cobblestone alleys.

"But imagine how noisy and inhospitable this place must have been a century ago when grain was milled here practically day and night," Drayton said.

"It's not that hospitable now." The mill was dark, and Theodosia felt as if shadows were flitting all around them. Maybe it was the flicker of torches from outside? Or just her imagination?

"All that chaff filling the air, making it difficult to see and breathe," Drayton continued. "And the noise and clatter of clanking machinery."

As if to punctuate Drayton's words, a low hum rose up from the nearby machinery. Then a leather belt started to vibrate.

Drayton took a cautious step back. "What just happened here?"

"Maybe someone threw a switch?" Theodosia said. She'd caught a faint scrape of footsteps behind her. "For a demonstration of some kind?" But when she turned and looked back over her shoulder, she didn't see a soul. "Huh, this is weird."

The noise increased in pitch, building from a low hum to a loud, repetitive *clickety-clack-clack* as chains and leather belts began to move. It was as if the machinery, untouched for decades, had suddenly been sparked to life. Now, with everything thumping and thrumming, Theodosia could barely hear anything at all.

"I don't think we should be in here," Theodosia shouted in Drayton's ear, feeling foolish even as she said it. Of course, they shouldn't be here. These old mill contraptions were dangerous. As if they could grab somebody and . . . the phrase *grind his bones* suddenly popped into her head. She spun hastily, ready to grab Drayton's sleeve and pull him away from this strange, shadowy place. But Drayton was rooted to where he stood, mouth open, seemingly dumbstruck. Then he slowly lifted a hand and pointed.

"What?" Theodosia shouted. When Drayton didn't answer, she said, "What?" a second time. Then she lifted her eyes, blinked hard, and did a kind of double take. Because something, Lord knows what, was caught in the giant heavy chains that pulled the leather paddles up toward the ceiling.

"What do you think that is?" Drayton asked her. "Rags? A bunch of old gunny sacks?"

Theodosia shook her head. "I don't know."

But the strange thing was, she *did* know. Because whatever was caught between those giant paddles had a definite shape to it. Two arms, a leg . . . maybe a head?

"Help!" Drayton shouted as he suddenly arrived at the same conclusion. He turned and sprinted for the doorway. "Help!" he called out. "There's been an accident, we need help in here!"

His plaintive cries brought a half dozen curious people.

A man in a white dinner jacket yelled, "What's wrong?" while behind him Theodosia's friend Delaine Dish screamed, "My Lord, is that a man dangling up there?"

The chains and leather paddles had pulled the body even higher. Now, the onlookers' screams blended with the noise of the machines and rose to a fever pitch. Their screams drew even more people who lifted their collective voices in a dreadful cacophony that seemed to billow through the ancient grist mill, matching the enormous clouds of dust being spun up by clanking machinery.

"Someone's caught in the gears," a man shouted.

"Somebody do something," a woman in a bright yellow gown cried.

Even Cricket Sadler ran in and started screaming for help.

But no one did anything. They simply stood there, horror-struck, too paralyzed to help or figure out the situation.

Theodosia didn't know *what* to do, but she knew she had to do *something.* She waved a hand in front of her face, trying to see through the swirl of dust and chaff, then edged over to what Drayton had pointed out earlier as bevel gears.

Reaching a hand out, Theodosia pushed one of the wooden levers, hoping to stop the machinery. Nothing. The clanking grew louder and the screams from the crowd increased in volume. She touched a hand to a second lever, pushed hard, felt it start to give, *want* to give. Blowing out a stream of air, trying not to choke as she cleared the terrible dust from her nose and mouth, she leaned hard into her task. Pushing with all her might, she managed to throw the lever hard-left. There was a deep shudder, a terrible screeching noise, and then the machinery finally, mercifully, ground to a halt.

"Get him down! Help him!" came countless cries. Now, a dozen hands reached up to try and free the trapped man, but no one could reach him. Seconds dragged by, then a full minute, before a ladder was found and lifted up. A young man in a green-and-yellow caterpillar costume scrambled nimbly up the ladder and worked feverishly to untangle the man from the chains. After two minutes of twisting and turning, he was finally able to free the injured man. Balancing precariously now, he bent forward to lower the victim into waiting arms. But at the last second, he fumbled and lost his grip. The victim cartwheeled away from him, plunging fifteen feet down and hitting the cobblestone floor like a sack of flour.

More screams of horror reverberated throughout the old mill as Theodosia stumbled her way through the crowd, pushing past a couple of the entertainers in their White Rabbit and Mad Hatter costumes. Her heart was in her throat, and she was hoping against hope that the man had somehow survived.

But wait. He'd been chewed up by those chains and paddles, then fallen and landed badly. Now, he was curled up like a bug in a cocoon, breathing shallowly and not moving a single muscle. His suit was ripped; his hands and feet were battered and bloodied. Worst of all, his head oozed copious amounts of blood that streamed down over his black mask and soaked into his tartan-plaid bow tie.

"Who is it?" a woman asked in a shaking voice, as the bleeding man's right foot seemed to tremble on its own.

Ever so gently, Drayton reached down and removed the man's mask.

Coughing, shuffling their feet, the crowd pressed closer to see if they could identify this poor soul.

And that's when Cricket Sadler took one look, moaned softly, and fainted dead away.

2

❧

The EMTs were the first to arrive—two men in blue jumpsuits with serious expressions on their faces. They piled in with oxygen, medical packs, and a stretcher. They laid Harlan Sadler out flat and worked feverishly. Bagged him to try to amp his respiration and administered CPR. When that didn't yield a favorable response, one of the EMTs filled a syringe with epinephrine and injected it directly into the man's heart.

Theodosia hugged a somewhat revived Cricket as everyone held their breath, hoping for a miracle.

They were still holding their breath when four uniformed officers arrived a few minutes later. The officers pushed back the crowd that had gathered, then gazed at the victim with serious cop expressions.

"Are you transporting him?" one of the officers asked the EMTs.

The EMT who was still kneeling pulled off his gloves and shook his head sadly. The other EMT, a young, sandy-haired man, leaned down and covered the man's body and face with a thin white blanket.

"No!" Cricket screamed. "Harlan can't be dead."

A dozen pairs of hands reached out to comfort her. Then, her son, Duke, arrived. The way he jostled his way through the crowd made it obvious that he'd been drinking heavily. He stared at the covered body, then knelt down and flipped back the white blanket.

"Who did this?" he bellowed.

When nobody responded, Duke stumbled to his feet. He was tall, at least six feet two, with broad shoulders and dark hair that hung over his forehead. His eyes were slightly wonky, and his mouth was set in a grimace.

He stared at an older couple who were standing nearby. "Did you see who did this?"

They shook their heads.

"Somebody better start talking!" Duke shouted. "Come on, people, don't go all stupid on me."

"Duke, stop!" Cricket implored. "Please!" She grabbed for her son, but he pulled away.

"We don't know what happened," Theodosia said, in what she hoped was a gentle, quieting tone.

"Somebody must know!" Duke snarled. "This kind of crap doesn't just happen out of the blue."

Cricket fumbled for Theodosia's hand. "He's upset. When Duke gets in one of his black moods, I don't know what to do," she whispered. "There's nothing anyone can do."

Duke was still yelling and posturing when the two investigators arrived. Detective Burt Tidwell, who headed Charleston's Robbery and Homicide Division, and his assistant D-2 Pete Riley. Theodosia knew both of them. Tidwell was her nemesis. Riley was her boyfriend.

"I need some answers," Duke huffed at Detective Tidwell.

PEACH TEA SMASH 13

"And who are you?" Tidwell asked, giving Duke his best dead-eyed stare.

"Duke Sadler," he responded.

"I see. Well, kindly step aside, will you?" Tidwell said. "It appears I have my work cut out for me."

Tidwell spun away from Duke. A rapid, well-choreographed movement for such a large man. Then again, Tidwell's size always fooled people. In his baggy jacket, loose-fitting slacks, and heavy cop shoes, some people—usually those who'd committed a crime—took him for a buffoon. But look past the soup stains on Tidwell's tie, and he was shrewd, quick-witted, and profoundly cunning. Simply no match for an ordinary intellect.

Now, Tidwell, operating in his own world of criminology, carefully studied the body of Harlan Sadler.

"Lacerations on his hands," Tidwell muttered. Then, as an aside to Pete Riley, "But look at the man's head."

Riley looked and nodded.

"Blunt force trauma," Tidwell intoned. "Could have been a hammer or the business end of a two-by-four."

Theodosia stepped forward, quick to offer her own take on the murder.

"You see that slightly rounded indentation?" she said as she pointed to Harlan Sadler's bashed and bloodied skull.

Curious now, everyone around her bent forward to take a more careful look—Tidwell, Pete Riley, uniformed officers, EMTs, Cricket and her son, Duke . . . even Drayton.

"I don't think that's your garden variety blow to the head," Theodosia continued.

Tidwell favored her with a hardened glare. "You say this why?"

"Because it looks to me as if Mr. Sadler was struck in the head with a croquet mallet."

"More like clobbered," Drayton murmured under his breath.

Tidwell frowned as he leaned in closer. "Croquet?" He sounded as if he wasn't familiar with the word.

"Yes, croquet," Theodosia said. "As in the lawn game."

Tidwell rocked back on his heels. "Huh. Maybe. Possibly. I'll ask the medical examiner what his thoughts might be."

"That's not all," Theodosia said.

Tidwell sighed and wiggled chubby fingers at her, as if he were impatient and short on time. Had somewhere more important to be.

"If the murder weapon was, in fact, a croquet mallet used in a game that was played here tonight . . . ," Theodosia's voice trailed off.

"Yes?" Tidwell said.

"It would point to one of the guests as the killer," Theodosia said.

There was dead silence for a few moments and then Drayton said, "Boom. I think she's got it."

This time Tidwell, Riley, the police officers, and EMTs all turned around to look at the guests. At least fifty sets of eyes peered back at them from behind ornate masks as they shifted about nervously in the dark. Those who were still holding their croquet mallets surreptitiously tossed them aside.

"Indeed," Tidwell said. He gestured at the uniformed officers. "You men detain everyone here, interview them, get names and addresses. Riley, give them a hand, will you?"

"Right, boss," Riley said as he helped herd the onlookers away from Harlan Sadler's body.

Theodosia stepped back as well, hoping against hope that someone, anyone, had seen something—had been a witness to this horrible crime. Then there was a sudden scuffle behind her as a bright light flashed on and lit up the entire crime scene. She turned, squinted, and spotted a familiar face.

It's Billy—no, Bobby—one of the cameramen from Channel Eight News.

Bobby was cradling a video camera in the crook of his arm and had a coil of black cord looped over one shoulder. Behind him, holding the brilliant light, was his lighting and sound guy, Trevor.

Theodosia hurried toward them and touched Bobby's arm to get his attention. "Bobby . . ."

Bobby recognized her instantly, and said, "Theodosia, the tea lady. Long time no see. Hey, you remember Trev, don't you?"

"I do," Theodosia said. "Good to see you guys again, even though the circumstances aren't that great." She'd met Bobby and Trevor a few months earlier when one of their team members, a female reporter, had been brutally murdered. Now, here they were at another murder.

"What happened?" Bobby asked.

"A fellow named Harlan Sadler got his head smashed in with a croquet mallet," Theodosia said. "Then we think his killer kind of hung him up on those old chains over there for everyone to see."

"Nasty," Bobby said.

"But interesting," Trevor said. "The cops gonna let us get some footage?"

"Don't know," Theodosia said. She watched as a newly arrived officer started stringing up black-and-yellow crime scene tape. "Maybe not."

"Rats," Bobby said. "Well, we can wait."

"How are you doing otherwise, Bobby?" Theodosia asked.

"Oh, can't complain. There's always plenty of crazy news to keep us hopping from one story to another. Crime, celebs, city events, political dustups, the same old same old." Bobby had curly dark hair, a crooked nose that was somehow endearing, and wore a battered leather jacket that looked as if it had come through World War II. Trevor, the blond-haired and blue-eyed lighting and soundman, wore a hoodie and jeans. He was skater-boy cute and had the earnest gawkiness of a teenager, even though he was in his mid-twenties.

"I'm glad you're keeping busy," Theodosia said. Then, when she saw Pete Riley motioning to her, said, "Excuse me."

Theodosia pushed through the crowd, weaving her way over to Riley. He was tall, fairly athletic, and carried a boyish demeanor about him. He was also blessed with an aristocratic nose, high cheekbones, and blue eyes a shade lighter than Theodosia's. Pete Riley was an up-and-coming detective on Charleston's police force and one of Tidwell's formidable weapons. Theodosia, of course, simply thought of him as Riley, her Riley. And he called her Theo. It was as easy as that because it suited them.

"This is awful," Theodosia said to him. "A terrible ending to what had been a perfectly lovely gala." She longed to slip into Riley's arms for a gentle embrace, but knew this wasn't the time or place. "How long do you think you're going to be here?" Theodosia had an ulterior motive. She was hoping Riley could break away early from this crime scene and come home with her. They could retreat to her cozy home, sit in the dark, hold hands, and drink a glass of wine. Forget all about murder and mayhem.

"The Crime Scene techs just arrived, like, one minute ago," Riley said. "So it's going to be a long night." He touched a hand to her shoulder. "Why don't you go home? There's nothing you can do here."

"You're going to keep me in the loop on this, right?" Theodosia said. Since discovering Sadler's body, she'd had a strange proprietary feeling about the bizarre circumstances of his murder. Why Sadler? Why such brutality? And why at this event?

But Riley was shaking his head. "Can't, Theo. I'm headed down to Savannah first thing tomorrow morning."

"What?!" It was the first she'd heard of this. "Why? What's going on?"

"An assignment just came up having to do with hijacked trucks that ended up at Charleston's commercial docks. Apparently, there are a couple of witnesses who need interviewing, and I drew the short straw."

"When will you be back?"

"I don't know, sweetheart. It all depends on how cooperative my witnesses' lawyers are."

"But you need to . . ."

Riley reached out and touched her nose with the tip of his index finger. "I need to what?"

"Work on this, of course. Help solve the murder!"

"There's no need for me to be involved," Riley said. "Not when I've got you."

Theodosia was slightly gobsmacked. "Wait a minute, you're the one who's always telling me *not* to get involved in murder cases."

"I don't mean *involved* involved," Riley said. "But I know you're familiar with most of the guests here at the party. You live in their neighborhood, and they frequent your tea shop."

"Are you asking me to be your covert operative?"

Riley smiled. "That sounds a little too Secret Squirrel."

"Then what?" Theodosia asked. For some reason this seemed out of character for him.

"Just do what you do best," Riley said.

"And what's that?" Theodosia asked.

Riley wiggled his brows at her. "Snoop. That way you can keep *me* in the loop."

3

❧

The atmosphere at the Indigo Tea Shop was fairly subdued this Monday morning. It was early, yet not quite nine o'clock, so Theodosia, Drayton, and Haley had the place to themselves. Seated at one of their rustic wooden tables, they were enjoying—or at least trying to enjoy—a cup of English breakfast tea with their morning scone.

With one ear cocked for her oven timer—because she had a batch of blueberry scones baking—Haley had been devouring the Charleston *Post & Courier*'s front-page story. Now, she was asking some rather pressing and direct questions about the murder of Harlan Sadler.

"Was his head really smashed in like it says here?" Haley asked. "This story makes it sound awfully gruesome."

"Because it was gruesome," Drayton said. He helped himself to a second lemon scone, split it crosswise, spread on a generous amount of lemon curd, then added a puff of Devonshire cream.

"Murder's never pretty," Theodosia murmured, almost to herself.

"So it was for sure murder?" Haley asked. "The reporter who wrote this story is playing it kind of cagey."

Drayton gave Haley an owlish look as he peered at her over his half-glasses. "My dear girl, do you really suppose poor Mr. Sadler struck *himself* in the head?"

"I guess not," Haley said.

"And then managed to tangle himself up in a mess of pulleys and chains?" Drayton said.

"Well, no," Haley said.

"There you go, it was a case of murder, plain and simple," Drayton said. He brushed an invisible crumb from the lapel of his Donegal tweed jacket, seemingly pleased with his pronouncement.

"But not so simple when it comes to finding the killer," Theodosia said. "Harlan Sadler is a social butterfly, just like his wife, Cricket. So he was probably running all over that party last night. Grabbing drinks, glad-handing friends, dancing, maybe even playing croquet."

"So you're saying anyone could have killed him," Haley said. "Any of the guests?" She wrinkled her pert nose and shook back her head of stick-straight, shoulder-length blond hair. Haley was young, impudent, a talented baker and chef. She could also be a little busy bee when she wanted to. Today was one of those times.

"Lots of guests, but probably only one killer," Theodosia said. "Someone who might have struck up a friendly conversation with Sadler then surreptitiously stalked him. You know, followed him around the party and then waited until he caught Sadler all by his lonesome."

"Lured him off the beaten path," Drayton put in.

"And then attacked him?" Haley said.

"Smashed him in the head with a croquet mallet," Drayton said. He pursed his lips, then popped them open fast, producing a loud WHOMPING sound.

"There's a possibility that the initial blow didn't kill Sadler like it was intended," Theodosia said. "Maybe that's why the killer dragged him into the mill and strung him up among those chains and paddles."

"Yipes," Haley said, hunching her shoulders. She liked to be frightened, but not *too* frightened.

"Then the killer threw the switch," Theodosia said. "Maybe he didn't intend to. Or maybe when Drayton and I came stumbling in, the killer panicked."

"Or maybe he decided to show off his handiwork," Drayton said. "By tangling Harlan Sadler in those chains and paddles."

"That sounds so awful," Haley said.

"Awful, yes, but that's the reality of the situation," Theodosia said. She crooked a finger at Haley, who quickly slid the newspaper across the table to her. Theodosia picked it up and glanced at the two-inch-high headline that said GRISLY GRIST MILL MURDER. And beneath that, in smaller type, MAD HATTER MASQUERADE DEAD-ENDS AS FUNDRAISER.

"This kind of bad publicity has got to damage the Opera Society's reputation," Theodosia said. Having worked in marketing and PR for several years, she knew about bad publicity and had seen it practically destroy small businesses and other organizations.

"I agree," Drayton said. "That headline is not exactly conducive to garnering money from donors. And I know the Friends of the Opera Society have a couple more fundraisers coming up this week." He thought for a moment. "A silent auction on Thursday and the opera Saturday night."

"Cricket's already under terrific stress, there's no way she can manage another couple of events," Theodosia said.

"After seeing that poor woman faint dead away, I doubt she's got any energy left at all," Drayton said.

"She's going to have to muster some strength because she has to plan her husband's funeral," Haley said.

"Dear Lord." Theodosia stood up from the table just as the phone rang. "A funeral. I can't imagine anything worse." She moved toward the front counter, grabbed the phone, and said, "Good morning, Indigo Tea Shop."

"Theo!" The bellow in her ear was so strident and harsh, it sounded like the trumpet of an angry elephant at full charge.

"Good morning to you, Delaine," Theodosia said. Delaine Dish was a society doyenne, serial dater, hustler, and local gossip. She was also Theodosia's friend and the dynamic powerhouse behind Cotton Duck, one of Charleston's premier women's clothing boutiques.

"How did you know it was me?" Delaine asked in a more mellow tone.

Theodosia smiled. "Just a lucky guess."

"We need to talk about last night."

"How so?" Theodosia asked.

"You know how so!" Delaine cried. (Did we mention that Delaine was also pushy and officious?) "Theo, you *have* to get involved. In the murder, I mean. You owe it to Cricket."

"I don't," Theodosia said. "I know Cricket, I like her, but I don't *owe* it to her."

"Well, maybe I do," Delaine said.

"What are you talking about?" Theodosia glanced at Drayton who was frowning and shaking his head. "Explain, please."

"Here's the thing," Delaine said. "I just got a call from Ned Grady."

"The man you've been dating. Who also serves on the board of the Opera Society."

"Right. And he says the police are interviewing all the board members. Asking lots of impertinent questions and really grilling them hard."

"That's what police do, Delaine."

"But you and I know that Harlan Sadler wasn't murdered by any of the board members. They all *loved* Cricket. They're the ones who voted her in as chair of the Mad Hatter Masquerade because she's so smart and well-connected."

"Hmm," Theodosia said, stalling for time.

Delaine ranted on. "So it *had* to be someone else, some outside person who hated Harlan Sadler. It could have even been someone who had a bone to pick with Elysian Bank."

"He was president there, right?"

"Actually, he was CEO."

Theodosia thought about all the dreadful things she'd read in the business section of the newspaper about the banking industry. Banks closing, depositors not getting their money, investors and bankers making foolhardy judgment calls . . . even outright fraud. It didn't seem like a happy industry in which to work, which meant there were probably lots of unhappy people. Okay, so maybe there *was* a motive there.

"Or it could have been someone who felt cheated by one of Sadler's land deals," Delaine said. "He was also senior partner in that real estate company, The Lanvesco Group."

"You make a good point," Theodosia said, trying to sound neutral.

"So am I getting through to you? Tickling your sense of justice? Of right and wrong?"

"Just spit it out, Delaine."

"Like I said before, Cricket needs your help. And you just happen to be Charleston's own Nancy Drew."

"I got lucky a couple of times."

"You got *smart,* chickadee."

"I still have to think about it," Theodosia said.

"Well think fast," Delaine said, her voice rising in volume again. "Because the police are looking in the absolute wrong direction while a stone-cold killer is out there laughing his socks off!" Then she hung up abruptly.

Theodosia turned, saw the look on Drayton's face, and said, "What?"

"I can see the wheels whirling in that clever brain of yours. I know what you're thinking," he said.

"What am I thinking?"

"That you're just as smart as Sadler's killer. That, given the proper input and gathering of information, allowing for some random snooping and a possible lucky break, you could possibly track this killer down."

"Should that happen, I'd point the police in his direction," Theodosia said mildly.

"Is that what you'd do? Really?" Drayton didn't look convinced.

"Sure. I mean I guess so." Theodosia wasn't all that convinced, either. A murder, right under her nose, was horrifically offensive. It did ignite her sense of justice and make her want to jump in and help.

On the other hand . . .

Theodosia decided she had much to think about. Delaine was the proverbial evil sprite sitting on her left shoulder urging her to go for it, while Drayton was an angel on her right shoulder whispering "take care." Meanwhile, the front door had just whapped opened and a woman in a red knit cap and matching poncho poked her head in.

"Are you open for business?" the woman asked. "For tea?"

Before Theodosia could reply, Drayton was up and striding across the tea shop, putting on a gracious smile and pulling open the door; welcoming their first customers of the day.

4

The phrase "tornadic activity" didn't do justice to their morning tea time. Theodosia took orders, greeted and seated another two dozen guests, made subtle tea suggestions (perhaps try the Satrupa Estate Assam then the heartier Kopili Estate Assam), and ran orders in to Haley. Haley's lemon scones proved to be a huge hit, as were her blueberry scones, strawberry muffins, and apple tea bread. Drayton, meanwhile, was happily ensconced behind the front counter, brewing tea as he constantly scanned his floor-to-ceiling shelves, trying to select the absolute perfect teas to please their guests. His fingers literally danced over hundreds of colorful, exotic tea tins that held fragrant tea leaves imported from China, Japan, Sri Lanka, Thailand, South Africa, Kenya, India, and Madagascar. Some of Drayton's more recent acquisitions included a Bitaco green tea from Colombia, and a rich black tea from Queensland, Australia.

Theodosia was so busy, she completely forgot about the murder for a while. Put it on a back burner to simmer away. But she wasn't so busy that she forgot to whisper a prayer of gratitude.

The hum of the tea shop, the fragrant aromas from the steamy, steeping teas comforted and nourished her, giving her a renewed sense of accomplishment at being able to open the Indigo Tea Shop all by herself and keep it going these many years. As a lucky strike extra, Drayton and Haley had become her tea family.

Theodosia knew that, for many people, promising careers eventually turned into day-to-day jobs, but she remained rapturously happy at being the proprietor of the Indigo Tea Shop.

"You're looking somewhat dreamy and lost in thought," Drayton said as Theodosia stood at the front counter, watching him prepare pots of Fujian black plum and orange pekoe.

"I'm thinking about how lucky we are. And how much I love this place." Theodosia gazed at the interior of her tea shop, struck by the golden light from the crystal chandelier, the warmth of the Aubusson carpets on the wood-pegged floor, and the general coziness of the place.

The Indigo Tea Shop, to put it bluntly, was Theodosia's pride and joy. She'd scrimped and saved for a down payment on the small, English-style brick building with its high-pitched roof, leaded windows, hunter green awnings, and rounded-at-the-top door that looked like it belonged on a hobbit house. Then she'd added a front counter, a dozen slightly battered tables, creaking but comfortable chairs, and antique highboys that held retail items, such as tea cozies, strainers, tins of tea, and jars of DuBose Bees Honey. Blue toile café curtains had been swagged in the front windows, and antique prints and Theodosia's handmade grapevine wreaths were hung on the brick walls. And though every piece she added—from a brass clock to an old ladder that displayed linen tea towels—was fairly eclectic, the tea shop came together beautifully, reflecting a slightly British, quasi-French charm.

"Excuse me," Drayton said again. "Earth to Theodosia." Those words finally brought her back to the here and now.

"Yes?" Theodosia said.

"This is the genmaicha for table three," Drayton said, sliding a Japanese cast-iron tetsubin across the counter. "And this is Formosa oolong for table four. But kindly remind them to let it steep for an additional two minutes, okay?"

"Right," Theodosia said. She picked up both pots and hesitated. "I've been thinking."

Drayton cocked his head. "So I noticed. What's been swirling about in that Hadron Collider mind of yours?"

"I was remembering Duke's rather violent reaction last night and wondering what your take was?"

"I think Harlan's son was justifiably angry and upset. He no doubt spouted off without thinking things through, which seems to be a fairly common occurrence these days." Drayton cleared his throat for emphasis. "Even among polite society."

"I see your point. I was just thinking . . ."

"What?" Drayton asked.

"Never mind. I need to think some more."

Drayton nodded. "Right."

By eleven fifteen, the tea shop had quieted down some, which was good, because that's when Bill Glass chose to darken their doorway. Glass was the writer/editor/publisher of a sleazy weekly gossip tabloid called *Shooting Star*. He was always on the prowl for news, gossip, hearsay, and innuendo, which meant he was guilty of sneaking into all manner of society events. If Bill Glass could weasel his way into a garden club party or crash a gallery opening, he'd snap copious photos and plaster them all over the front page of his tabloid. The snarky rumor around town was that Bill Glass would go to the opening of an envelope.

Bill Glass sauntered toward Theodosia dressed in a ratty khaki jacket, sloppy dark green slacks, and orange tennis shoes. He looked, she decided, like a grunged-out scarecrow. Of course, Glass had come here to see if he could pick her brain about last night's murder.

"Hey, tea lady," Glass said. A tumble of dark hair spilled over his heavy brows and olive complexion, and a cheesy, too-friendly smile was pasted on his face. "Long time no see."

"And isn't that a blessing," Theodosia said under her breath. Normally, she hustled Bill Glass out of the tea shop with minimum fanfare. Her demeanor always remained polite but firm as she dropped a single scone into a blue bag and poured tea into a take-out cup. Then, she'd escort Glass to the door in a sort of genteel bum's rush.

But today, something inside Theodosia made her wonder if Bill Glass might not be privy to information that linked back to last night's murder. And, lucky for her, Glass kicked things off with a great opening line . . .

"That Sadler murder last night?" Glass said. "I bet you were there."

"I was there," Theodosia said.

"My invitation must have gotten lost in the mail," Glass said. Then he snickered. "But I still managed to get the inside scoop."

"Really?" Theodosia said. "What have you heard?"

Glass rested an elbow on the counter and leaned toward her, bristling with intensity. "That Sadler dude was supposedly a bad guy. People are saying he could have finally gotten his comeuppance."

This line of conversation *was* interesting. "How do you mean?" Theodosia asked while Drayton edged a little closer, the better to hear.

"When I worked for the *Goose Creek Sentinel,* before I started my own paper, I covered a nasty story that featured none other than Harlan Sadler," Glass said. "The dead guy du jour."

"Go on," Theodosia said. She lifted the cover off a glass cake saver and plucked out a scone for Glass while Drayton hurriedly poured him a cup of tea. This time, they wanted to keep him here and talking.

"Hey, thanks loads," Glass said. He took a big bite of scone, chewed noisily, and continued. "To give you a little background, Harlan Sadler was once part of a so-called 'horse mafia.'"

"What on earth is that?" Drayton asked.

"It was a consortium of Charleston fat cats who owned racehorses," Glass said. "You know, like the long-legged Kentucky Derby kind? Anyway, this inner circle of men—Sadler included—had a falling-out with this guy, Jeb Stacks, who sold them a horse under false pretenses. It was touted as a racehorse from Argentina that'd won all these fancy stakes races on the South American circuit. But when they took the horse to Churchill Downs, the horse turned out to be a dud, just an ordinary nag. Anyway, not long after, Jeb Stacks disappeared and the horse mafia was suspected of killing him and burying his body somewhere out in the country."

Drayton let loose a low whistle. "So Harlan Sadler wasn't exactly a Boy Scout. He has a checkered past."

"The thing is, the police could never *prove* that Sadler and his cronies murdered this guy Stacks, so the horse mafia guys were never prosecuted," Glass said.

"Let me guess," Theodosia said. "Your theory is that Harlan Sadler's murder last night was some sort of retribution or revenge."

Glass tapped an index finger against the side of his head. "That's *exactly* what I'm thinking. Somebody close to Jeb Stacks, maybe even a family member, finally exacted their pound of flesh. And since you two attended that gala, I was wondering if you had any inside poop as well." Glass took a noisy slurp of tea, then smacked his lips together. "Ah, tasty."

"All we know is that the police are questioning all the Opera Society board members," Theodosia said.

Glass shook his head. "That's wrong, they're way off base. It was an outsider."

"Are you going to tell the police about the Jeb Stacks murder?" Theodosia asked.

"Honey, they already know," Glass said. "I got it confirmed this morning from one of my contacts at CPD."

"And the police aren't rushing to question Jeb Stacks's family or business associates?" Theodosia asked.

"Not that I'm aware of," Glass said. "Maybe they'll get around to it, but who knows?"

"Seems like the first place I'd start," Theodosia said.

"There you go," Glass said gleefully. "So would I."

Drayton added three scoops of dragonwell tea to a Brown Betty teapot, then poured in a stream of hot water. "This is starting to get complicated. A murder to avenge another murder?"

"Twisty, huh?" Glass said. He seemed to relish the idea.

"So what are you going to do?" Theodosia asked Glass.

"Put on my thinking cap and try to figure out who benefits from last night's murder," Glass said. "And then try to scare up a nice juicy story for next week's paper."

"Spoken like a true Christian," Drayton said.

"Will you, um, keep us in the loop?" Theodosia asked. The words tasted sour in her mouth, considering what a scoundrel Bill Glass was. Still, if he continued to feed her information . . .

"You got it, babe," Glass said. He cocked a finger at her, then grabbed his tea and headed for the front door.

"He worries me," Drayton said as the door banged shut on Glass's retreating figure.

"Why?"

"Because he's starting to make sense."

"Sadler and his fat-cat friends get cheated by this guy Jeb Stacks, so they hold a kangaroo court and decide to have Stacks killed," Theodosia said slowly.

"We don't know that for a fact. I remember reading about that disappearance and no dead body ever turned up. No *habeas corpus*, which translated from Latin literally means 'show me the body.'"

"But what if Bill Glass's theory is right on point?" Theodosia said. "What if Sadler was killed in a kind of revenge murder?" She stopped to consider this. "But by who? Someone in Jeb Stacks's family? Another horse trader? Someone with a warped sense of justice?"

"Your guess is as good as mine." Drayton grabbed a pink Belleek cup and saucer, poured tea into it, and pushed it across the counter to Theodosia. "Here you go, my special blend of chamomile and jasmine. You look as if you're in dire need of a calming cup of goodness."

"I am, thanks." Theodosia took a sip and said, "Do you think Sadler's killer was a guest at the party last night?"

"Probably."

"On the other hand, it could have been someone who skulked in with the rather large contingent of decorators, caterers, bartenders, and entertainers."

"The entertainers," Drayton said, "were all grease-painted-up and wearing fancy costumes."

"And all the guests wore masks."

Drayton looked suddenly unhappy. "So it could have been anybody."

"I don't remember seeing a security guard at the entrance. So, you're right, any lowlife could have slithered in and mingled with the crowd."

One of Drayton's brows rose and quivered. "Reminds me of the character Death in Poe's 'Masque of the Red Death.'"

"Something like that, yes," Theodosia said. "A masked intruder with a vendetta. This is turning into a tricky case."

"Please tell me you're not going to let yourself get pulled into Harlan Sadler's murder." Drayton gave Theodosia a questioning gaze. "Are you?"

"I don't know, I have to say, the whole thing gives me goose bumps and is fairly intriguing. Especially with this Jeb Stacks information that Glass just gave us."

"I wish you'd tamp down that curiosity gene of yours and remember we have a busy week ahead of us. We've got our Regency Tea tomorrow, then the Chocolate Stroll on Wednesday, and our Book Lovers Tea on Thursday." Drayton sighed. "And, against my sage advice, you went ahead and scheduled a Silk Road Tea for Friday."

"That one's almost sold out."

"Lucky us."

"We can handle the pace, we always do," Theodosia said.

"Lord knows how. Obviously, we have to ask Miss Dimple to come in and help. And maybe Haley's cousin, Beth Ann."

"Miss Dimple's already scheduled to work tomorrow through the rest of this week."

"Thank heavens for small miracles," Drayton said. "But Harlan Sadler's murder is still going to be hanging over our heads like the proverbial dark cloud."

"Maybe, maybe not." Theodosia was already spinning ideas in her head as she picked up her teacup and walked down the hallway. She ducked past the celadon green velvet curtain that separated the tea room from the back of the shop and went into her office. Well, actually, it served as both an office and a store-room. And right now the space was packed to the gills with stacks of felt hats, boxes of tea cozies, crates of DuBose Bees Honey, tins of tea, seasonal decorations, flower vases, and an abundance of favors and trinkets for guests.

Still thinking about the murder, Theodosia plopped into her leather desk chair and set down her tea. She idly surveyed the stacks of invoices, magazines, and tea catalogs that littered her desk, then pushed everything aside. Drawing a deep breath, Theodosia let the events of last night rumble through her brain for a few minutes. Then she picked up her phone and called De-laine.

5

❧

"*I changed my* mind," Theodosia said once she had Delaine on the line. "I do want to help. But I have to talk to Cricket first."

"Blessings on your head!" Delaine shrieked. "I knew you wouldn't leave that poor woman twisting in the wind. You really do want to don your Sherlock Holmes hat, don't you? See if you can figure out who Harlan's killer was . . . is?"

Theodosia leaned back in her chair. "I suppose that would be the general idea." She just hoped it was a *good* idea.

"Tell you what. Things are cray-cray here, what with customers and planning a trunk show for my new line of slubbed silks, but I'll still make time to bring Cricket by your tea shop. Maybe even this afternoon. Would that work for you? Hmm . . . would it?"

"I think that'd be perfect," Theodosia said.

"Not that one, the dark *blue* one," Delaine suddenly shouted. "With the narrow lapels and gold buttons. Right. Balmain, not Balenciaga."

"What?"

"Nothing," Delaine said. "Just talking shop." She dropped her voice. "Trying to please a demanding customer. Okay, we'll see you in a bit. Ta-ta, darling."

Morning tea segued into a fairly busy lunch rush, but Haley was more than ready. Today, her menu featured sweet potato bisque, curried chicken salad tea sandwiches, roast beef and cheddar cheese brioche tea sandwiches, and mushroom quiche.

"And for dessert?" Theodosia asked when she popped into the kitchen to grab two plates of apple tea bread.

"Blueberry tartlets and shortbread cookies," Haley said. "And I for sure baked enough of everything to last well into afternoon tea time."

"That's based on the idea that *I* last into afternoon tea time." Theodosia chuckled.

"Hold tight, sister, we've got Miss Dimple coming in tomorrow to help."

"Thank goodness for that."

Theodosia served steaming bowls of bisque, ferried endless pots of tea to her guests, and overheard more than her share of gossip concerning last night's murder.

"Everyone's whispering about the murder," Theodosia said to Drayton when she stopped at the counter.

He looked up from his reservation book. "Who's everyone?"

"Our guests. All the people who were here for morning tea, our luncheon customers, and probably our afternoon tea guests as well."

"I'm not surprised. Rumors have always spread like wildfire here in the Historic District."

"When do you think we'll hear something legitimate?" Theodosia asked.

"As soon as Delaine brings Cricket in and you launch your shadow investigation."

Theodosia did a kind of double take. "How did you know Cricket was coming in? And that I agreed to help out?"

Drayton tapped pen to paper. "Because I know *you*."

Twenty minutes later, Bud Jasmer from Quality Arts Printing stopped by the Indigo Tea Shop and thumped a heavy cardboard box down onto the front counter.

"Guess what I brought," Jasmer said. He was a chubby, cheerful, redheaded guy who wore a too-tight pink polo shirt with a Quality Arts Printing logo over the front pocket.

"Let me guess," Theodosia said. "Candy labels?"

"Yes, ma'am. And are they ever beautiful," Jasmer said.

Drayton handed Theodosia a sharp knife so she could slit the tape holding the box shut. And when she opened the box she let loose a sharp gasp. "They're gorgeous," she said, lifting out a bound stack. "Drayton, go get Haley. Tell her the labels for our chocolates arrived."

Haley came rushing out, wiping her hands on her apron. "How do they look?" she asked.

"Gorgeous," Jasmer said.

"They're perfect," Theodosia said as she lifted a stack of labels out of the box. She'd tapped the creative skills of an artist by the name of Tye Holt, and he'd done wraparound labels for their milk chocolate sea salt bars, as well as stick-on labels for boxes to hold their caramel-pecan turtles and truffles.

Haley peered at the labels. "Okay, I like them, I like them a lot. That line drawing of the front of the tea shop is to die for. And even though I loved the name Sweet Caroline . . ."

"Too bad it was taken," Drayton said.

"Gotcha," Haley replied. "But now I'm fairly smitten with the name Church Street Chocolates. It's got real punch."

"What kind of truffles are you doing?" Jasmer asked.

"We're starting out small with chai, cinnamon, and amaretto truffles," Theodosia said. "If those go over well, if we have actual sales, then we'll add in some tea-infused flavors."

"And you're going to sell them here at the tea shop?" Jasmer asked.

"Here and a couple of gift shops for starters," Theodosia said. "But the real test will be the Chocolate Stroll on Wednesday."

"I heard about that," Jasmer said. "Sounds wonderful."

"We hope it will be," Drayton said.

"Okay, folks, enjoy," Jasmer said as he turned to leave. "Let me know when you're ready for reprints."

"Will do," Drayton said. "Though we need to sell all the chocolates stored in our cooler first."

"But first we need to add wrappers and glue on labels," Theodosia said. "Which is going to be a job and a half."

"I've already got that covered," Haley said.

"You do?" Theodosia said.

"I took a cue from you," Haley said. "I called Beth Ann to see if she could come in and help this week, 'cause like Drayton says, we're gonna be ferociously busy."

"I hope we intend to pay your cousin," Drayton said. "Instead of take advantage."

Haley gave an impish grin. "Can't we do both?"

"You," Drayton said to Haley, "are a troublemaker of the first magnitude."

"Gosh, I hope so," Haley replied with wide-eyed innocence.

Drayton pointed with his finger. "Hark thee back to your kitchen, please." Once Haley had scampered away, he turned to Theodosia and said, "That girl is a sassy little pill."

Theodosia put a hand on her hip and threw him a challenging look. "What do you want me to do? Upset the apple cart and fire her?"

Drayton looked utterly horrified. "Heavens, no. I love Haley to death!"

At two o'clock, Delaine Dish came steaming into the Indigo Tea Shop with a somewhat reluctant Cricket Sadler in tow. Delaine was glammed up in a red skirt suit with a pink Chanel bag, and her dark hair was pulled into a sleek chignon, the better to set off her heart-shaped face. Cricket looked sedate in black slacks and a fitted black jacket. On her lapel she wore a bejeweled flamingo brooch. Theodosia wondered if it was a genuine Cartier, like the Duchess of Windsor had worn, or just a really good copy.

"I feel it's only fair to warn you," Cricket said as she sat down at a table. "The police issued a very stern warning about me not talking to anyone about Harlan's murder."

"Honey, Theodosia's not just anyone," Delaine cajoled as she sat down next to her. "She's our dear, dear friend. Charleston's very own Nancy Drew. The thing is, Theo's got a red-hot track record when it comes to figuring out all sorts of crazy crimes and misdemeanors."

Cricket still wasn't convinced. "Detective Tidwell was particularly insistent I remain quiet about this."

"He's always crabby like that," Delaine said, waving a hand as if she could magically wish Tidwell away. "He's your basic Johnny Law, so he has to assume that tough guy facade."

"Well, if you two really think it's okay," Cricket said. Her eyes darted between Delaine and Theodosia, wondering, starting to look a little hopeful.

"Of course, it's okay," Delaine said. She gazed across the table at Theodosia. "Tell Cricket it's okay," she urged.

"It's okay," Theodosia said. Then added, "But only if you *want* to talk about it. Honestly, Cricket, if you don't feel comfortable sharing any information about your husband, the masquerade party, about anything—then you don't have to. I can sit on the sidelines, lend whatever support you need, and let the police do their job."

Cricket's chin quivered, then she started to sob.

"That's right, honey," Delaine said. "Let it all out, it's good for you. Helps release your inner toxins." She pulled a lace hanky from her bag and passed it to Cricket.

"This couldn't have come at a worse time," Cricket said, wiping and sniffling. "My new shop, Wildflower, was supposed to open next week."

"You can just push your grand opening date a teensy bit into the future," Delaine said. "Until this matter is . . . um, resolved."

Delaine had always been big on pushing things into the future. Theodosia figured she was afflicted with Scarlett O'Hara syndrome—the old "I'll think about it tomorrow" attitude.

Theodosia reached across the table and took Cricket's hand. "Tell me about Wildflower."

"It was . . ." Cricket interrupted herself with a loud hiccup. "It was . . . I mean, I was stocking Wildflower with an entire line of botanical beauty products. You know, all-natural products." She wiped at her tears and gave Theodosia a tentative smile. "One of the face creams even had green tea in it."

"That sounds lovely," Theodosia said as Drayton set a tea tray on their table, then quietly backed away.

"I think so, too," Cricket said. "Having a shop like that has always been a dream of mine."

Theodosia poured a stream of tea into a teacup and handed it to Cricket. "Do you think you could tell me a little about the party? The Mad Hatter Masquerade?"

Cricket nodded. "What do you want to know?"

"Let's start with the guest list," Theodosia said. "How many people received invitations?"

Cricket closed her eyes, thinking, then said, "Around two hundred."

"And they were . . . ?"

"Donors and prospective donors."

"The donors being people you know," Theodosia said.

"And people I trusted," Cricket said, though Delaine rolled her eyes skyward.

"Tell me about *prospective* donors," Theodosia said. "And please do drink your tea. It's chamomile and really quite soothing."

Cricket took a sip of tea, nodded her approval, and said, "There were certain people we *hoped* would get involved. Another tear slid down her cheek and she wiped it away with her hankie.

"You're talking about people with money," Theodosia said. It was a statement, not a question.

"Correct," Cricket said. "We have a small pool of loyal sustaining members, but our Friends of the Opera organization is always out for new blood." When she realized what she'd said, Cricket grimaced. "You know what I mean. New members who could bring in an infusion of cash."

"And you have a list?" Theodosia asked. "Of members and prospective donors?"

Delaine opened her handbag, pulled out several sheets of paper, and officiously handed them over to Theodosia.

"Before I take a look at these lists, I want to ask you about your husband," Theodosia said.

Cricket nodded.

"This is going to sound strange and kind of awful, but do you know if he had any enemies?"

"I don't think so. People loved Harlan. He was so caring and generous. An all-around good guy."

"Nobody comes to mind?" Theodosia said.

Cricket drew a deep breath. "Well, possibly a few disgruntled customers at Elysian Bank."

"He was the CEO, right?" Theodosia said.

"For almost fifteen years. But Harlan was planning to step aside next year. We were going to travel . . . go to Rome and . . ." Cricket's voice trailed off and she broke into sobs again.

Theodosia and Delaine let Cricket go on for a while, then Delaine said, "There must have been a few clients who were more than unhappy."

"How about your husband's business associates?" Theodosia asked. "Any problems there?" She knew there had to be more behind Harlan's murder than hard feelings about overdraft fees.

"Oh," Cricket said. "I don't know . . . maybe."

"And those maybes would be . . . ?"

"Well, I suppose you could look at Ray Crispin, his partner in The Lanvesco Group. Lanvesco was Harlan's real estate business on the side. But I think he mostly got on well with Crispy."

"Anybody else we should be looking at?" Theodosia asked.

Cricket fidgeted with her bracelet. "Maybe one."

"Who's that, honey?" Delaine asked.

"Well, there's Emily Bates." Cricket's face took on a sudden hard look. "She heads Unity One Bank."

"And that was a rival bank of Harlan's?" Theodosia asked.

"Yes, but his bank's parent company, Copernicus Financial, has been negotiating to buy it."

"So a takeover," Theodosia said.

"I suppose you could call it that."

"A *hostile* takeover?"

Cricket scrunched up her face. "Everything's hostile when it comes to Emily Bates."

"Tell me about her," Theodosia said as Delaine leaned in closer, eager to hear a bit of juicy gossip.

"We both go way back with Emily," Cricket said. "She and I went to school together at Emory University in Atlanta. In fact, Harlan even dated her for a short time."

"But he married *you*," Delaine hastily pointed out.

"Which is probably what started the rift between us. Then Harlan and Emily both went into banking and ended up here in Charleston. And even though they worked at rival financial institutions, they somehow traveled in the same social circles." Cricket dabbed at her eyes.

"I have to ask, was Emily Bates at the Mad Hatter Masquerade last night?" Theodosia said.

Cricket nodded. "Emily's a past donor, so of course she was invited."

"How interesting." Delaine's green eyes glittered fairly with interest.

"Did you have any interaction with Emily?" Theodosia asked. "Did you exchange words?"

"Are you kidding? I was so dang busy, I never even *saw* her," Cricket said. She leaned forward. "Do you think Emily could have killed Harlan? Because of the bad blood between them?"

"Emily's kind of small and puny," Delaine said. "I don't think she could have overpowered Harlan."

"She could have hired someone," Theodosia said. "So I will look into that. But right now I just want Cricket to paint a few broad strokes, like she has been doing."

Cricket nodded.

"And answer a few more questions." Theodosia decided to dredge up what seemed to her like unfinished—or at least unresolved—business. She squared her shoulders and said, "What do you know about your husband's issue with the racehorse?"

Cricket sat up straight in her chair as if she'd been jabbed with an electric cattle prod. "You *know* about that?" She looked stunned.

"A little," Theodosia said. "Enough to want to know more."

"Well, there's nothing to know. Absolutely *nothing*. And that's all I'm going to say."

Which led Theodosia to believe Bill Glass's racehorse story might be something to look into after all.

They talked a little more then, but Cricket still didn't have any ideas about who might have murdered her husband.

"You can't think of anything—anybody else?" Theodosia asked.

"Not really," Cricket said.

"Then I'll start with what you've given me," Theodosia said, even though she had a few ideas of her own.

"Thank you," Cricket said. "You're a true friend." She stood up from her chair and gave a wan smile; did her best to look plucky. Then her shoulders sagged. "Unfortunately, this is still Opera Week, with our cocktail party and silent auction on Thursday, and Opera in the Park on Saturday night."

"Those are big events to deal with," Theodosia said.

"That's how you raise money," Delaine said.

Theodosia stared at Delaine. "Sure, but there's no way Cricket can manage both those events *and* plan a funeral."

Delaine wrinkled her nose as she considered this. "I suppose that would be tough. Okay, I can step in and honcho the silent auction, and I'll sweet-talk Ned Grady into handling Saturday's Opera in the Park."

"Thank you," Cricket said to Delaine, tears oozing from the

corners of her eyes again. Then she turned to Theodosia and said, "Delaine's been singing your praises to high heaven, making it sound as if you're the FBI and CIA all rolled into one clever little bundle. So I'm counting on you to help shed some light on Harlan's murder."

"I'll do what I can," Theodosia said as she gave Cricket a quick hug. "By the way, is there any chance of getting a list of all the musicians and entertainers?"

"That might be tricky," Cricket said. "Considering there were so many committees in charge of so many things."

"There has to be some way to get a handle on this information," Theodosia pressed.

"We'll ask around," Delaine said.

"Oh," Cricket said. Her mouth had suddenly formed a perfect *O* and her eyes widened in surprise. "I just remembered something."

"What's that, honey?" Delaine asked.

"The entire event was videotaped," Cricket said.

"Whoa!" Theodosia cried. "You mean to tell me . . . there's actual *footage* of the party?"

6

~✤~

"*Do you remember* seeing two fellows walking around with cameras?" Cricket asked.

"Sure, but I thought they were taking snapshots," Delaine said. "You know, for publicity purposes."

"Right," Theodosia said. She'd seen the two young men wandering around the grist mill grounds with cameras, but hadn't given them a second thought.

Cricket shook her head. "Those guys were *videographers*. Using those cute little handheld video cameras."

"So there's an actual record of the event," Theodosia said. She felt a tug inside her. Here was a way to virtually turn back the clock and hopefully see what Harlan Sadler had been up to at the party—and maybe even figure out who'd been shadowing him.

"The videographers were supposed to shoot as much of the party as possible," Cricket said.

"Then the million-dollar question is . . . has anyone looked at that raw footage yet?" Theodosia asked.

"I don't know," Cricket said. She touched a hand to her heart. "Wow, I guess you're thinking there might be an important clue buried in all that footage. And, silly me, I forgot all about the videotape until this very moment!"

"So the police aren't aware of this footage?" Theodosia asked.

"I don't think so," Cricket said. "At least *I* didn't tell them."

"Well, somebody has to inform them," Theodosia said. She was stunned that video footage of the Mad Hatter Masquerade existed at all. If they were lucky, scanning through that footage would help get a bead on Harlan Sadler's killer.

Theodosia was suddenly aware that Cricket and Delaine were staring at her with expectant looks.

"Let me guess," Theodosia said. "You want *me* to tell the police about this?"

"Would you?" Cricket said. "That'd lift an enormous weight from my shoulders."

"Okay, I can do that," Theodosia said. "But in the meantime, can you call your videographers and have them e-mail that footage to me?" Theodosia asked.

"I think so. It should be simple enough," Cricket said.

"Please," Theodosia said. "Make that call."

Once Cricket and Delaine left, Theodosia hastened over to the front counter.

"I take it you overheard our conversation?" she said to Drayton.

"Videotape," he said. "Sounds like a lucky break." He held up an index finger. "But you must inform the police that this footage exists."

"I intend to do exactly that."

"When?" Drayton asked.

"After I take first crack at it."

"You're playing with fire."

"What's the harm if I look at the video first?"

Drayton blinked. "Did it ever occur to you that somebody else may be vying to get their hot little hands on that footage? Namely the killer?"

Theodosia took a step back from the counter. "I hadn't considered that possibility."

"Perhaps you should."

"Drayton, you worry too much."

"And you don't worry enough."

"I'll be careful, I promise."

"I'm going to hold you to that, my dear. I mean, where would the Indigo Tea Shop be without you? You're its beating heart."

"Oh, Drayton, you're either trying to guilt me or make me cry."

"Good. It's working then."

Theodosia turned and took a quick look around the tea shop. Since it was already midafternoon, there were only three tables of guests left. "Can you handle things for a few minutes?"

"Of course. But what have you got up your sleeve now?"

"I need to duck into my office and catch up on a few things."

"If you're as smart as I think you are, you'll call Detective Tidwell immediately," Drayton said. "Inform him about that tape."

But Theodosia didn't call Detective Tidwell. She decided she'd call him *after* she reviewed the video footage. But first . . . there was some other information she wanted to dig into.

Theodosia sat down at her computer and ran a quick Google search to see if she could find anything about the so-called horse mafia, as well as their connection to Jeb Stacks's death. It took a bit of searching, but she finally found an article about Jeb Stacks's disappearance. The police had treated it as a missing person's report and never bumped it up to a murder charge because no body had ever been recovered. No *habeas corpus,* as Drayton had said. Plus, there was a rumor that Jeb Stacks left town on his own to escape financial difficulties.

Hmm, not much to go on.

Then, almost by accident, Theodosia stumbled upon a mention of Jeb Stacks's son, Ethan Stacks. Interestingly, Ethan Stacks was a partner in an antique shop by the name of Stacks & Soames.

Is this something? Maybe it's something.

Theodosia thought for a minute and had, what she considered, a mega-brainstorm. She hastily scanned the list of invitees that Delaine had given her, and there, toward the bottom of the list, was Ethan Stacks's name.

Bingo.

Theodosia hurried out to the tea room. "Did you know that Ethan Stacks, the son of the horse trader guy Bill Glass told us about, was a guest at the masquerade last night?"

Drayton stared at her, a look of surprise on his face. "Are you serious?"

"Small world, isn't it? Also, have you ever heard of an antique shop by the name of Stacks & Soames?"

"I . . . I think I might have purchased a set of oyster plates from them at one time," Drayton said. "I know they usually have a booth at Charleston's annual Fall Antique Fair. Wait, you're not thinking that . . ."

"Actually, I *am* thinking that Ethan Stacks might have had a serious axe to grind. If he believed that Harlan Sadler helped murder his father . . ."

"Perhaps it's just a strange coincidence that the son was in attendance."

"Strange isn't the word for it. More like incriminating," Theodosia said.

"I guess this means you're going to pay a visit to Ethan Stacks?"

"It's at the top of my to-do list." Theodosia glanced at her watch. "In fact, it's not that late. If I wrap things up here, there's still time to visit that shop."

"Isn't it strange that the father was a horse trader while the son became an antique dealer? Occupations that are basically polar opposites."

"Maybe not that different, seeing as how they're both in the business of wheeling and dealing."

"I suppose that's one way to look at it," Drayton said. "Where's this antique shop located?"

"Over in Mount Pleasant." Theodosia knew it was a little out of her way, but what's a few miles when you're trying to get a bead on a stone-cold killer?

At four o'clock, Haley bid them goodbye, scooting upstairs to the apartment above the tea shop that she shared with Teacake, her orange-and-brown cat. Then, Drayton rushed off to a meeting at his beloved Heritage Society, which left Theodosia to lock up, set the security alarm, and then jump in her Jeep—which she always kept parked in the back alley. She knew if she booked it hard, she could probably make it to Stacks & Soames before they closed for the day. And maybe, if she was super lucky, she could have a conversation with Ethan Stacks himself. She wasn't sure what she was going to ask Stacks, but figured she'd wing it. Try to figure things out when she got there.

But getting there was no picnic. Theodosia hit a huge backup trying to get onto the Ravenel Bridge, then had to detour around a street maintenance crew on Coleman Boulevard. She passed the Vicious Biscuit where she'd once had a beignet that brought tears to her eyes, then hung a left on Japonica Road.

When Theodosia finally pulled up in front of Stacks & Soames, the lights were still on, and she could see someone moving around inside. Looks like luck was with her.

The words STACKS & SOAMES FINE ANTIQUES were stenciled in gold paint on the front window of a red brick building that looked cute, cozy, and antiquated. A window display included an assortment of crockery, a large brass clock, a few pieces of marble statuary, and several smaller oil paintings resting on easels.

As Theodosia entered the shop, a bell over the front door *ding-ding*ed, announcing her arrival.

"Hello," she called out, as her eyes roved over brass lamps, carnival glass, collections of sterling silver flatware, antique clocks, a cast-iron letterpress, and wall sconces. There were larger items, too—a butter churn, a Charleston joggling board, a wood and marble console table, and a mahogany sugar chest.

"Good afternoon," Ethan Stacks said as he emerged from a back office. He was tall with dark bushy hair, round, wire-rimmed glasses, and a scruffy goatee. He wore a dark green canvas jacket over nondescript gray pants and reminded Theodosia of old pictures she'd seen of the Russian revolutionary Leon Trotsky. She wondered, just for a split second, what his politics might be.

"How can I help you?" Stacks asked her. He lifted a hand to indicate a jewelry case and said, "I just returned from a superb auction at Crispin's in New York and brought back a veritable treasure trove of jewelry. Rings, necklaces, even a few watches— all from the jewelry boxes of Upper East Side society women.

These days, everyone seems to want to cash out. You see this?"
He picked up a tank watch with a leather strap. "Vintage
Cartier."

"Gorgeous," Theodosia said. Then, "You're Mr. Stacks, right?"
She wanted to make sure she was buttonholing the right guy.

Ethan Stacks nodded. "That's right."

"I'm actually looking for a little information."

Curiosity flickered in his dark eyes. "Yes?"

"You were a guest at the masquerade party last night?"

"You're with the police?" Ethan Stacks asked. "May I please
see some identification?"

"No, no," Theodosia said, waving a hand, trying to look
friendly and nonthreatening. "I'm making inquiries for a friend.
Well, actually . . . for the victim's wife."

Now Stacks looked confused. "I'm not sure I understand the
nature of . . ."

"I just need to ask you a couple of questions."

"Concerning?"

"The murder of Harlan Sadler."

Stacks's demeanor changed immediately. He took a step backward and his eyes turned marble hard. "Now I understand. I'm
guessing you've heard the rumors about Panchesco?"

"Pardon?"

"Panchesco, the racehorse that my father supposedly sold to
Harlan Sadler."

"The racehorse, yes." Theodosia smiled. "It seems we've arrived at the crux of the matter rather quickly. So I'm wondering,
Mr. Stacks . . . do you believe Harlan Sadler had a hand in
murdering your father?"

Stacks was shaking his head. "I'm not interested in discuss-
ing anything relating to my family. Especially when it involves
hearsay or rumors."

"But you *were* in attendance last night," Theodosia said, trying to keep the conversation inching ahead.

"Of course I was. Because of the nature of my business, I make it a priority to stay connected to my customers. Their interests are my interests."

"As is their money?"

"I suppose you could look at it that way." Ethan Stacks gave her a smug look. "I'm lucky to have some loyal, well-heeled clients that I also count as dear friends."

"Did you kill Harlan Sadler?" Theodosia blurted out.

Stacks gazed at her with a world-weary expression. "I left the party early, so I didn't even *know* the man was dead until I read about it in this morning's newspaper."

"How do you feel about Sadler's murder?"

"I feel nothing, except maybe to say good riddance to yet another arrogant, pompous banker."

"So you actually *do* feel something," Theodosia said.

"Don't," Stacks said. "Don't you dare try to hang this on me. I'm not—I have never been—associated with Harlan Sadler."

Theodosia decided to take a chance. "Then who should I be looking at?"

Ethan Stacks picked up a blue velvet ring box that was sitting on the counter in front of him. Flipping it open to reveal a stunning blue sapphire and diamond cocktail ring, he seemed to ponder her question. Then he said, "Have you looked at Duke?"

"You're talking about Harlan's son," Theodosia said. His pointing a finger at Duke Sadler gave her a little jolt. Because somewhere, deep inside, she'd been thinking about Duke, as well.

"Duke," Ethan Sadler said. "Please believe me when I say he's a conniving thief and a skillful con man. He's constantly embroiled in real estate deals that he swears on a stack of Bibles will make a pile of money for his investors and kick back returns of over two hundred percent. I'm embarrassed to say that Duke suckered two of my friends into a debacle of a land deal a few years ago."

"You actually think Duke could have murdered his own father?" Theodosia asked.

Ethan Stacks grimaced. "From what I've heard, his father was a hard-nosed, cutthroat banker. What pundits today are calling a 'bankster.' So maybe . . . like father, like son?"

The bell over the door *da-ding*ed as two affluent-looking women strolled into the shop. Ethan Stacks looked at them with anticipation, then shot Theodosia a perfunctory glance and said, "I rather think we're done here."

7

On her way home, Theodosia mulled over the possibility that Duke Sadler might have had a hand in his own father's death. It sounded both crazy and preposterous. Then again, stranger things were known to happen. Wives murdered husbands; mothers took the lives of their own children. It was a messy, sometimes murderous world out there.

Looking at her watch, Theodosia decided she had time to swing over to Duke's office and try to talk to him. The operative word being *try*. Maybe she could offer Duke a dab of sympathy and couch her probing questions in deep concern for his well-being. If Duke was wallowing in grief—or even false grief—he might not notice how hard she was poking around.

When Theodosia got to King Street, she pulled over to the curb and googled Duke's office address. And learned that it was located in the same office building as his father's business, The Lanvesco Group. That should be easy enough to find. She turned at King Street and headed down Donegal. The autumn sun was just beginning to dip low in the sky, casting golden shadows on the many brick buildings in this part of town. And the offices for The Lanvesco Group was one of them. Theodosia found a parking spot nearby in front of a cute little boutique with the name Wooly Bug. After salivating over the lush cashmere sweaters, shawls, and scarves displayed in their front window, she headed next door to Duke's office.

The offices of The Lanvesco Group looked more like a posh architectural firm than a real estate company. White walls, modular desks, gray industrial carpeting, and colorful slashes of expressionist paintings hung on the walls. It also appeared to be in complete disarray. Two people were shouting into phones while a pretty blond woman in a blue pin-stripe blouse, navy pencil skirt, and killer high heels was hurriedly packaging up a stack of papers.

"Excuse me, I wonder if you could help me?" Theodosia said.

When the woman looked up, Theodosia saw that her face was lined with tension and her eyes were red. It was obvious she'd been crying.

"I'm Rita Reitner, the office manager," the woman said. "What can I do for you?"

"You work for Harlan Sadler of The Lanvesco Group?"

The woman let loose a shudder. "I did." Her eyes bounced around the office. "I don't know what's going to happen now. I guess it's all up to Mr. Crispin, his partner."

"I'm very sorry for your loss," Theodosia said. "I happened to be at the Mad Hatter Masquerade last night . . ."

Rita's mouth twisted in a grimace. "Oh no."

"Which was a pretty awful scene," Theodosia said. "And I'm sure Mr. Sadler's death has been terribly hard on you." She looked over at the other two employees. "On all of you."

"Mr. Sadler was a sweetheart," Rita said. "We all just loved working with him." She touched a hand to her throat. "We're *devastated* and can't imagine who on earth would want to kill him."

"I know," Theodosia said. "I feel the same way." Then, "I'm also a friend of Cricket's, of Mrs. Sadler's."

"Ooh, I spoke with Mrs. Sadler this morning," Rita said. "The poor woman sounded positively gutted."

"The thing is, I've agreed to look into a few things for Cricket," Theodosia said. "One of them involves checking on Duke's well-being. So I was wondering . . . is Duke around? His office is here, right?"

"It's down at the end of the hallway, but I'm afraid you just missed him," Rita said. "Duke took off a few minutes ago. I told him he should go home and take it easy—that losing a close family member can be a terrible blow to your system—but Duke didn't listen to me. He said he needed to file some papers with the city clerk's office and then stop by one of his properties. Apparently, he's having problems with one of the tenants."

"I really need to talk to Duke," Theodosia said. "Do you know which property he was headed for? Maybe I could catch him . . ."

"Let me think," Rita said. "I believe he was headed for the property on Floral Drive just off Magnolia. One Six Five Floral."

"Thank you," Theodosia said. "And I really am sorry about Mr. Sadler."

It was another trip out of her way, but Theodosia was so intrigued by Ethan Stacks's remark about Duke that she was willing to delay her dinner for the time being. After all, Duke hadn't been at his best last night, so tonight might prove to be a different story. Reality might have kicked in, and Duke's attitude might be more somber and reflective. Along with that, Duke might also have some ideas as to who his father's enemies might be.

Theodosia did find it somewhat unusual that Duke was carrying on with business as usual the day after his father's murder. On the other hand, she knew that people mourned in different ways. And life, though precious and sometimes fleeting, does go on.

Theodosia found the property on Floral Drive easy enough. She pulled up in front of a seedy fourplex that had definitely seen better days. The front porch sagged, shutters on two windows hung awry, and the landscaping was almost nonexistent. Walking up the cracked front sidewalk, she could hear Duke Sadler before she could actually see him.

He was yelling at someone, ranting about how they were three months late with their rent. A woman, her voice high and quavering, pleaded with him, but Duke simply shouted her down. Theodosia couldn't help it—the words *slum landlord* ran through her brain.

Two kids were standing outside the apartment, looking scared.

Theodosia stopped to talk to them. "Is that your mom in there?" she asked.

The older kid, a sandy-haired boy of about eight in a tattered jacket and jeans, nodded his head. He looked frightened to death as he clutched the hand of his younger sister, who wore a pink T-shirt and yellow overalls.

Doggone, Theodosia thought as she stepped onto the porch. *This is so not good.* She opened the outer door and stepped into a dingy-looking entry. The carpet was frayed, wallpaper had come unstuck in several spots, and four black mailboxes hung from a wall. Duke and whoever he was shouting at were standing halfway down the first-floor hallway.

"Excuse me," Theodosia said in a loud voice as she strode down the corridor, her heels ringing out sharp as castanets. She fully meant to interrupt their "conversation," if that's what you'd call it.

Duke turned to look at her and frowned. "Who are you?" He was taller than Theodosia remembered, with the kind of wide shoulders you get from seriously working out. A curl of brown hair hung over one brow, and she saw he was a good-enough-looking man. But his eyes were lizard flat.

"I'm Theodosia Browning," Theodosia said. "A friend of your mother's."

"That's nice," Duke said as the woman he'd been yelling at cowered in the doorway of her apartment. She was thin with straw-colored hair and frightened gray eyes. She wore a pink dress with a white lace collar and a white apron tied around her waist. Theodosia figured she probably worked as a waitress at a nearby restaurant.

"Excuse me," Theodosia said again as she addressed Duke. "But we need to talk. Like, right now."

Duke hesitated for a moment, then turned back to the frightened woman and said, "Three days, you've got three days." Then he took a step toward Theodosia and said, "Let's go outside."

Once they were out on the sidewalk, safely past the children, Theodosia said, "I don't know if your mom had a chance to tell you, but I've agreed to look into a few things for her."

Duke fixed her with a hard gaze. "Who are you again?"

"Theodosia Browning. I was at the Mad Hatter Masquerade last night."

"Huh." Duke seemed to carefully weigh his next words. "Are you with the police?"

"No, no, people keep asking me that, but it's nothing like that. I run a tea shop."

"So you're a private investigator on the side?" Now Duke looked almost amused.

"Nothing quite that formal."

"I don't get it," Duke said. "What is it you want from me?"

"If you don't mind, I'd like to ask you a few questions."

"Questions?" Duke's attitude shifted from barely tolerant to belligerent and he glowered at her. "You know what? I very much *do* mind. I have absolutely no intention of answering any questions. Furthermore, I seriously doubt your ability to assist my mother in any way, shape, or form. So you know what, Little Miss Tea Shop Lady? I think you should go back to wherever you came from and mind your own sweet business."

"One quick question," Theodosia said.

"No." Duke exhaled loudly, then cocked his head to one side when he realized Theodosia exhibited no fear whatsoever and wasn't about to move. "What?"

"How much back rent does that woman owe?"

Duke shook a finger at her. "Don't get involved, this is none of your business!"

Theodosia took a step forward and put some grit in her voice. "I asked you *how much*?"

"Eight hundred dollars," Duke spat out. "And I seriously doubt I'll ever see a penny of it."

"And if you don't?"

"Then she's out on her can."

8

Theodosia arrived home later than she'd planned, feeling a little down and a tiny bit depressed. But when Earl Grey greeted her joyfully at the kitchen door, her mood lifted enormously.

Woof!

The dog threw himself at Theodosia, almost knocking her over, at which point Theodosia gladly knelt down to fully embrace her sweet dog. But Earl Grey's excitement could barely be contained. He poked at her hair with his muzzle, snuffled her ear, then administered a complete set of sweet doggy kisses. Theodosia couldn't help it—now she was smiling from ear to ear.

"I know Mrs. Barry stopped by to walk you," Theodosia said once she was able to stand up again. "But did she feed you?" Mrs. Barry was Earl Grey's dog nanny—a retired schoolteacher who'd joined the gig economy as a dog walker, dog nanny, and dog babysitter.

Theodosia peered in Earl Grey's aluminum bowl and saw a few uneaten chunks of kibble.

"Yup, she fed you alright. And gave you cold water, too?" She dipped a finger into his water bowl and found it to be nice and cold. Check. "So how about we head out for a quick run?"

Now Earl Grey was swishing his tail back and forth like crazy, ready to rocket on out of there.

"Whoa. First things first, okay, fella?"

Earl Grey padded after Theodosia as she walked through her dining room and tossed her bag on the Sheraton buffet. She continued into her living room and opened the front door where she grabbed a handful of mail out of a brass mailbox that hung on the brickwork next to her front door.

"Not much," Theodosia murmured as she looked through the envelopes and flyers. "Mostly bills and stuff. Nothing for you to worry your furry little head over." She smiled to herself as she casually glanced around her living room. She'd recently had her sofa recovered in a nubby terra-cotta-colored fabric, and it looked great sitting on her blue and persimmon-colored Oriental carpet. Of course, she loved the look of the entire room. Keying off the warm brick of her fireplace and the exposed beams, Theodosia had made some careful purchases that included a mixture of French and English furniture, a mirrored cocktail table, and a vintage tea trolley that she used as a sideboard for wine and cocktails when she entertained. The fireplace mantle held a row of silver mint julep cups, all antique, as well as two small oil paintings on brass easels.

Tucking the bills in her pocket, Theodosia suddenly remembered the video footage that Cricket was supposed to have emailed, and wondered if it had arrived yet. She sprinted upstairs to her bedroom / sitting room / walk-in closet retreat and hastily checked her e-mail.

Nope. No video footage yet.

As Theodosia changed into a hoodie, yoga pants, and running shoes, she worried that something might have gone wrong.

Maybe Cricket had changed her mind. Or the police had found out about the video and confiscated it. Or something equally dire had happened.

Theodosia shook her head and told herself, *No, Cricket promised to send it and she will. I'm just jumping the gun. Like I always do.*

Back downstairs, Theodosia took time to gnaw an apple and a piece of cheese, and took a few glugs of Fiji water. Then she snapped a leash on Earl Grey and they were out the door.

It was full-on dark as they sprinted down the back alley. Theodosia noted that the Granville Mansion, the very large home next door—the one that practically dwarfed her home— was still dark. The owner, a man named Robert Steele, a hedge fund guy, had gone off to London and arranged with a real estate company to rent the place out. One man, an obnoxious investigative reporter, lived there for a month or so, then hightailed it out of there. No new tenants had shown up since.

Good. Maybe it'll stay that way.

As they ran along, trees shuddered in the stiff breeze, and dry leaves tumbled down the middle of quiet streets that were lit by old-fashioned wrought iron lamps. Theodosia's neighborhood was an amalgam of old-line mansions and vintage cottages with the occasional Charleston single house tossed in for good measure. Of course, it was all lovely and quite elegant, with palmetto trees fronting stately, well-preserved homes, many of which were painted in a French palette of pink, cream, and eggshell blue. Along the way, remnants of cobblestone streets and sprawling live oak trees added more character. Charleston had earned the nickname "the holy city" because of its steepled skyline, and Theodosia could see almost a half dozen or so flood-lit church steeples rising in the darkness.

Theodosia hadn't intended to run past the old Pendleton Grist Mill, but that's where she and Earl Grey ended up some twenty minutes later. She slowed as she approached the entrance, then stopped dead in her tracks. It was dark and spooky, the stone walls rising like jagged teeth, other parts of the mill looking like crumbled battlements.

Do I dare go in? Especially since the crime scene tape is still up?

The decision was made for Theodosia when Earl Grey pulled on his leash and tugged her forward. Ducking under the black-and-yellow tape, they walked through a low arched doorway and into the old mill.

It was exactly as Theodosia remembered it—dusty and grimy with old-fashioned machinery that looked dangerous, as if it might spring to life at any second.

No, that's not going to happen.

They walked swiftly through the business part of the mill, then down a narrow corridor and out into a grassy area where remnants of the party lay strewn like debris in a tornado's path. Theodosia saw masks, glassware, cocktail napkins, and even what looked like a few articles of clothing. One of the papier-mâché mushrooms had been punched in and tipped sideways. Wandering over to the croquet court, she saw that the croquet hoops were still in the ground, and a few croquet mallets were lying about. She walked over and picked up a wooden mallet. Hefting it, she swung it hard with all her might and was amazed at how fast it whizzed through the air.

Yes, one of these mallets could definitely disable someone.

Theodosia got out of there then. Turned and headed for home, jogging at a good clip, but looking back over her shoulder, too.

When Theodosia and Earl Grey arrived home, Theodosia jumped into the shower while Earl Grey jumped into his doggy bed. She soaped, steamed, and thought for a while, as hot water pulsed down onto her neck and shoulders. Five minutes later, she was wrapped in a plush robe and anxiously looking through her e-mail.

And wouldn't you know it? The video footage of the party had finally arrived!

Wonderful.

Theodosia hit a button, and there, on her screen, was a replay of Sunday night's Mad Hatter Masquerade. She watched as guests came and went, greeted each other while servers served drinks, and . . .

The BRIIIING of her phone interrupted her. She glanced at her phone's screen and saw it was Riley.

"Hey," Theodosia said as the footage continued to play. "How are things in Savannah?"

"Good. Slow," Riley said. "Great food, though. I just had dinner at The Olde Pink House."

"How was it?"

"Let me put it this way, they were named one of the most romantic restaurants in America by *Food & Wine* magazine, and the place looks it. Oh, and FYI, The Olde Pink House has also been called the most haunted landmark."

"Right up my alley," Theodosia said. "Dare I ask what you ordered?"

"Corn bread fried oysters and pork tenderloin with bourbon molasses."

"Yum. Good to know you're well fed."

"Not nearly as good as your cooking," Riley said.

Theodosia chuckled. "Liar."

"So what kind of trouble are you in so far?"

"Not much. Right now I'm just checking my e-mail." Theodosia continued to scan the video footage as she talked to Riley, feeling slightly guilty that she hadn't revealed the existence of the tape to him. Then, suddenly, a figure jumped out at her, one she wasn't expecting to see. Her eyes crossed and she let out a startled "Eek!"

"What just happened?" Riley asked. "Did you see a mouse or something?"

"What *did* I just see?" Theodosia yelped, basically talking to herself now.

"I don't know," Riley said. "Um, are you talking to me?"

"Hang on a minute." Theodosia stopped the footage, reversed it, and watched it play again. "I don't believe it!" she murmured.

"Theo, what are you *doing*?" Riley asked. "And don't try to tell me you're lazing on your bed painting your toenails hot pink. Something's going on, something big. Now spit it out."

"If you must know, I'm looking at video footage from last night's masquerade party," Theodosia said, feeling almost breathless as she ran the footage back and forth.

"There's video footage!" Riley shouted. "Why haven't you . . ."

"Hang on a doggone minute," Theodosia cried into the phone. "I can't believe what I . . ."

"What did you see?" Riley asked. He was sounding a little hot and bothered.

"This is going to sound completely wacked, but it looks as if there were *two* Mad Hatters at last night's party."

There was silence on the phone for a few seconds, then Riley said, "Two Mad Hatters? What do you mean?"

"I mean there was a *real* Mad Hatter, an actor portraying the Mad Hatter, and a second one. Like . . . a *fake* Mad Hatter."

"And you're thinking what?" Riley asked. "That one of the Mad Hatters might have been the killer?"

"I'd say it's a possibility," Theodosia said.

"You'd better send me that footage," Riley asked. "So I can take a look."

"Will do. As soon as we hang up."

"And, Theo, you need to send that video footage to Detective Tidwell, as well."

"But . . ."

"No, no," Riley said. "This is nonnegotiable. You *have to* e-mail that footage directly to Tidwell. Like, immediately!"

"Okay, okay," Theodosia said. "I'll do that." She paused. "But what happens if Tidwell gets himself in a heckuva twist and calls to scream at me?"

Riley chuckled. "Sweetheart, that's a risk you'll have to take."

9

❧

Detective Tidwell didn't call Theodosia on Monday night. But he did burn up the phone lines this Tuesday morning and left her a scathing voicemail. Something to the tune of *How could you possibly hold back critical video evidence when you know we're blah blah blah.*

Theodosia decided that, rather than return Tidwell's somewhat rude call, she'd bring Drayton up to date on her visits to Ethan Stacks and Duke Sadler. And, of course, tell him about her discovery of the two Mad Hatters she'd seen on the video. Drayton, being a true Southern gentleman, would probably listen carefully, ask a few succinct questions, then quietly commiserate. In other words, he wouldn't scream at her.

"Drayton?" Theodosia crooked a finger as she sat down at one of the front tables. Drayton hurried over with a tea tray, poured them each a steaming cup of Darjeeling, then listened attentively as Theodosia told him about yesterday's visit to Ethan Stacks.

"So you probed Stacks about possibly killing Sadler in

retaliation for his father's murder," Drayton said. "And he denied it?"

"Of course, he did. Stacks basically swore on a stack of Gideon Bibles that it wasn't him—that he wasn't even interested in Harlan Sadler anymore."

"Did Ethan Stacks believe that his father *was* murdered? Or had just skipped town?"

"He said he didn't want to talk about it—that it was none of my business."

"So we don't know if the father is dead or alive?"

"That's right," Theodosia said.

"Then what happened?" Drayton was listening carefully to Theodosia's every word.

"Then Ethan Stacks asked me if I'd considered Duke Sadler as a suspect. Well, he didn't say it in those exact words, but that's what he implied."

"That could have been a smoke screen. Trying to keep you from taking a hard look at him."

"I thought of that."

"But you stopped to see Duke anyway?" Drayton said.

"Right. There's something about Duke that doesn't feel right to me. Anyway, Duke wasn't at his office, but I was able to catch him at one of the apartment buildings he owns. He was there, screaming at one of his tenants about back rent. The poor woman looked scared to death."

"How awful."

"It *was* awful," Theodosia said. "Especially since the poor woman's kids were right there."

"So you're telling me Duke Sadler has a miserable temper."

"He basically went ballistic over a couple months' back rent."

"A short fuse could be indicative of someone who could commit murder," Drayton said.

"Or it might just mean Duke's a miserable jackhole."

"Such a pity that he has to treat his tenant so harshly. Especially when so many people are struggling to make ends meet in this economy." Drayton took a sip of tea and said, "But what I really want to know is . . . did Cricket send you the video footage?"

"She did."

"And you looked at it?"

"I was in the middle of reviewing the footage when Riley called. And then I got all excited and kind of spilled the beans to him."

Drayton ran a hand across the top of his head and squinted at her. "Oh no."

"Oh yes. When Riley detected—he *is* a detective, you realize—that Detective Tidwell hadn't seen the footage yet, all hell broke loose."

"I can imagine."

"Riley was totally ticked off at me. He told me this was a full stop situation and that I should ignore the rest of the footage and send it to Detective Tidwell immediately. That their Crime Scene lab would review it and take over from there."

"So did you stop looking at the videotape?"

"Excuse me, have we met?" Theodosia said.

"I'll take that as a no," Drayton said, a wry smile creasing his face. "So. What did you see? Did something jump out at you?"

"It's the strangest thing, but there appeared to be *two* Mad Hatters running around that night."

"No way!" Then Drayton lowered his voice and said, "Do you think one of them was a fake? That he might have been the killer?"

"I think it's possible. But before I skew my investigation in that direction, I need to talk to whoever was in charge of booking the entertainers."

"Do you know who that is?"

"No, but Cricket will know. We'll see her at her husband's visitation tonight, so I'll ask her then."

"You might be onto something," Drayton said. Then the front door rattled loudly, and his calm expression evaporated. "Don't people ever read our sign and take it seriously? Can't they see that our tea shop doesn't open for another fifteen minutes?"

But the annoying rattle continued until Theodosia went to the door and parted a curtain to peer out the window. And saw . . . Detective Burt Tidwell.

"Rats," Theodosia said, ducking back behind the curtain. She didn't know if she should hide, flee the premises, or let him in.

After the door shuddered a fifth time, she let him in. She couldn't take the pounding anymore.

Tidwell's face was a thundercloud as he stalked into the tea shop. He raised a hand and pointed his index finger at Theodosia. "You," he said. "You withheld key evidence from a police investigation. That video footage should have been turned over to us immediately."

"I sent it to you, like, two minutes after I got it," Theodosia said.

"You did not," Tidwell said.

"Look, I didn't even know it existed until late yesterday." That was a little white lie, but Theodosia figured she could get away with it.

"Doesn't matter. Time is critical in a murder investigation."

"I understand that, I really do," Theodosia said. "And I apologize." When Tidwell continued to glower at her, she said, "Here now, why don't you sit down and let me bring you a scone and a pot of tea. I'll bet you haven't had breakfast yet. You're probably starving to death."

Her words mollified Tidwell enough that he did take a seat. He never could resist a tasty, fresh-baked scone.

Theodosia winked at Drayton who immediately prepared a pot of tea for Tidwell while Theodosia scurried into the kitchen.

"What's on the docket as far as scones today?" she asked Haley.

"I just baked a batch of apple-walnut scones and some lemon–poppy seed scones," Haley said. "Which one would you like?"

"Better give me one of each. Tidwell's out there and he's in a mood."

"Gotcha," Haley said.

Haley plated the scones while Theodosia added small cups of Devonshire cream and lemon curd. Carrying everything into the tea room, Theodosia grabbed a pot of tea and set it down in front of Detective Tidwell.

His nose twitched immediately at the delicious aromas, so Theodosia poured him a cup of Lapsang souchong tea, pushed the plate of scones in front of him, and sat down across from him.

"How is the investigation coming along?" Theodosia asked.

Taking his own sweet time, Tidwell cut his scone in half, slathered on an inordinate amount of Devonshire cream, and took an enormous bite. Finally, he said, "Slowly. The wheels of justice always turn slowly."

"Does that mean you don't have any viable suspects?"

"Oh, we have suspects," Tidwell said. "Just not a substantial amount of direct evidence to tie them to the murder."

"Direct evidence versus circumstantial evidence."

Tidwell nodded as he chewed.

Theodosia decided to take a chance. "With Harlan Sadler involved in the banking business as well as real estate, he must have made a few enemies along the way."

When Tidwell didn't respond, she prompted him again with, "I'm guessing Sadler was no angel?"

"What's the old saying?" Tidwell said. "You have to crack a few eggs to make an omelet."

"Cracking one of those eggs, I understand that Harlan Sadler was a suspect in a murder case several years ago."

"I'm not at liberty to divulge any details concerning that case," Tidwell said.

"Actually, I already know quite a few details. It's the racehorse murder, right?"

"Who told you about that?"

Theodosia folded her arms across her chest. "A source."

Tidwell peered at her. "You really have been snooping, haven't you?"

When Theodosia didn't answer, Tidwell said, "Of course you have. Kindly look but do not touch. I don't want your sticky little fingers mucking up any part of my investigation."

"What if I could help shed some light?" Theodosia asked.

"Absolutely not," Tidwell said.

"I could talk to Duke and . . ."

"Stop!" Tidwell shouted. His hand smacked down on the table, making his teacup jump and clatter in its saucer.

"Why? Do you think Duke is dangerous?" Theodosia asked.

Tidwell lifted his teacup and peered at her over the rim. "Let me put it this way, he's not *not* dangerous."

"That's all you can say?"

"That's all I'm going to say," Tidwell said.

As guests began to arrive for their morning cream teas, Theodosia tried to pry a little more information out of Tidwell, but it was a no go. So she thanked him for dropping by, then went to the front counter, grabbed three scones from the glass pie saver, and put them in a to-go bag. She thought about her precarious situation with Tidwell and added two more scones.

That should keep him happy.

Even so, Detective Burt Tidwell didn't look one bit satisfied as he grabbed his bag of scones and stomped out the door, his heavy cop shoes making a clatter as he left.

Theodosia blew out a glut of air and dusted her hands together. Then her day began in earnest.

Miss Dimple, their octogenarian bookkeeper and sometime server arrived at nine fifteen. Standing a little under five feet, with pinkish-blond hair and a perpetual smile on her face, Miss Dimple was always thrilled when she was asked to fill in.

"Your call couldn't have come at a better time," Miss Dimple told Theodosia as she looped a black Parisian waiter's apron around her neck and wound the strings around her ample waist. "I was reduced to watching daytime game shows for lack of anything better to do." She gave a girlish shiver. "Guessing the retail price of a floor mop isn't exactly stimulating to one's brain cells."

"We're delighted to have you," Drayton called to her from the counter. "Plus, we really do need your assistance."

She looked around the already bustling tea room. "I bet you've got some tea for me to deliver?"

"Two pots of fresh-brewed tea," Drayton said. "The green teapot goes to table six, the floral teapot to table three."

"I'm on it," Miss Dimple said as she got to work.

Miss Dimple's helping out gave Theodosia some much-needed think time and breathing room. And by the time Beth Ann arrived at ten o'clock, she was feeling positively giddy.

"This is the life," Theodosia said to Drayton as she lounged against the counter. "Two assistants to take our guests' orders, grab scones, deliver tea, and clear tables. I'm loving it."

"Don't get too comfortable," Drayton said. "You still have to decorate for our Regency Tea and act as genial hostess."

"Who says I'm acting?" Theodosia said.

"Well, you know what I mean."

By eleven fifteen, the tea room was starting to empty out and Beth Ann approached Theodosia with an expectant look on her face.

"Haley said you're going to start decorating pretty soon for the Regency Tea. Can I help?"

Beth Ann was five years younger than Haley, slim with dark hair, and a junior at Clemson where she was majoring in marketing. Beth Ann had taken this quarter off—a gap quarter instead of a gap year—to get some practical, real-life experience.

She was also a type A who loved to keep busy.

"Your words are music to my ears," Theodosia said. "In my office are a couple boxes of silk wisteria vines. You can start by draping those vines across the ceiling for a kind of romantic garden effect."

"Got it," Beth Ann said as she took off.

"What can I do, honey?" Miss Dimple asked.

"Let's get out the lace tablecloths and start setting our tables," Theodosia said. "We'll probably want to use our Grantham by Royal Doulton teacups and plates, since Royal Doulton was a popular Regency-era pottery house."

"And then?"

"I'll pull out the Elizabeth Tudor sterling silver flatware and the Baccarat crystal," Theodosia said.

They all worked together for a good fifteen minutes, decorating the tea shop and making the tables sparkle.

"What else?" Beth Ann asked.

"Check for a pail of pink asters and some greenery that should have been delivered to the back door. Place a few stems in crystal vases and then add a few fluffy feathers."

"Anything I can do?" Miss Dimple asked.

"Grab the ceramic honey pots that Drayton filled and add wooden dippers."

"How perfect!" Miss Dimple squealed.

With more and more touches of Regency layered on, Theodosia was feeling pleased about the atmosphere in the tea shop. The swags of wisteria vines, in particular, lent a wonderful, vintage air. And the colors they'd chosen were all genteel pastels.

"Aren't you forgetting something?" Drayton asked.

"Your tea caddies?" Theodosia said.

"I didn't drag in half my collection for nothing."

Together, Theodosia and Drayton placed an antique tea caddy on each of the tables, which seemed to add the perfect touch.

Miss Dimple fingered one of the tea caddies. "Is this one real old?"

"That tea caddy, my dear lady, is from seventeenth-century England," Drayton said. "Mahogany inlaid with decorative marquetry."

"And inside?" Miss Dimple asked.

"Take a look-see."

Miss Dimple opened the tea caddy. "Three compartments?"

"Three *lidded* compartments, which would have housed three different teas, all of which the butler would have blended to the owner's taste."

"Well la-di-da," Miss Dimple said. "It's like touching actual history."

"And one more historic twist," Theodosia said.

"I think I know what's coming," Beth Ann said. "The dresses that are hanging in your office?"

Theodosia nodded. "That's right, we'll be wearing costumes today."

"Ooh." Miss Dimple clapped her hands together. "What are they?"

"They're basically high-waisted, Regency-era dresses," Theodosia said. "But they're easy to slide into because they button in back."

"Dibs on the pink one," Beth Ann cried.

"Is there a yellow dress?" Miss Dimple asked.

With a twinkle in her eye, Theodosia said, "Go check it out for yourself."

10

Wouldn't you know it? Delaine showed up early for the Regency Tea. With her niece, Bettina, in tow.

"Good heavens!" Delaine cried when she saw Theodosia in her Regency-style dress with her hair pinned up in a graceful topknot. "What Jane Austen book did you just crawl out of?"

"I'll have you know, it's the latest in Regency style," Theodosia said.

Delaine wrinkled her nose. "A lesson in why most styles eventually go *out* of style."

"Be nice," Bettina warned as she flashed an apologetic smile at Theodosia. "This is, after all, a Regency Tea that we bought tickets for."

"Yes, yes," Delaine said as she seated herself at a table and sighed. "I'm sorry, I'm all kerfuffled because something very strange happened to me this morning."

"What's that?" Theodosia asked.

"My phone was stolen," Delaine said.

"Stolen where?" Theodosia asked.

"From out of my house, I think." Delaine pushed her lips out, making her trademark lemon face. "It's the weirdest thing ever. I was positive I had my phone this morning. I mean, after I counted out my six almonds and twenty blueberries for breakfast, I left it on the kitchen counter and went upstairs to get dressed. When I came back down it wasn't there."

"Are you saying somebody broke in and stole just your phone?" Theodosia was fairly sure that hadn't happened.

"I don't know," Delaine said. "It sure seems that way."

"You probably just left it somewhere," Bettina said. "You tend to be a bit untethered at times."

Delaine looked stunned. "How can you *say* that when you *know* I'm an organizational whiz!"

Sensing a family dispute in the making, Theodosia quickly changed the subject.

"How are your wedding plans coming?" Theodosia asked Bettina. Much to Delaine's consternation, Bettina had recently become engaged to a young man by the name of Jamie Wilkes.

But Delaine jumped in before Bettina had a chance to answer.

"I wanted Bettina to wait and have a Christmas wedding," Delaine said. "Think how fabulous it would be to have a church wedding with hundreds of flickering white candles and strings of green garland sparkling with frosted red berries. And to top it off, a white horse and carriage waiting outside to carry them off to an elegant, fantasy-like reception."

"But I pushed the wedding up a bit," Bettina said. "To next month!"

"So soon," Theodosia murmured.

Bettina grinned. "Jamie and I don't want to wait."

"They're the Now Generation," Delaine said, somewhat peevishly. "They want it all right now."

"I'm sure it'll be a lovely wedding," Theodosia said. "Were you able to find your perfect venue given such a short time frame?"

"They want to do it *outside*," Delaine said, her voice tinged with bitterness.

"Right now we're deciding between an apple orchard and a flower farm," Bettina said.

"An autumn wedding," Theodosia said. "Sounds gorgeous."

"I think so," Bettina said, her eyes shining with happiness. "I'm thinking all jewel tones with an outdoor arch of white pampas grass and bright red bittersweet. Maybe a bridal bouquet of golden mums and dark red roses."

"And a horse-drawn carriage," Delaine said.

Bettina shrugged. "Sure. Why not. Who doesn't love the aroma of horses clinging to your wedding veil on the most important day of your life?"

With yet another family squabble simmering below the surface, Theodosia excused herself and went to join Drayton at the front door. Two guests had just arrived. He welcomed them heartily, then skillfully passed them off to Beth Ann so she could escort them to their table.

The floodgates opened then, and a horde of guests descended upon the Indigo Tea Shop. Brooke Carter Crocket, a local jeweler and owner of Hearts Desire, arrived along with Leigh Carroll, the entrepreneurial owner of the Cabbage Patch Gift Shop next door. Then a gang of regulars arrived that included Jill, Kristen, Allie, Judi, Lynda, and Jessica. Angie Congdon from the Featherbed House B and B arrived with two of her guests, followed by a women's garden tour group that was staying at the nearby Dove Cote Inn.

When all the guests were seated, Theodosia squared her shoulders and walked to the center of the room. This was the part she liked best, and this was also the part that gave her the jitters, because you never knew how a menu would be received. Yes, they'd enjoyed great success so far, but there was always a first time an event—or an experimental menu—could fall flat. Theodosia tucked a hand into the folds of her long dress and crossed her fingers for luck. Hopefully, this would prove to be a successful tea party.

"Welcome, dear guests, to the Indigo Tea Shop," Theodosia said. "We're delighted you could join us today for our Regency Tea." Her words, met by warm smiles and an encouraging spatter of applause, gave her the impetus to continue. "As you may know, the Regency era was ruled by elegance and etiquette. It was made even richer by the poetry and prose of Byron and Shelley, and the paintings of Constable and Turner. Romanticism was the watchword, and it was often said that the Regency era was a time of low morals and high fashion." Theodosia grabbed her skirts and gave an impromptu curtsy that drew another round of applause. "To give you a taste of the Regency era, we've created a special menu for you today. For our first course, our chef has baked apricot scones as well as traditional Bath buns. If you're not familiar with Bath buns, they're sweet, doughy buns that originated in Bath, England. Ours are topped with raisins and a sprinkle of crushed sugar. Both our scones and Bath buns will be served with Devonshire cream and a trio of fruit jams. Our second course of tea sandwiches includes a dill and cucumber tea sandwich and a Stilton cheese and chutney tea sandwich. For your main entrée, our chef has created a Welsh rarebit with cheddar cheese sauce. Dessert—if you still have room—will be a traditional British quaking pudding that's flavored with almonds and is similar to our modern-day panna cotta. And since this is a tea shop, with a resident tea sommelier, obviously there will be copious amounts of tea." Theodosia looked over at Drayton. "Drayton, will you do the honors?"

Drayton strode to the middle of the room with the urgency of a minister about to deliver a sermon. He inclined his head slightly, then said, "The favored tea during the Regency era was Chinese black tea. So that is what we shall be serving." He held up a finger. "But . . . I have also created a special blend of tea that I call my Regency Rose Blend. This is a black tea flavored with rose petals and a hint of vanilla. It's medium bodied and highly aromatic."

Drayton paused, which was the signal for Miss Dimple and Beth Ann to step forth with steaming hot teapots and begin filling teacups.

"And since our servers are ready and willing, please do enjoy your tea as well as your romantic Regency luncheon," Drayton said.

From then on it was a breeze. The scones and Bath buns were served and became an instant hit, then the tea sandwiches arrived. These were oohed and aahed over, and several guests even asked for recipes.

Some guests asked questions, as well.

"Excuse me," one of the women said to Theodosia. "The tiny pats of butter you put out for the Bath buns . . . they tasted so different from the butter I'm used to buying at Harris Teeter."

"That's because we serve English butter," Theodosia said. "English butter is churned for a longer time in order to achieve a higher fat content. That's why it has a slight tang and richer taste."

Another woman wanted to know the difference between herbal teas and tisanes.

"The term is basically interchangeable," Theodosia explained. "An herbal infusion or tisane is any plant-derived drink other than true tea."

Theodosia answered a few more questions, chatted with

guests, and checked in with the kitchen. Haley was just plating the entrées.

"You need help serving?" Theodosia asked.

"Negative," Haley said.

"We got this," Miss Dimple said as she hovered nearby with Beth Ann.

"You look like you're having fun," Theodosia said.

"I always have fun when you guys stage one of your special event teas," Miss Dimple said. "I remember when you had your Murder Mystery Tea." She turned to Beth Ann and said, "They hired genuine actors and had an entire cast of characters. Then, when the lights went down . . . kaboom! A murder took place and the guests had the fun of figuring out whodunit."

"Sounds great," Beth Ann said.

"It was a blast," Miss Dimple said as she loaded plates onto her tray and swept out of the kitchen.

The Welsh rarebit was enjoyed by everyone. And because Haley had made extra portions (she always did), Theodosia wolfed hers down in the kitchen.

"You sure you have enough Welsh rarebit left for Drayton?" Theodosia asked Haley.

"I'm sure," Haley said. "I wouldn't forget Drayton. I'd feel terrible if the poor dear went hungry."

Theodosia paused. "Now you're putting me on."

"You think? But seriously, there's gazillions of food, so I guarantee that Drayton won't starve."

The quaking pudding was served and more tea was poured. A couple of guests inquired about a dessert tea, so Drayton brewed pots of vanilla chai and cinnamon spice. As conversation wound down, candles guttered in their holders, and the luncheon tea wore down as well. A few people left to return to work. Others wandered around the tea room, greeting friends at other tables and shopping for gifts. Theodosia was kept busy at the front counter wrapping purchases that included tins of tea, tea trivets, jars of honey, and teacups and saucers. Everything was carefully wrapped in either bubble wrap or their signature indigo blue tissue paper, then placed in indigo blue bags.

Drayton tallied up the checks, accepted cash and credit cards, and made change. With his tortoiseshell half-glasses and careful manner, he looked like an old-timey bookkeeper keeping tabs on the receipts.

As the last of the guests milled about, checking out the grapevine wreaths that hung on the back wall, Theodosia edged closer to Drayton and said, "How much money do we have in cash?"

He blinked. "You mean actual funds in the till?"

"Yes."

"As of right now?"

"Right."

"Well, we cleared a little over twelve hundred on today's Regency Tea, and we probably have another nine hundred in cash. Why? Are you thinking about making a bank run?"

"Something like that," Theodosia said.

"Okay, but maybe wait until I take care of these last few guests."

"Got it."

Theodosia helped Miss Dimple and Beth Ann clear tables. Then, when the final guest exited the tea shop, she stepped behind the front counter. Opening their cash drawer, she silently counted out a series of twenties and fifties. She put the money in an envelope, then tucked the envelope in her purse for safe keeping.

"You got the money?" Drayton asked a few minutes later.

"Some of it," she said. "Did you get your Welsh rarebit? Haley said she saved a serving for you."

"I know she did and I'm going to chow down in about two minutes," Drayton said. "Before we get busy again with afternoon tea."

"Take your time," Theodosia said. "I'll play hostess to any arrivals. In the meantime, I'm going to set up the tables and restock shelves."

"Good. Our luncheon guests shopped us pretty hard."

"And thank goodness for that." Theodosia made a shooing motion. "Now go. Eat. Drink. Be merry. Well, maybe not all that merry since there's still work to be done."

Miss Dimple had cleared all the tables near the front door, so that's where Theodosia started. She put down white linen tablecloths and set out plates, cups, and saucers. She added glass teapot warmers that held small tea lights, then grabbed sugar bowls and small pitchers of cream.

As Theodosia worked, she thought about Duke Sadler. When Tidwell was in this morning, he'd been coy about Duke. Which led her to believe that Duke might have a somewhat checkered past.

All the more reason for me to attend the visitation for Harlan Sadler tonight.

Theodosia knew she could do some nosing around and even ask a few impertinent questions. Since it was a visitation, people would be polite and more inclined to talk to her, right? At least she hoped so.

"Theodosia?"

Theodosia turned to find Miss Dimple gazing at her.

"Yes?"

"What are we offering for afternoon tea? In the way of goodies, I mean?"

"Let me find out."

Theodosia scurried into the kitchen where Drayton was sitting on a stool, eating his Welsh rarebit, and talking to Haley.

"Haley," she said. "What baked goods are we offering for afternoon tea?"

"We've still got Bath buns and apricot scones," Haley said. "And I've got two pans of banana bread baking in the oven, which should be ready in . . ." She checked her timer. "Five minutes. Oh, and there are apple-walnut and lemon–poppy seed scones from this morning. Still plenty fresh, of course."

"Wonderful," Theodosia said.

Haley held up a finger. "If you want to do a kind of combo, I've got an entire brick of cheddar cheese left over, so we could do a cheddar cheese and chutney tea sandwich paired with a scone."

"Add a pot of tea to that," Drayton said. "Our guests always love a good combo."

"Then that's what we'll do," Theodosia said.

Back in the tea shop, she went to their chalkboard, wrote down all the offerings, and then, at the very bottom, did a funky line drawing of a scone and a tea sandwich on a plate nestled next to a small pot of tea. Under that she wrote, AFTERNOON SPECIAL: TEA, SCONE, & TEA SANDWICH $12.95.

"That's a good deal," Miss Dimple said as she looked over Theodosia's shoulder approvingly.

By midafternoon, with business humming along nicely, Theodosia said to Drayton, "You think you can manage without me?"

Drayton nodded. "Probably. Where are you off to? More investigating?"

"I just need to bug out for a quick errand and then I'll be back."

"Okay. But . . ."

"What?"

"You're going dressed like that?"

Theodosia looked down. "Oh, good grief." She was still wearing her Regency-era gown. "No, I'll for sure change."

Ten minutes later, back in her street clothes, Theodosia climbed into her Jeep and headed for Floral Drive. She wasn't sure if she could find the exact location of the apartment building again, but knew she had to try. After a few twists and turns, Theodosia figured she was in the basic vicinity. Then she had a bad moment when she made a wrong turn down an alley and two men working on a pickup truck gave her threatening looks. But Theodosia backed out of that alley and, two minutes later, found the intersection of Floral and Magnolia and the apartment building she'd been searching for.

Theodosia parked at the curb and sat there for a few minutes, listening as the engine ticked down. Then she grabbed her purse, climbed out of her Jeep, and walked up the cracked sidewalk.

Theodosia had no idea what she was going to say, and figured that words might make this exchange a little awkward. With that in mind, Theodosia knocked on the door and, when the woman opened the door to her small apartment, simply handed her the envelope.

The woman wore a fearful look on her face, as if she was being served with legal papers that heralded bad news. She shifted from one foot to the other and was dressed in the same pink uniform with the white lace collar and apron. This time she had a name tag that said CYNTHIA.

"What's this?" Cynthia asked in a trembling voice.

"It's a little help," Theodosia said, finally finding her voice. "It seems as if you and your kids could use a break."

The woman's eyes widened in surprise as she tore open the envelope and saw the stack of green bills. Then she shook her head as she stared at the money and said, "I can't accept this."

Theodosia smiled. "You already did."

"But . . ."

"For the kids," Theodosia said.

Cynthia clutched the envelope tightly to her chest as if it were a lifeline, which it probably was. "For the kids," she repeated. Then, "God bless you for your kindness." She reached for Theodosia's hand and squeezed it tightly.

Theodosia was still smiling as she climbed into her Jeep, but there were tears in her eyes, too.

Back at the Indigo Tea Shop, Miss Dimple and Beth Ann had left for the day, and Haley was sitting in Theodosia's office, her feet on the desk, reading a cookbook.

"How does a Toulouse-style cassoulet strike you?" Haley asked.

"Sounds complicated," Theodosia said.

"It is. This dish requires white beans, five different cuts of pork, and duck confit. But I think it would make a dandy entrée for our Moulin Rouge Tea."

"We're having a Moulin Rouge Tea?"

"Why not?" Haley said. "That's if Drayton gives his stamp of approval."

"Are you kidding? Drayton will adore the idea. He's a Francophile at heart. Loves French shoes, French antiques, and French wine. You should see his wine cellar. Vintages from all the great regions—Bordeaux, Champagne, Provence, the Rhone Valley."

"So you'll talk to Drayton about scheduling the tea?"

Theodosia tossed her jacket on the coatrack. "Count on it." She walked into the tea room where she found Drayton rearranging his shelves of tea tins. Sometimes he did them alphabetically, sometimes by country of origin. For all she knew, he could do it according to astrological signs.

"I'm supposed to schedule a Moulin Rouge Tea with you," Theodosia said.

Drayton turned and gave a cursory smile. "I've already got it on the calendar for mid-October."

"You're always a step ahead, aren't you?"

Drayton let out a long, thoughtful, "Mmmm." Then said, "Where'd I put my tin of toasted coconut tea? Oh, there you are, you little rascal." Then he focused on Theodosia and said, with all sincerity, "Can I go to Harlan Sadler's visitation dressed like this or should I go home and change?"

Now it was Theodosia's turn to give an appraising "Mmmm." Drayton wore a Harris Tweed blazer, blue oxford shirt, gray slacks, Church's shoes, and his trademark bow tie. He looked like he'd just stepped off the pages of *GQ* magazine.

"You want my opinion?" Theodosia said, "I think you should go home and put on a Nike hoodie and your sloppy tennis shoes."

"I don't have any sloppy tennis shoes." Then, "What's a Nike hoodie?"

"I rest my case."

11

At seven fifteen, they pulled into the parking lot of Francis Brothers Funeral Home and parked in the last row.

"Lots of people here for the visitation," Drayton remarked.

"And on such short notice," Theodosia said.

Drayton studied Theodosia in the dim light of the console. "You think Cricket wanted to speed things up? Get her husband in the ground before anybody started asking tough questions?"

"The idea had occurred to me," Theodosia said.

"How very suspicious of you."

"Not really. I'm ninety-nine, maybe ninety-eight percent sure Cricket didn't have her own husband murdered," Theodosia said.

"But someone wanted him dead."

"Now we just have to figure out who."

"We?"

Theodosia shut off the engine. "Come on, Drayton, you know we're in this together."

"Maybe we are."

They climbed out of the Jeep and threaded their way through an ocean of cars.

"It does seem like an awful lot of people showed up," Drayton said.

"Harlan probably had lots of friends and business associates. And there are always a few curiosity seekers," Theodosia said.

"I read somewhere that it's not unusual for random strangers to show up at visitations and funerals," Drayton said. "Funeral directors refer to them as 'professional ghouls.'"

"How macabre."

"You know arsonists sometimes show up at fires, just to watch the drama and excitement brought about by their own handiwork."

"Are you going somewhere with this?" Theodosia asked.

"I was thinking that perhaps a murderer might show up at their victim's visitation or funeral."

"Thank you for that lovely thought," Theodosia said. "It's something to keep in mind."

Stepping into the lobby of the funeral home, they were immediately assaulted by an odor that Theodosia thought of as sixty percent floral and forty percent chemical. But that was the extent of her analysis. She wasn't interested in pursuing it any further.

"Nice," Drayton said as he looked around. "Bright and homey, but without that overdone decorator touch."

Theodosia jabbed an elbow into Drayton's ribs. The place was funereal with a capital *F*. Wine-colored carpeting, floral chairs and sofas, innocuous landscape paintings featuring lots of hopeful, glowing sunsets, and low cocktail tables that held no cocktails—just boxes of tissues.

"We're here for the Sadler visitation," Drayton told a morose-looking, black-suited attendant who was straightening a vase of gladiolas that didn't need straightening.

"Slumber Room B," the attendant intoned.

They walked into a large room filled elbow to elbow with people. The decibel level was so high it sounded like a magpie convention. People argued, shouted, laughed, and talked on their phones.

"This is positively awful," Drayton said. "Makes me want to turn around and leave."

"Try not to let it get to you," Theodosia said. "I guess visitations aren't as formal and sedate as they once were."

"More bad behavior, pointing to a complete and total societal breakdown."

"You'll get no argument from me."

But as they walked toward the front of the room where Harlan Sadler's coffin rested on a mahogany bier, the noise level dropped. This was the quiet part of the room.

It was also the part of the room that Theodosia didn't much care for. She wasn't a fan of the open coffin, and this coffin was definitely open for business.

"Oh sweet dogs, he's wearing gloves," Drayton whispered as they approached Sadler's coffin.

"Because his hands . . ."

"Don't say it!"

"Okay, okay," Theodosia said as she fixed her gaze on poor Harlan Sadler. He looked pale, waxy, and well dressed. Sadler was being laid to rest in one of his two-thousand-dollar banker's suits, which made Theodosia wonder if the undertaker had to cut it up the back to make it fit. Then she shivered and tried to shake off that awful thought.

The coffin was surrounded by an ocean of white lilies with

two pillar candles at each end. A red velvet kneeler was parked in front of it, should someone be inclined to kneel down to pray, and there was a wooden stand with a guest book and fountain pen.

Theodosia was not inclined to kneel, but did sign the guest book. Drayton did neither, but instead headed straight toward Cricket to offer his heartfelt condolences.

Cricket was seated in a plum-colored, high-backed chair, and wore a black skirt suit, diamond earrings, and classy black stilettos. Theodosia wondered if they were the same Louboutins she'd worn the other night at the masquerade party.

"Drayton, Theodosia," Cricket said as she dabbed at her eyes. "Thank you for coming." Her voice was rough, as if she'd been crying.

"Of course," Drayton said.

"We wouldn't miss it," Theodosia said.

Cricket indicated the two older women who were seated next to her. "These are Harlan's cousins from Seagrove, Lenore and Verna."

"My condolences," Drayton said to them as he shook their hands. "So you ladies hail from South Carolina's pottery country."

"Indeed, we do," Verna said, seeming pleased. "We have more than fifty pottery shops, galleries, and studios along Highway 705."

"Or what we like to call the Pottery Highway," Lenore added.

"So many wonderful artists," Drayton said. "I'm always impressed by all the raku, stoneware, and salt-glazed pottery that's produced there. I, myself, have a Joseph Sand teapot in my collection."

"Lucky you," said Verna.

Theodosia shook hands with the three women and murmured her condolences as well. Then she glanced up to find Delaine frantically waving at her.

"Theodosia!" Delaine called out in a stage whisper. "Over here."

Theodosia and Drayton eased their way through the crowded room to join Delaine. Then, as if by magic, Delaine suddenly produced a tall, barrel-chested man from out of the crowd. "Theo, Drayton, this is Ned Grady," Delaine cooed. She turned to Grady and batted her eyes shamelessly at him. "You remember, dear, that I told you all about my very dear friends Theo and Drayton?"

"Yes, indeed," Grady said. "It's nice to finally meet you both. Put faces to names, even though we're meeting under such sad circumstances."

"You knew Harlan Sadler well?" Theodosia said.

"We were great friends," Grady said.

"And I understand you're on the Opera Society's board of directors," Drayton said, shaking Grady's hand.

"More like I got shanghaied by this one." Grady nodded at Delaine and smiled. "But I have to say, I am enjoying it immensely." Ned Grady was turned out tonight in a pink sport coat with a pale blue shirt and tan slacks. His eyes were a watery blue and his brownish-blond hair was combed straight back and worn longish. He had a snappy black Rado on his left wrist and a gold pinky ring on his little finger. For Delaine's sake, Theodosia decided not to hold the pinky ring against him.

As Drayton and Ned Grady chatted, Delaine pulled Theodosia aside and whispered, "What do you think?"

"Good looking, seems very sweet. I think you picked a winner this time," Theodosia said. "What's he do for a living?"

"He's a big-time broker at Connaught and King."

"Impressive."

"I'll say. And not afraid to show a girl a good time. After this he's taking me to dinner at High Cotton."

"Lucky you. I understand they recently won an award from the National Restaurant Association."

"We'll probably order something positively sinful, as well as a bottle of champagne. Hopefully Dom Pérignon."

"Only the best for Delaine," Ned Grady said, catching part of their conversation as he and Drayton came over to join them.

Theodosia kept a tight smile on her face and said, "Delaine's always had a penchant for champagne and caviar."

"I'm beginning to see that," Grady said.

"By the way . . ." Theodosia touched Delaine's arm. "Do you know who was in charge of hiring the entertainers for the Mad Hatter Masquerade?"

"That would be me," Grady said. "But all I basically did was outsource it to the Westside Theatre Company. They're the ones who auditioned the characters and dressed them up in costumes."

"Do you remember who you worked with there?" Theodosia asked.

"Sure, it was the company's executive director, Peter Tolboth."

"Thanks," Theodosia said.

Delaine gazed up at Grady and said, "Time to honor those dinner reservations, sweetie?" She clamped her best death grip on his forearm and yanked him away.

"Like a lamb to the slaughter," Drayton said. "That poor man doesn't have a clue as to what he's in for."

"Maybe he'll figure out how to handle her," Theodosia said. Then she laughed and said, "No, he won't. Dealing with Delaine is like riding an angry longhorn steer. All you can do is hang on and hope for the best."

"Perhaps we should pay a visit to the refreshment table?" Drayton suggested.

"Why not?"

But as Theodosia passed a woman in a severely tailored navy blue suit, she couldn't help but overhear part of her conversation, which was . . . "The only reason I'm here tonight is to make sure the old pirate is really dead."

"Emily?" Theodosia stuttered out. "Emily Bates?"

The woman's head swiveled in Theodosia's direction. "Yes?" She was polite but wary.

"Could we talk for a moment?" Theodosia was shocked that she'd run into Emily Bates like this. It was bizarre but also serendipitous.

"You have me at a disadvantage," Emily said. She had a thin, almost bird-like face, thin lips, and short dark hair that looked more chopped than styled. "You apparently know who I am, but I don't know you. Or at least I don't recognize you."

Theodosia touched a hand to her chest. "I'm Theodosia Browning. I own the Indigo Tea Shop over on Church Street."

Emily gave an acknowledging nod, but her expression was cool.

"I've agreed to look into things for Mrs. Sadler."

"I see." Now Emily's tone was cool as well.

"I guess what I really meant to say was . . . I'm looking into her husband's murder."

Emily raised her brows in a show of faux confusion. "Who did you say you were again?"

"Theodosia Browning."

"And you brew tea and investigate murders? In that order? How very clever of you." Now Emily Bates was being downright dismissive.

Theodosia decided she could show a little flint and be just as tough as this woman was—or thought she was.

"I wanted to speak to you because I know you and Harlan Sadler didn't exactly see eye to eye. Especially when it concerned Copernicus Financial's interest in merging with your bank."

"Harlan Sadler tried to engineer a hostile takeover of Unity One!" Emily spat out.

"From what I read in the Business section of the newspaper, your board of directors was actually in favor of a merger."

Emily closed her eyes for a second, then opened them and focused squarely on Theodosia. "Is there a point to this conversation?"

"I don't think I can be any more clear," Theodosia said. "I'm talking to . . . interviewing . . . the people who most wanted Harlan Sadler out of the way."

Emily was completely aghast. "And you think *I'd* stoop to murder? Just to get a pathetically megalomaniac banker out of the way?"

"I don't know. Would you?"

"This discussion is over!" Emily snapped.

"But the investigation isn't," Theodosia said as Emily turned away. "Not by a long shot."

Emily turned back to her, eyes blazing, practically baring her teeth. "Since you're barking up the wrong tree, I'm going to give you a friendly kick in the *right* direction."

"And what might that be?"

"You see that man over there? The older, white-haired man in the windowpane-check jacket?"

Theodosia turned to look.

"That's Ray Crispin, Harlan Sadler's partner in The Lanvesco Group. He and Harlan were in the process of splitting everything up."

"You mean the company?"

"The company, the assets, everything." Emily's eyes gleamed. "Now, Crispin is probably dancing a jig that everything belongs to him. So *that's* who you should be talking to!" Emily shot a triumphant look at Theodosia and walked stiffly away.

Drayton returned a few minutes later with a glass of sherry for Theodosia. "Who was that lady?"

"That was no lady. That was Emily Bates."

Drayton stifled a laugh. "The banker?"

"President at Unity One."

"Which kind of sounds like it should be a political organization." He held up a glass of sherry. "Care for a glass of sherry? I checked the label and it's Valdespino Solera. Fairly decent wine, usually goes for around fifty dollars a bottle."

"Hang on a minute, Drayton. I need to talk to someone else, okay?"

"Since you're the one who's driving, I don't really have a choice."

"Five minutes, okay?"

He held up one glass, then the other. "Two glasses of lovely dry sherry? No problem. Take another thirty minutes if you like."

Ray Crispin looked like he was getting ready to leave as Theodosia hurried over to greet him.

"Mr. Crispin, could I possibly have a few minutes of your time?"

Ray Crispin stopped and flashed a friendly smile. "Call me Crispy. Everyone does."

"Crispy, then."

"What can I do for you, young lady?" Ray Crispin had keen gray eyes, a ruddy complexion, and a shock of white hair. He was probably in his high seventies, but looked as if he kept in shape—maybe worked out, probably played golf or tennis a couple of times a week.

"This might sound a bit presumptuous," Theodosia said, once she'd introduced herself and mentioned her relationship with Cricket Sadler. "But Emily Bates just told me that you and Harlan Sadler were in the process of splitting up your business."

Crispy eyed her. "Did that crazy witch insinuate that I had something to do with Harlan's murder?"

"I'd say she was trying her best to nudge me in that direction."

"Well of course I didn't kill Harlan. He and I were partners in our real estate company for almost twenty years."

"But you *were* splitting up?"

Crispy shook his head. "More like slowly cashing out, taking our well-earned profits. We owned a lot of land, and prices have gone sky-high lately. So we started selling off parcels to developers, so we could finally reap the benefits. Fact is, neither of us were spring chickens anymore."

"So selling off the properties and taking profits was really a retirement strategy."

"Exactly. And we weren't planning on firing anyone at the office. Just, hopefully, moving them over to Duke's company."

"Sounds like you had a smart exit strategy," Theodosia said. "But what about Harlan's share?"

"That goes to Cricket. And, I suppose, to Duke, depending on how Harlan set up his will or trust or whatever he had. I don't really know all the details." Crispy paused. "Now. About Emily Bates. That lady is one slippery she-devil. She resisted the idea— no, she *hated* the idea—that her bank could be taken over by a larger banking corporation."

"You're talking about Copernicus Financial."

"For sure. And the sad thing is, a takeover, or merger, or

whatever you want to call it, would have surely benefited her customers."

"How so?" Theodosia asked.

"Deeper pockets would mean more loans available to small businesses that are just getting started, as well as loans to existing businesses seeking to expand their enterprise."

"So, favorable for commercial accounts."

"Good for consumer accounts, as well. It would have meant Unity One could offer brokerage capabilities, estate planning, trusts . . . really all sorts of smart financial tools."

"So Emily Bates holding out was also holding back progress."

"Essentially, yes." Crispy cocked an eye at Theodosia and said, "You seem to have taken quite an interest in Harlan's murder."

"Like I said, I promised Cricket that I'd look into things for her."

"'Look into' means what exactly?"

"Snooping around, asking questions . . ."

"Running a shadow Investigation?" Crispy said. He seemed intrigued by the idea.

"I suppose you could call it that."

"Are you one of those Internet people who dig around for clues and try to crowdsource solving a crime?"

"No, it's just me. And at this point, it's mostly informal digging."

"Have you taken a hard look at Duke?" Crispy asked.

"At Harlan's son?" Theodosia pretended to be surprised.

"He wasn't really Harlan's son, you know."

Now Theodosia was surprised. "Excuse me?"

12

"*Duke's not Harlan's* biological son," Crispy said. "Duke is Cricket's boy from her first marriage to Earl Donaldson. But Harlan was always like a father to Duke. Raised him as his own, paid for his fancy education at Princeton where he was eventually expelled. Bailed him out of all sorts of trouble, and still bankrolled Duke's real estate company."

"A generous man," Theodosia said, even as she was reeling from this latest revelation.

"Maybe too generous," Crispy said. "Still, Harlan took Duke under his wing and tried to teach him a few things."

"Did it work?"

Crispy offered a downturned face and swept a hand in the direction of the refreshments table. "Take a look at him over there." His brows knit together. "What do you think?"

Theodosia turned to see Duke Sadler yucking it up with one of the pretty young women who'd been hired to serve glasses of sherry and slices of imported cheese. As they watched, Duke whispered something in the girl's ear, then put his hand on her shoulder and squeezed.

"A ladies' man," Crispy said.

"If that's what you want to call it," Theodosia said. Then, "I've heard more than a few rumors about Duke scamming people in real estate deals."

"It's not a rumor. It's fact," Crispy said. "Duke's office is next to mine, so I got an occasional earful. I remember one fellow Duke got involved with—a guy by the name of Wes Lenkov. Duke burned Lenkov and two of his buddies big time on a condo deal over on James Island. Lenkov put in all the legwork and sweat equity. He found a parcel of land and started the wheels turning on financing. While he was waiting for his loan to be approved, he obtained permits, hired an architect, and began talks with building contractors. Then Duke waltzed in, flipped Lenkov off, and offered a cash deal to the landowner. Yup, Lenkov got burned big time."

"Interesting. Where's Lenkov now?"

"He exited the real estate business fast. Now he sells and customizes high-end sports cars. He's got a fancy showroom and garage not too far from here." Crispy shrugged. "Anyway, if you're looking for suspects—and it appears that you are—maybe take a second look at Good Time Charlie over there. He's not endeared himself to a whole lot of people, as far as I can see."

"Thank you," Theodosia said. "I will take a hard look at him."

A few minutes later, Drayton drifted over to her, a half-empty glass in hand and a smile on his face. "Are you ready to leave?"

"I think so," Theodosia said. "But . . . I need to ask Cricket one quick question, okay?"

"Go for it."

Theodosia made her way over to where Cricket was sitting. She was by herself now. The cousins must have left.

When Cricket saw Theodosia, she said, "This is such a nightmare, sitting here next to my dead husband . . . knowing that, after his funeral tomorrow, I'll never see him again."

Theodosia knelt down and took Cricket's hand in her own. "I know. And I'm truly sorry for your loss. My heart aches for you, and I wish there was something more I could do."

"You've done plenty," Cricket said, as a tear trickled down her cheek. She squeezed Theodosia's hand, then let it go. "Just knowing you're out there asking questions, running your own version of an investigation into my husband's murder, fills me with hope."

"I wanted to ask you something," Theodosia said. "About Duke."

"Sure," Cricket said. She reached down and picked up a tartan-plaid handbag. "What is it you want to know?" She dug into her bag for a fresh hankie.

But Theodosia was momentarily startled at the sight of the tartan-plaid handbag. She recognized it as the exact same plaid as Harlan Sadler's bow tie—the bow tie he'd worn at the Mad Hatter Masquerade.

"Your tartan bag," Theodosia said. "This is meaningful to you?"

"This is Harlan's family tartan," Cricket said proudly. "There's a crest, too. See?" She flipped her bag around to reveal an embroidered gold crest. "And we used tartan-plaid ribbon to decorate the wreath over his coffin."

Theodosia spun around to look at the coffin. She hadn't noticed the tartan-plaid ribbon or even the wreath before. Now it stuck out. Stuck in her brain, too.

"Harlan was wearing a tartan-plaid bow tie at the Mad Hatter Masquerade, wasn't he?" Theodosia asked.

"Yes, he was. He adored that plaid bow tie. Said it grounded him, connected him to his ancestors."

"Um, what about Duke?"

"I had to talk him into it, but Duke wore a matching plaid bow tie that night as well."

"Ohmigosh!" Theodosia cried, as an idea exploded in her brain with the force of a newly gestated star.

Cricket's eyes fluttered in nervous confusion. "Why are you asking? What's wrong?"

"What if your son, Duke, was the intended target?"

"What!" Cricket looked startled. Her face turned deathly pale, then she touched a shaking hand to the base of her throat and let loose a series of choking sounds.

"Hear me out," Theodosia said, as this new hypothesis quickly congealed. "It was dark at the masquerade, with lots of entertainment happening all around us. Harlan and Duke were basically dressed alike in tuxedos and tartan-plaid bow ties. Maybe, just maybe, in the dim, flickering light, the killer mistook Harlan for Duke."

"You mean someone wanted to kill my *son*? That's preposterous!" In the blink of an eye, Cricket had gone from frightened to indignant.

"Is it really?" Theodosia asked.

"Well . . . uh." Cricket's mouth snapped shut as she thought about it some more.

"Please tell me," Theodosia said. "Has Duke been in trouble? Does he have any enemies?"

Cricket sat there silently for a few moments, her hands moving, worrying the diamond rings on her fingers. Then she said, "I don't think so."

"Are you sure? If you really want my help, then you have to be completely upfront about this."

"I mean, well . . . I don't know," Cricket said.

"Does the name Wes Lenkov mean anything to you?"

"Maybe. The name *sounds* familiar."

"There was a lawsuit," Theodosia prompted.

"Could have been."

"Maybe I should ask Duke directly," Theodosia said.

"Please don't frighten Duke or threaten him or do anything to make him upset," Cricket begged. "He's . . . he's really quite sensitive."

Theodosia wondered where Duke's sensitivity was when he was yelling at his tenant about the rent, but she held her tongue.

"I'm sorry," Cricket said. "I find it totally improbable to believe that Duke was the intended target." She put a hand over her mouth and rocked back and forth as tears began to stream down her face. When she finally managed to get her emotions under control, she looked at Theodosia and said, "How can you even *say* such a thing?"

Theodosia sighed. "Because it might be true."

"Okay," Drayton said, once they were ensconced in Theodosia's Jeep and wending their way home. "Tell me what was going on back there. Who was the white-haired guy you were talking to? And why did Cricket look so devastated after you went and talked to her this last time?"

"The older gent was Ray Crispin, also known as Crispy. He was Harlan Sadler's real estate partner who opened my eyes to quite a few things."

"Like what?"

"Like Duke is not Harlan's biological son," Theodosia said.

"What!" Drayton just about levitated out of his seat.

"He's from Cricket's first marriage. Harlan kind of semi-adopted Duke and brought him up with a silver spoon in his mouth."

"That changes everything," Drayton said.

"Just wait. I also found out there was a bad business deal between Duke and a car dealer named Wes Lenkov. I got the feeling the two men hated each other."

"So why would Lenkov attack Harlan instead of the son—or the non-son?"

"Here's the kicker to the whole evening," Theodosia said. She turned down Meeting Street, passed The Peninsula Grill where, per tradition, the lanterns in the courtyard were always lit by hand. She drove past the Meeting Street Inn, Miss Sassy's Cork and Fork, and Cleo's Oyster Bar.

Once Theodosia had her thoughts straight, she told Drayton about the tartan-plaid bow ties that both men had worn to the masquerade, and how Duke might have possibly been the intended target.

"You detected all this while I was sipping sherry and talking to boring Mr. Greenburg who owns the wallpaper store down the block from us? Listening to him go on about paste versus pre-glued?"

"Yup. Lots of weird twists and turns kept popping up. Which means lots more for us to think about, huh?"

"Almost too much," Drayton said. "Where do we even start?"

"First off, we need to know more about Wes Lenkov, this car guy. Maybe I'll run an Internet search on him. Then I'll try to find out if Duke has any more enemies besides Lenkov. See if Duke was involved in any more lawsuits."

"How are you going to manage that?"

"I'll do an Internet search. If that doesn't turn up anything, I'll resort to the old-fashioned way . . . ," Theodosia said. "Go to the courthouse and look at records."

"Ah."

"I'm also going to attend the funeral tomorrow and for sure keep my eyes and ears open," Theodosia said. "It's amazing the things you overhear."

"I'm going to pass on the funeral," Drayton said. "We've got the Chocolate Stroll and I want to be ready."

"Drayton, you were born ready."

"I know, but I want to be extra ready."

Theodosia chuckled.

"Okay," Drayton said. "I'll admit it. I'm a little OCD. There, does that make you happy?"

"Drayton, I'm ecstatic." Theodosia cut over to Horlbeck Alley, heading for Drayton's home.

"Here, I almost forgot." Drayton passed her a paper napkin folded into a square envelope.

"What's this? What's in here?"

"Cheese," Drayton said. "I noticed you didn't eat a single bite at the visitation."

"I didn't have time." But Theodosia was already biting into one of the cheese squares. "Thanks loads, this is delicious. Creamy and kind of tangy at the same time."

"That's blueberry Brie from Blue Horse Farm in Oregon," Drayton said. "There's some nice sharp cheddar there, too."

Theodosia nibbled and chatted as she wound her way through the Historic District, finally pulling up in front of Drayton's home. He lived in an elegantly refurbished brick home that had once been owned by a Civil War doctor. Now, it boasted a historically accurate exterior and a gorgeous interior that featured hand-painted wallpaper, oil paintings, English furniture, and French antiques.

"Do you want to come in?" Drayton asked. "I can fix you something more substantial than a few squares of cheese."

"Thank you, but I want to get home and do a little research."

"And you're attending Sadler's funeral tomorrow morning?" he said.

"I think so, yes."

"Alright, then, good night and good luck."

13

~✿~

Theodosia had come away from the visitation with one additional name to check out, and that was Wes Lenkov, the man
who'd been suckered by Duke Sadler. So as soon as she arrived
home, she kicked off her shoes, changed into comfy clothes, and
took Earl Grey out into the backyard for his nightly sniff. The
evening had turned cool, and there was a scatter of stars in the
blue-black sky. If she squinted, she could just make out Cygnus,
the swan, and Aquila, the eagle. And was that Sagittarius hanging low in the western sky? She wasn't sure. Looked like it
might be.

Now that Theodosia had given herself a crook in her neck,
she lured her dog back inside with a jerky treat, locked up the
house, and turned off all the lights.

Gotta button everything up. Can never be too careful these days.

Five minutes later, Theodosia was upstairs, reclining on her
bed with her laptop, starting her research on Lenkov.

The first thing she found was a short article from the Charleston *Post & Courier.* Turns out, Wes Lenkov owned a company

called Sport Luxe located over on Society Street. According to the article, Sport Luxe bought and sold high-end sports cars, such as Jaguars, Porsches, Ferraris, and Alfa Romeos. Getting interested now, Theodosia clicked over to the Sport Luxe website. It had a glitzy splash page that featured a driver's through-the-windshield view of a Porsche 911 zipping around the track at Myrtle Beach Speedway.

Huh, pretty cool. Definitely appealing to sports car nuts.

Other sections included an inventory of new and used cars for sale, car customization options, and a list of upcoming road rallies and car shows. Just for fun, Theodosia looked up the price on a used Porsche 911, a car she had always coveted. And found that a 2017 model was priced at—*holy buckets*—seventy-eight thousand dollars! How could a *used* car cost so much? How many scones, how many cups of tea, would she have to sell to afford that baby?

Anyway. Wes Lenkov looked like a businessman who had lots of bases covered and was definitely on the way up. Of course, Theodosia wanted to pay him a visit, so she could get that all-important firsthand impression.

Theodosia rolled her chair back, wiggled her shoulders, and massaged the back of her neck where a dull pain had started to insinuate itself. She was tired and still had to select an outfit for the funeral tomorrow. Still, she had a burning curiosity about Duke Sadler. The more she saw of him, the more she learned about the man, the less she liked him.

Could Duke have murdered his stepfather? Maybe. Possibly. The jury was still out on that.

Theodosia went back to work, this time focusing her Internet research on Duke. And, lo and behold, after more digging, discovered that Duke did indeed have a few more enemies—if that's what you wanted to call them. It seems that Duke Sadler had been involved in a hellacious lawsuit two years ago. He'd crashed his speedboat, a Sea Ray 250, on Lake Moultrie and killed his girlfriend, a woman named Susan Markham. Theodosia hunted around but couldn't find anything that told her how that lawsuit had turned out.

Then, besides the Wes Lenkov suit that Crispy told her about, she found another real estate lawsuit filed against Duke Sadler. He had allegedly owed $2.5 million to two ex-partners— guys by the name of Tom Dudley and Barry Milne. They sued him over a failed real estate development, but somehow that suit had been either dropped or settled out of court.

"Two point five million," Theodosia said out loud.

Earl Grey looked up at her from where he was curled up, nose to tail, on his overstuffed, overpriced doggy bed.

"That sounds like two point five million reasons to kill someone," she said. "And why did the lawsuit just go away? Could it be that an influential banker had stepped in to grease a few palms?"

A half hour later, Theodosia was still scouring the Internet as Earl Grey snored softly in his sleep.

Tweedle-deedle, tweedle-deedle.

"What?" A groggy Theodosia rolled over in bed and groaned. *Tweedle-deedle.*

"Is that my stupid cell phone? What time is it anyway?"

Theodosia sat up in bed and grabbed her cell phone off the nightstand. With a note of trepidation in her voice, because no good calls ever came in the middle of the night, she said, "Hello?"

"Theo, we got problems!" cried a just-this-side-of-hysterical Haley.

Now Theodosia sat bolt upright in bed. "What's wrong?"

"Somebody broke in downstairs!" Haley cried. "They're rummaging around in your office!"

"They're there now?" Theodosia's heart thudded in her chest as her brain bonked into overdrive. Who could it be? What did they want? Would Haley be okay?

"I can hear them moving around downstairs," Haley said in a hoarse whisper.

"Is the door to your apartment locked?"

"Yes!"

"Have you called the police?"

"Just did. The dispatcher said they're on their way."

"You did all you could. Now grab Teacake and lock yourself in the bathroom. I'll be there in ten minutes."

"Promise?" Haley said.

Theodosia was already out of bed and getting dressed. "I'm on my way."

By the time Theodosia pulled into the alley behind the Indigo Tea Shop, the initial excitement had died down. A blue-and-white cruiser was there, its red and blue lights twirling lazily, as if to convey that the incident was no longer code red. The back door of the tea shop stood partially open, the lights were on in her office, and Haley was talking to two uniformed officers. Haley's orange-and-brown cat, Teacake, was cradled in her arms.

The first words out of Haley's mouth when Theodosia came rushing in were, "You came!"

"Of course," Theodosia said as she grabbed Haley and hugged her tightly. Then she kissed the girl's cheek, and asked, "Haley, are you okay? You didn't get hurt, did you?"

"I'm still a little shaken up," Haley said. She was big-eyed and talking a little too fast—probably the result of too much adrenaline in her system. "But, all things considered, I'm pretty fine."

Theodosia gave Teacake a gentle pat on the head, then turned her attention to the two officers.

"Did they hit the cash drawer?" Theodosia asked. "Is that what this was about?"

"Ma'am," said the taller of the officers, a young, earnest-looking man whose name tag read T. ERWIN, "I don't think they even made it into your café."

"Tea shop," said Theodosia.

"Tea shop," said the other officer, an older Black man with a shaved head and clipped mustache, whose name tag read J. PURDY.

"Then what did they want?" Theodosia asked. "I've never heard of a robbery where the perpetrators weren't interested in money."

There was a long pause, and then Officer Erwin said, "Looks more like vandalism."

"What?" Theodosia said.

"I'm afraid your chocolate bars are all busted up." Officer Erwin stepped aside to reveal a half dozen cases of chocolate bars upended and smashed on the floor. Labels were torn off, in some cases the foil protecting the bars had ripped open, and chocolate had been ground into Theodosia's Oriental carpet.

"Who would do such a thing?" Theodosia wondered out loud.

"Kids?" Officer Purdy offered.

"Maybe," Theodosia said slowly. But she was suddenly thinking about her shadow investigation into Harlan Sadler's death, and the childish behavior exhibited by several of the people she'd earmarked as suspects. Could one of them have done this? Maybe. Did they know her tea shop was supposed to take part in the

Chocolate Stroll tomorrow? Well, since it was after midnight, today? Possibly. Worst-case scenario, was somebody trying to knock her off-balance? Could be. Was it working? Not on your life.

The officers waited while Theodosia called an all-night hardware store. Then, while she was still on the phone, recommended she order a more substantial door with a double lock.

"You might consider installing better lighting in your alley, too," Officer Purdy suggested.

"I'll do that," Theodosia said. "Thank you." She walked the officers to the door, thanked them again, and waved goodbye. Turning back to Haley, she said. "You're shaking."

"I guess I'm still a little bit scared." Haley's chin quivered as she spoke.

"You want to come home with me? Spend the night at my house? Or maybe go over to Ben's place?" Ben was Haley's boyfriend.

Haley shook her head. "No, I'll be okay." Then, "You're going to stay here until the hardware store guy comes, aren't you?"

"Of course," Theodosia said. "And thank you for being so brave."

A single tear trickled down Haley's cheek. "I'm sorry all your chocolate bars got smashed."

"No, Haley," Theodosia said, embracing Haley again. "The most important thing is that *you're* safe. It's the only thing that really matters."

14

❦

The morning dawned overcast and a little cool. Perfect weather for a funeral. Theodosia wore her good black skirt suit—the one she thought of as her funeral suit—and drove over to the intersection of Broad and Meeting Streets where St. Michael's Church was located. She found a parking spot a block and a half away, then walked past St. Michael's Alley and a small cemetery, heading for the church. As she walked, she called Drayton on her cell phone.

When Drayton answered, Theodosia said, "It's me. You saw what happened to the chocolate bars?"

"Yes. Haley's been filling me in on the whole mess. Awful. But thank goodness we've managed to salvage some of the bars where the foil wasn't ripped. Lucky you had extra labels printed."

"Pretty strange, huh? A break-in but no robbery?"

"It *does* seem strange that the only point was vandalism."

"Did you look around? Is anything missing?"

"Everything seems to be in place. The cash drawer hasn't

been touched," Drayton said. He hesitated. "What do you think last night's agenda really was?"

"I think someone knows we've been investigating Harlan Sadler's murder and they're trying to throw us offtrack. Send us a warning."

"That means we've made someone very uncomfortable," Drayton said.

"Touched off a vibration in their spiderweb," Theodosia said.

"Which means we're going to have to be a whole lot more careful."

"Don't I know it," Theodosia said as she suddenly found herself surrounded by a throng of mourners. "I gotta go, Drayton, I'm at the church. See you in a couple of hours."

Theodosia silenced her phone's ringer as she walked into St. Michael's Church. It was one of the oldest surviving religious structures in Charleston, boasted a massive steeple, and was fronted by four large columns. She elbowed her way through the door and saw that, just like last night's visitation, the joint was jumping. Which caused Theodosia to wonder, once again, *Who are all these people?*

But as she looked around and saw how most of the mourners were dressed, she decided they were probably employees of Elysian Bank, Copernicus Financial, and The Lanvesco Group . . . and maybe a few real estate clients and country club cronies, as well. So that would definitely account for such a large crowd.

Theodosia sat down in one of the box pews near the back of the church and looked around. Built in the seventeen fifties, it was a lovely church. The clean lines and box pews lent a true Colonial feel, and the enormous brass chandelier overhead imparted a warm glow. A Tiffany stained glass window had been added in 1905 and gave St. Michael's a true sense of grandeur.

Just as Theodosia was counting the number of saints in a row of stained glass windows, trying to remember their names, the organ music started up. It rose in a curtain of sound, swelling to the opening notes of "How Great Thou Art."

Everyone who was sitting suddenly stood up. Everyone who was still filing in scurried to take a seat.

Then the funeral procession began. Theodosia turned to see a sliver of casket as it was nosed up the aisle. Then, quick as a jackrabbit, Bill Glass darted ahead of the casket, looking somber in a rumpled blue suit and intense in his mission. He spun in his tracks and began walking backward ahead of the casket as it rolled along on a metal carriage, a camera lifted to his face. Glass was either taking photos nonstop or shooting video—Theodosia wasn't sure which. She just knew that Glass looked annoying and intrusive. On the other hand, he must have gotten Cricket's permission, because nobody had tossed him out yet.

Then the full casket came into view, topped with a spray of red roses entwined with tartan ribbon. Cricket followed behind her husband's casket, supported, both physically and emotionally, by Delaine. While Cricket cried and dabbed at her eyes, Delaine managed to look both chic and fashionable in a short black leather jacket and tapered silk slacks. Cricket's two cousins followed behind, sniffling loudly, wearing all black and looking like a pair of Sicilian widows. Duke drew up the rear, scowling and looking generally unhappy.

The procession continued up the aisle to the front of the church where the casket was gently seesawed into place between two standing sprays of white orchids and green bear grass. The music rose to a crescendo, then dipped low as a minister stepped up to a wooden podium. Wearing a dark suit and a Roman collar, the minister carried a Bible in his hands. When the music ended and all the mourners were seated, the minister began. He gave a blessing, recited a short prayer, then segued into a soliloquy about Harlan Sadler. The minister talked about Harlan Sadler's long and stellar career in banking, and how he'd held great regard for his fellow man. He detailed Sadler's many contributions to the community, as well as to the church.

Then it was Duke's turn at the podium. He made a big deal of unfolding a piece of paper—his speech, no doubt—then began reading. And even though it was written out, it sounded disjointed and rambling. Theodosia wondered if Duke had either lost his place or decided to go off script. Thank goodness Duke's speech was blessedly short. But as Duke delivered his closing lines, he broke down in sobs. Theodosia was skeptical and wondered if this was all for show.

Then Ray Crispin strode to the podium and delivered a heartfelt, genteel eulogy that brought everyone to tears. He talked about how he and Harlan Sadler had been partners for years—how they'd started from scratch, buying their first Charleston single house, and then moved on to commercial property, and then, finally, to raw acreage. He praised Sadler's upward trajectory in the banking industry and how the man was truly an inspiration, a leader, and a bold innovator.

The minister stepped back in and led everyone in a recitation of the Lord's Prayer. Then, from up in the balcony, a female singer began an a capella rendition of "You Can Close Your Eyes" by James Taylor.

The casket was wheeled back down the alley, followed by Cricket, Delaine, Duke, the two sisters, and Ray Crispin. As Theodosia waited for her turn to step out into the aisle, she listened to the soloist, whose voice rose high and sweet, singing those heart-stopping, tear-inducing lyrics: "Only close your eyes / You can close your eyes / It's alright . . ."

As Theodosia stepped out from her pew box, she was startled

to see Emily Bates moving down the aisle, carried along by the throng of mourners. Emily flashed cold eyes at Theodosia, then looked away.

By the time Theodosia got outside the church, Emily was nowhere to be seen, and she wondered if Emily had really been in attendance or if her eyes had played tricks on her. Then a hand touched down on Theodosia's shoulder and she spun around quickly, positive it was Emily Bates. But it was Delaine.

"Did you see her? Was that Emily Bates?" Theodosia asked, her eyes still searching the crowd.

"Who?" Delaine said. She'd pulled out a silver compact and was powdering her nose.

"Emily Bates, the banker from Unity One Bank."

"Don't really know the woman all that well. Don't care to," Delaine said. She snapped the compact shut. "Listen, are you coming to the cemetery? If you are, you're welcome to ride with Ned and me." She dimpled prettily. "Cricket reserved a couple of stretch limos."

"Sorry, no, I've got to hurry back to the tea shop," Theodosia said. "Today's the day we . . ." She stopped abruptly as, nearby, voices rose in anger.

Theodosia and Delaine both turned to see Duke Sadler physically shove a cameraman out of his way. And that cameraman wasn't Bill Glass. It was Bobby from Channel Eight. She recognized him instantly, since his news crew had shown up almost as fast as the police had after Harlan Sadler's murder.

"What is their *problem*?" Delaine wondered in a petulant tone. "Doesn't that news crew know it's a *funeral*?"

"They know," Theodosia said. "And they're not the problem. Look."

Now Duke Sadler had his hands on Trevor's shoulders, shaking him from side to side, kind of pushing him away. And all the time Duke was shouting, "Get out. Get away. You're not welcome here!"

"Take it easy, man," Bobby yelled back, trying to pry Duke's hand off Trevor. "We've been respectful, kept our distance. Now we just want to get a little footage."

"I said get out!" Duke screamed.

"Keep rolling sound," Bobby shouted at Trevor. Then with a hand on Duke, trying to calm him down, said, "You could give us a quote if you'd like. Something hopeful, maybe an appeal to the public to come forward with information that might help solve your stepfather's murder."

"You're not hearing me!" Duke cried. "Leave me alone!" He was red-faced and practically frothing at the mouth. He'd slowly backed off from harassing Trevor, but his fists were tightly balled, and he looked like he was ready to throw a punch.

"That boy has anger issues," Delaine observed with a drawl.

"He's sure making it tough on himself," Theodosia said. "Which he's going to deeply regret when he shows up on the five o'clock news looking like a smoldering wreck."

Trevor backed up, trying to remain calm. "Come on, man," he urged.

Duke pulled his elbow back, cocked a fist, and let it fly at Trevor. At the last second, Trevor ducked to one side and caught Duke's fist just behind his ear.

"Hey!" Trevor shouted. "That hurt!"

"Enough!" came a loud rumble. Then Ned Grady came steaming through the crowd. Without hesitation, he grabbed Duke's right shoulder, spun him around, and yelled, "Stop it, Duke. You gotta cool down."

Caught in a blind rage, Duke simply stared at Grady, his eyes bulging, his tongue hanging out.

"What would your *mother* say?" Grady cried.

Duke continued to stare at Grady, but the steam seemed to be going out of him.

"That's right," Grady said. "Be cool, man. Now let's get you to the car. Come on, come on along with me." As he led Duke away, Grady looked over his shoulder at the news team and said, "Sorry guys."

"I hope Duke's not riding with you," Theodosia said to Delaine, who was still big-eyed and startled by what she'd just witnessed.

"No." Delaine shook her head. "If that boy is riding with us, I'll *walk* to the cemetery." And off she went, tagging after Grady, probably hoping to convince him to stash Duke in one of the other limos.

"Hey," Bobby said, noticing Theodosia and lifting a hand to wave. "Good to see you again." He paused and said, "At least I think it is."

"Why was Duke so hot and bothered?" Theodosia asked as Bobby walked toward her.

"Oh man, we were just trying to do an interview," Bobby said.

Trevor came over to join them. "The news director sent us. Wanted some kind of meaningful quote. The police are trying to shake something loose and garner any additional information they can about the murder. You know how that plea to the public works—if you saw something, say something."

"So you guys were really just trying to do your civic duty," Theodosia said with a wry grin. "And get a tasty sound bite to boot."

"Something like that," Bobby said. "What, um, do you know about that guy Duke?"

"Not much," Theodosia said.

Bobby cast a sideways glance at Trevor. "We heard, informally and off the record, of course, that Duke Sadler might possibly be under investigation for his stepfather's murder. Is that something you can confirm?"

"I can probably confirm it, but I don't know if the police have any hard evidence against Duke."

"Too bad," Bobby said. "When this breaks, it's probably going to be a juicy story."

"With the footage you just shot, it's plenty juicy now," Theodosia said.

Theodosia was back at the Indigo Tea Shop by ten thirty. She slipped in through the back door—which had thankfully been replaced—took off her jacket, and put on an apron. Then she peeked in the kitchen where Haley and Miss Dimple were fussing over a half dozen plates of scones.

"Everything okay, ladies?" she asked.

"Hunky-dory," Miss Dimple said. She was famous for her quirky, old-fashioned phrases. *Hunky-dory* was one of them. So were *Ain't that the berries* and *My stars and garters*, though Theodosia had no idea how stars related to garters.

Haley greeted her with a dip-and-glide hand motion—a gesture meant to convey she was on cruise control.

"Need any help in here?" Theodosia asked.

Both women shook their heads.

"You should have called me last night," was the first thing Drayton said when he spotted Theodosia.

"No sense, both of us losing sleep," Theodosia said.

"It makes sense when it concerns Haley," Drayton said. "And the tea shop."

"I thought about calling you, but by the time I got here the damage was done. And, honestly, from what I saw last night and what you told me earlier, it wasn't all that much damage."

"It still shakes a person up," Drayton said. "To know your space has been violated like that."

"I hear you," Theodosia said. "How's Haley doing? I wanted her to come home with me last night, but she insisted on staying, so we propped a chair against the door and waited for the hardware store guys."

"She's a tough cookie." Drayton poured a cup of tea for both of them, then said, "How did the funeral go?"

"Not bad. A little sad."

"Not surprising, considering it *was* a funeral." Drayton flipped the lid off a tea tin and added six scoops of Keemun to a glazed green teapot. "How did Cricket hold up?"

"About the same as expected, though Duke got rather emotional. And showed off that fiery temper of his again."

"He is a hothead," Drayton said. "Does that worry you?"

"Probably more than it should. I sincerely hope Duke didn't have his stepfather murdered. Then again, you never know."

"So you're going to keep looking at him."

"As hard as I can," Theodosia said.

"Changing the subject, were you able to do your research last night?"

"Sure did. And I learned that not only did Duke burn Wes Lenkov, the sports car guy, in a real estate deal; there were a couple of other guys that he cheated in a condo deal."

"Sounds like our Duke is a bad, bad boy," Drayton said.

"That's not the half of it. Turns out Duke also killed a girl in a boating accident a couple years back."

Drayton was stunned. "No!"

"There was a lawsuit over her death, but I couldn't find out if it had been settled or not."

"Perhaps it was settled out of court. Maybe Harlan Sadler stepped in and made it all go away."

"Not just the stepdaddy, but the step-in-daddy," Theodosia said.

"Hah," Drayton said, but he wasn't laughing. "What are you going to do with this new information? Pass it on to Detective Tidwell?"

"I thought I'd try to talk to the condo guys first. See if I can piece together a few more details."

"You're going to talk to both of them?"

"Sure, why not?"

But ten minutes later, Theodosia found it wasn't quite that easy. Several Internet searches and dead-end phone calls later, she found that one partner, Tom Dudley, had moved to Glendale, Arizona, where he was presumably involved in another real estate deal—hopefully nothing shady. The other one, Barry Milne, had apparently dropped off the face of the earth. Or he didn't have a Facebook or LinkedIn page, at least.

So Theodosia moved on to Wes Lenkov, the owner of Sport Luxe.

Lenkov took her call but sounded busy. "Yeah," he said, when Theodosia asked if she could come and see him about a used Porsche. "You can talk to my sales manager, or we can take a meeting if you'd like. But today's a crazy day. I've only got, like, ten minutes."

"When?" Theodosia asked.

There were a few moments of silence followed by a clicking of keys. Then Lenkov said, "Two thirty today. That work for you?"

"Perfect."

Contacting Peter Tolboth at the Westside Theatre Company was also fairly easy. Tolboth picked up the phone right away, and when Theodosia told him she was doing a favor for Cricket Sadler, immediately agreed to put her in touch with the actors he'd provided for the Mad Hatter Masquerade.

"But you don't think one of my actors was responsible for the murder, do you?" Tolboth asked rather breathlessly.

"Not at all," Theodosia said. "It's more like interviewing them to get different points of view. Trying to figure out what they saw and when they saw it."

"We're casting for a new play today," Tolboth said. "So everyone's a little tied up. Could you possibly drop by this evening?"

"Sure," Theodosia said. "What time's good?"

"Six thirty? Seven o'clock?"

"I'll see you then."

By the time Theodosia emerged from her office, she figured the Chocolate Stroll was well under way. Most Chocolate Stroll guests would start at small bakeries and chocolate shops that were first on the tour, then head for the Indigo Tea Shop. They'd sold umpteen tickets for what they were calling their Chocolate Tea Luncheon, so guests should be arriving fairly soon.

"Sorry I was on the phone for so long," Theodosia said to Drayton and Haley as she rushed out into the tea room to help.

Then Theodosia skidded to a stop when she saw that the tables were exquisitely set, and that small chocolate favors had been tied in silk pouches and set out for each guest. And here she thought she'd be galloping around at the last minute. How nice to be proven wrong.

"Wow, this place looks great," Theodosia enthused.

"Thank you, ma'am, but 'twas nothing on my part," Drayton said. "Haley, Beth Ann, and Miss Dimple did it all."

"Mostly Beth Ann and Miss Dimple," Haley said as she set a tray of applesauce brownies on the counter. Then she glanced at the clock and said, "You better be ready. Our guests will be here any moment."

"How is this supposed to work again?" Drayton asked Haley.

"Didn't we already go over this?" Haley asked.

"Indulge me," Drayton said.

Haley gazed at Theodosia and raised her brows as if to say, *Really?*

Theodosia gave a little nod as if to say, *I know it's a pain, but please run through it again.*

"There are six venues on the Chocolate Stroll, including us," Haley said. "Nutmeg Bakery, the Terrace Cafe at the Lady Goodwood Inn, Gilden's Chocolate Shop, Nancy's Patisserie, and the Dove Cote Inn."

"And us," Drayton said.

"And us," Haley said.

"So the Chocolate Stroll people are supposed to wander from one venue to another?" Drayton asked.

"That's why it's called a Chocolate Stroll," Haley said. She was antsy to get back to her kitchen.

"One more quick question," Drayton said. "How will we know which guests are participating in the Chocolate Stroll?"

"Tickets," Haley said as Beth Ann flew past them and set a tray full of chocolate chip scones on the front counter. "The Chocolate Stroll people will be clutching pink tickets in their hot little hands."

"And if they're not ticket holders but still want chocolate goodies?"

Haley shrugged. "We'll serve it to them anyway. And charge them for it."

"You're sure we have enough?"

Haley flipped her hair back and stared at Drayton. "Excuse me, but I've been baking my brains out for, like, *days*. We have enough chocolate scones, brownie bites, and chocolate bread to feed an entire army of chocoholics."

"What about our chocolate bars and truffles?" Theodosia asked. "So many of them were damaged last night."

"While you were at the funeral, Beth Ann was working wonders," Haley said. "She salvaged the bars that were intact except for ripped labels and redid them. I think we'll actually be okay."

"And we're still offering a chocolate-themed luncheon?" Drayton said.

"That's what the pink tickets are for," Haley said. "That's what I've been working on."

"Got it," Drayton said.

Haley stared at him. "I think you're more shook up about last night than I am."

"No," Drayton said. "I'm just . . ."

"What?" Haley said.

"Relieved that *you're* safe and sound."

"Drayton," Haley said. "You're like a good French baguette. Crusty on the outside and all warm and soft on the inside."

"Haley," Theodosia said, chuckling as Drayton actually blushed. "You're running on only a few hours' sleep. Do you need my help in the kitchen?"

Haley shook her head. "So far so good."

15

Wednesday's Chocolate Tea Luncheon at the Indigo Tea Shop went off without a hitch (*thankfully!*) and was so chocolicious, the end result really could have been death by chocolate. Thanks to help from Miss Dimple and Beth Ann, Haley had rallied heroically to serve a fanciful menu. There were chocolate chip scones with clotted cream infused with chocolate and orange zest as a starter. Then, tea sandwiches that included chocolate bread with cream cheese and strawberries, and chocolate zucchini bread with cardamom custard and figs. Dessert was brownie bites and bourbon chocolate pie. And, should anyone be craving even more chocolate, there were also chocolate-almond biscotti and chocolate-dipped strawberries.

"Our guests are loving this!" Theodosia told Drayton as she took a break at the front counter once all the ticketed guests had been served.

"Tell me about it," Drayton said. "I'm standing here blending chocolate teas like crazy. I thought we had enough of the chocolate-blackberry, but no. People want to buy tins to take home. And when I mentioned chocolate chai to a few people, they darned near went crazy. Wanted to buy several tins of that, too." He threw up his hands. "I couldn't help but oblige them."

"I hate to tell you this," Miss Dimple said as she scooted up to them. "Because we're so dang busy . . . but we've got a bunch of folks waiting around outside who are hoping to come in."

"Are they with the Chocolate Stroll?" Drayton asked. "Do they have pink tickets?"

"That's the thing," Miss Dimple said. "They don't. They're kind of hangers-on who heard about our chocolate luncheon and are all whipped up about the chocolate chip scones and chocolate tea."

"And we've got enough scones?" Theodosia asked.

"I checked with Haley and we're good to go," Miss Dimple said. "As far as chocolate tea goes . . ." She grinned at Drayton. "This gent is a regular Houdini when it comes to blending more tea on demand."

"Then as soon as we have a free table . . ." Theodosia looked around. "Wait, we *do* have a couple of free tables. Great, let's bring them in."

Theodosia stood at the front counter wiping out teapots while she watched Miss Dimple and Beth Ann welcome the new guests, lead them to their tables, and reel off the Indigo Tea Shop's chocolate menu by heart. The guests seemed delighted and charmed to order à la carte scones, brownie bites, chocolate peanut butter pie, and chocolate tea bread to go along with their tea.

When Theodosia was positive everything was under control, that guests were all seated and being served, she headed out the door. After all, she had an appointment with Wes Lenkov at Sport Luxe.

*   *   *

The first clue Theodosia had that this was no ordinary car dealership was the frizzy-haired blond receptionist in the white bodycon dress sitting at a glass reception desk. The second was the glitzy showroom with the gleaming white floor, finely curated collection of sleek sports cars, and pyramid of video monitors all playing racing videos.

Wes Lenkov's office wasn't much different. All sleek chrome and glass with sports car posters, awards, and framed photos of him posing with local politicians and D-list celebrities in front of expensive sports cars.

"Hiya," Lenkov said to Theodosia as the receptionist escorted her in. He gave her a friendly look but didn't bother to get up, just pointed to a black leather and chrome chair that faced his desk. "What can I do for you?" He pursed his lips, thinking, then snapped his fingers and said, "Oh yeah. You were interested in a Porsche, right?"

"I am interested in a Porsche 911, if you've got one I can afford," Theodosia said as she carefully studied Lenkov. He was a big, good-looking guy, mid-thirties, with dark hair worn slightly long, piercing dark eyes, and a square jaw. He spoke with a slight accent and looked mildly European, as if his ancestors had emigrated from Croatia or maybe even Turkey. He wore a yellow cashmere sweater over faded blue jeans and had a Breitling Chronomat on his left wrist that had to go for at least twenty grand. Theodosia figured business must be good. Real good.

"My inventory's dismally low right now," Lenkov told her. "The 911 that's listed on my website just got sold this morning. Some big shot collector down in Florida."

"Oh no," Theodosia said. But she was secretly thinking, *Good, now I can steer the conversation to Duke Sadler.*

"The good news is I've got an almost-cherry 911 Carrera coming in from Dallas in the next couple of days. A 2023, Guards Red, under ten thousand miles."

"How much?"

"Ninety grand, give or take."

"Ouch."

Lenkov gave her an appraising look. He took in the black suit and low-heeled shoes she'd worn to the funeral that morning, then closed one eye and said, "Something tells me you're not really here to buy a Porsche."

"Not at that price, no." At which point Theodosia decided honesty was probably the best policy.

"Then what *do* you want?"

"Maybe a little information?"

"Concerning?"

"Here's the thing," Theodosia said. "I'm a friend of Cricket Sadler . . ."

"The woman whose old man was murdered the other night."

"Right. And I'm trying to build a dossier on Duke Sadler."

"On Duke Sadler or against him?" Lenkov asked.

"That's still up in the air."

"Duke. Hmm. You think Duke knocked off his old man?" Lenkov had looked mildly bored up to this point. Now he looked interested.

"I don't know. Somebody did," Theodosia said.

"You obviously know that Duke and I have a history. That's why you're here."

"Well . . . yes," Theodosia said.

"But, truth be told, I don't give that little piece of rat crap a moment's thought anymore. Not since he took me for an absolute sucker."

Theodosia lifted a single eyebrow. "You lost a lot of money?"

"And time," Lenkov said.

"And that unlucky foray into real estate is what spring-boarded you into the sports car business?"

Lenkov considered her words. "Not exactly. Cars were always my first passion, but I did learn a valuable lesson from my boon-doggle with Duke."

"Which is?"

"Never trust anyone. If a deal *looks* too good, *sounds* too good, then you're probably going to get mousetrapped. I tell you, it's a dog-eat-dog world out there. People are ruthless and vicious."

"That's a fairly negative point of view," Theodosia said. She believed in the good in people and had learned, firsthand, that business didn't have to be underhanded and cutthroat. There could be a respectable give and take—a professional exchange between both parties.

Lenkov gave an indifferent shrug. "Yeah, whatever." He leaned back in his fancy leather chair and rested one foot on his desk. Theodosia noted it was a Gucci loafer. Lenkov may be rough around the edges, but at least he dressed well.

"So now you run your own company," Theodosia said. "And do things your way."

"My way or the highway. You come to work for me you'd better be ready to drink the Kool-Aid. I'm the one who sets the vision."

Theodosia thought the vision part sounded sort of bullshitty—kind of like all those corporate fat cats who talked about teamwork and integrity but were really only interested in the bottom line—but she responded with an agreeable, "I can see that."

"Because we sell luxury sports cars," Lenkov said, "we have to be acutely perceptive about the taste and whims of the market. With that in mind, we still need to build relationships."

"And you have a service garage." Theodosia had noticed a large garage with at least a half dozen bays where technicians worked on what she figured were temperamental and capricious sports cars.

"Well, sure, we repair cars and do custom work."

"What kind of custom work?"

"Paint jobs, leather upholstery, high-end sound systems. You name it, we can probably do it."

"For the right price."

Lenkov smiled for the first time. "Always for the right price, yes." He stood up suddenly. "Look, you're a good-looking woman. You buy a Porsche, your street cred suddenly shoots up about a million percent." He winked at her. "You get what I'm saying?"

Theodosia gritted her teeth and smiled pleasantly. "I get what you're saying."

By the time Theodosia got back to the Indigo Tea Shop, there were only two tables of guests left, and Drayton was swishing out teapots.

"How'd your meeting with the sports car guy go?" he asked.

"Okay. Lenkov basically hates Duke Sadler," Theodosia said.

"That's what you picked up?"

"That's what he told me."

"What about Harlan Sadler?"

"I got the feeling Lenkov didn't really know him."

"Did your Mr. Lenkov think Duke could have killed his stepfather?"

"He didn't come right out and say that, but he was leaning in that direction," Theodosia said.

"So he might have helped in building your case against Duke, right?"

"Maybe. But there's still no clear-cut evidence, only hearsay that Duke is a liar and a cheat and took huge advantage of his stepfather's money and power."

"Mmn. Maybe you'll glean some better information when we talk to the actors at the Westside Theatre tonight. What time are we supposed to be there?"

"Six thirty, seven," Theodosia said. "We've got time to kill." She looked around the tea shop. Miss Dimple was stacking clean dishes in the cupboard, and Beth Ann was sweeping the floor. "Did Haley finally poop out?"

"About a half hour ago. She went full throttle, made a batch of crab-stuffed mushrooms and some veggie tea sandwiches for our afternoon guests, then kind of dropped in her tracks. I suspect she's upstairs in bed, dead to the world."

"If you don't need me here, maybe I'll wander down to Antiquarian Books and pick up a few titles for our Book Lovers Tea tomorrow. Chat up Lois for a while. You okay here?"

"Go on ahead. I'll pour refills for our guests and help with the cleanup."

Visiting Antiquarian Books was always a joy for Theodosia. Just a few steps down Church Street, the shop was a narrow little jewel box set between two red brick buildings. Hand-lettered gold script on the front window announced ANTIQUARIAN BOOKS, and this week's window display was a collection of books about Charleston—books detailing its founding and early years, volumes featuring Charleston's distinctive art and architecture, books on Charleston's churches . . . even colorful large-format books with photos of Charleston Harbor, the Historic District, the French Quarter, and nearby grand plantations.

Pumpkin's sharp bark welcomed Theodosia the minute she opened the door and stepped inside.

"Hello, sweetheart," Theodosia said. She knelt down to pet Lois's adorable little long-haired dachshund and said, "I think I might have . . ." Theodosia dug in her pocket as Pumpkin's bright eyes watched her every move. "Yes, I *do* have a treat. Would you like it?" Pumpkin wagged her tail and immediately sat down, an expectant look on her furry face.

"That sounds like Theodosia," a voice called from overhead. "Is that you, Theodosia?"

"It's me," Theodosia said. "Are you in the loft?"

"I've been shelving books like mad. Give me a minute to get down there."

Lois Chamberlain's scuffed brown clogs appeared first as she wound her way down the wrought iron circular staircase that connected the first floor to the loft. Then her jeans and red-and-purple tunic top put in an appearance. Finally, the whole of Lois emerged—a short, slightly stocky woman in her mid-fifties who wore her long salt-and-pepper hair in a single plait down her back. Lois was a retired librarian with a love for books, whose love was readily apparent on her cherubic face.

"Hey there," Lois said, obviously pleased to see Theodosia. Then, "Uh-oh, is Pumpkin begging for treats again?"

"Not at all. I offered a treat, Pumpkin accepted. We both felt we struck a fair bargain."

"If you say so."

Theodosia looked around the bookshop that Lois had recently updated. Lois had brought in an antique library table to use as a front counter, hung Tiffany-style lamps from the ceiling beams, and put worn but still serviceable Oriental carpets on the floor. Wooden bookshelves were stocked floor to ceiling with books and carried labels that read FICTION, HISTORY, LOCAL LORE, COOKING, ROMANCE, MUSIC, ART, BUSINESS, and RELI-GION. Upstairs in the loft were the MYSTERY and CHILDREN'S sections.

"I love this place," Theodosia said. "It's got such a cozy, magical feel."

"Because it *is* magic," Lois said. "Opening a book is like being sprinkled with fairy dust—you can be transported anywhere."

"That's what Drayton says about his teas. One sip can take you to Africa or Asia or even South America."

"So," Lois said, placing her hands flat on her library table. "I'm guessing you're here to pick up a few books for your Book Lovers Tea tomorrow."

"That was my original idea. But now that I think about it, you should really be there to sell them."

Lois's eyes lit up. "Oh yeah? You'd let me do that?"

"I *want* you to do that."

"So it would be a kind of pop-up shop."

"Right. If we stock the Indigo Tea Shop with stacks of books tomorrow, I'm fairly sure our book-loving guests will be in a buying mood, and you'll come away with a tidy sum."

"Then let's do it," Lois said. "In fact, why don't you start picking out a few books and we'll carry them down there right now. If you need more, we can always make another run in the morning."

So that's what they did. Grabbed books and packed them into boxes, then carried them down to the tea shop. Pumpkin rode along tucked inside Lois's bookbag, bouncing against her hip.

"Knock knock," Theodosia said when they reached her front

door. She shifted the heavy boxes in her arms and called out, "Need some help here." Pumpkin, with just her little head sticking out of Lois's bookbag, pitched in with a loud YIP.

Drayton heard them and came running. "What's this?" he asked as he opened the door and grabbed the top box off Lois's stack.

"We're not just going to display books at our Book Lovers Tea," Theodosia said. "Lois is going to *sell* them."

"Great Caesar's ghost," Drayton said. "What a fine idea."

They stacked all the boxes in a corner and decided to definitely make another book run in the morning.

"It only makes sense," Drayton said, dusting his hands together, "that book lovers would want to *purchase* books, too." Then he looked at Lois and said, "Say now, how would you like a cup of tea, a chocolate chip scone, and a chocolate bar for the road?"

"The tea sounds wonderful," Lois said. "But I really shouldn't indulge in sweets."

In the end, Lois accepted the scone and chocolate bar anyway.

16

⚜

At six o'clock sharp, Theodosia and Drayton piled into Theodosia's Jeep for their appointment at the Westside Theatre. The sun was barely a ribbon of gold edging the western sky, and soft yellow globes housed in antique wrought iron lampposts were starting to wink on.

"This area's looking better and better," Drayton remarked as they drove past a red brick building that housed Neily's Fine Arts and a white clapboard building that was home to Palmetto Bookshop and Logo Press.

"This area's gotten artsy," Theodosia said.

"Where's the theater located?"

"Charlotte Street, just east of the Cooper River. So we should be . . ."

"There it is," Drayton said. "Just up ahead. See, the marquee is even lit."

"Of course."

They found a parking spot a few spaces down from the

entrance to the Westside Theatre and walked back to what essentially looked like a movie theater. But instead of advertising the current movie attractions, the marquis said WESTSIDE THEATRE: HOME TO THE WESTSIDE THEATRE COMPANY.

Inside, the lobby looked exactly like a plush theater lobby. Maroon carpet, brass wall sconces, and the kind of art deco design that vintage theaters often had.

"I love that they kept the old-fashioned ticket booth," Drayton said.

"And the concession stand," Theodosia said, gazing at a glass case holding neatly lined-up candy bars. "But no corn popper. Looks like they just sell soft drinks and Swiss chocolate bars to the theater crowd."

"Mmn, who doesn't love aspartame and milk chocolate?"

"Be nice," Theodosia said, laughing. But she had to admit that Drayton had a point.

"Such a pity they no longer show films here," Drayton said.

"I think so many streaming services have emerged that everyone is watching movies at home now."

"I'm not," Drayton said.

"Because you're the exception to the rule. But look at it this way, the theater was put up for sale and the Westside Theatre Company was able to purchase it for a song."

"So it's been repurposed," Drayton said. "I guess there's a fair amount of synergy in that."

"Hello!" a female voice called out.

Theodosia and Drayton turned to face the entrance to the theater proper where a young woman was posed, an expectant look on her face. She was early twenties, wearing frayed jeans, huarache sandals, and a T-shirt that said "There will be Drama." Streaks of green ran through her short blond hair, giving the impression of an artfully arranged artichoke.

"I'm Jolie," the woman said, giving her name a French inflection. She looked Drayton up and down and said, "And you must be the dialect coach."

"Excuse me?" Drayton said.

"For our new play," Jolie said. "We're doing Oscar Wilde's *The Importance of Being Earnest*."

"Why would you assume I'm the dialect coach?" Drayton asked.

"Because you're dressed like somebody from the House of Lords," Jolie said.

Amused, Theodosia said, "It's the British shoes. And we're actually here for a meeting with Peter Tolboth."

"Oh, okay," Jolie said. "My bad." She waved a hand in front of her face as if to erase her mistake. "If you'll just follow me?"

"Welcome to our humble theater," Peter Tolboth said as he stood on the bare stage in front of a purple velvet curtain, smiling as Theodosia and Drayton walked down the center aisle. Tolboth was thin and wiry, with a thin face and slicked-back hair. He was dressed all in black, and from his pose, looked almost like a rather serious dance instructor. "Miss Browning, I assume?"

"And my tea sommelier, Drayton Conneley," Theodosia said.

"Welcome," Tolboth said. He lifted a hand and indicated a stairway up to the stage. "Just walk around to the side and we can get started."

Peter Tolboth led them to a cramped backstage office that looked like it could be the set from an old *Perry Mason* TV show. There was an old-fashioned metal desk, small metal filing cabinet, and a squat black vintage typewriter. Theodosia looked around, almost expecting to see a Dictaphone.

"So you're doing a little investigating on Cricket's behalf?" Tolboth asked.

"Looking into a few things for her," Theodosia said.

"About the murder, I assume." Tolboth offered a sad face. "So terrible what happened to her husband. They've both been such staunch supporters of our theater."

"Cricket is very civic minded," Drayton said.

Tolboth looked thoughtful for a moment, then said, "Right, so let's get to it." He sat down on an uncomfortable-looking secretarial chair with rollers and navigated it unsteadily to the nearby file cabinet. Theodosia and Drayton hovered in the doorway, as there was no room for them inside his office. As they studied the crinkled playbills peeling off the walls, Tolboth pulled open a metal drawer that groaned in protest, and grabbed a stack of papers.

"What I did was gather head sheets for all the actors who were hired to play roles at the Mad Hatter Masquerade," Tolboth said. "Those roles being the Mad Hatter, Red Queen, White Rabbit, Mock Turtle, Caterpillar, four fairies, and, of course, Alice herself."

"We're most interested in talking to the fellow who played the Mad Hatter," Theodosia said.

"That would be Renee Garcia," Tolboth said. He picked through his stack of head sheets and handed Theodosia an eight-by-ten, black-and-white sheet that pictured a smiling middle-aged man.

Theodosia studied it, noting that Renee Garcia had an angular face, high cheekbones, expressive eyes, and a mouth that seemed curled in perpetual amusement. His hair was curly and, in real life, had to be either reddish or dark blond.

"Renee's giving a workshop on stage movement right now, but he should be finished in ten minutes or so," Tolboth said.

"Great," Theodosia said. "We'll wait." She handed the head sheet to Drayton, who glanced at it, then turned it over to reveal four smaller photos of Renee Garcia portraying different characters, as well as an impressive list of past productions that Garcia had been in.

"Is there anyone else you want to talk to?" Tolboth asked.

Theodosia thought for a minute. "Maybe the Red Queen?"

"That would be Lucy," Tolboth said. "She's not here right now, but I can give you her number." He wrote something on the top sheet, then handed the entire stack to Theodosia.

Theodosia and Drayton sat on chairs outside Tolboth's office, going through the head sheets and waiting for Renee Garcia. When Garcia finally showed up, he headed toward them with a bouncy gait. Garcia was thin with sparse red hair and skin so white it was practically translucent. He was wearing jeans and a faded orange button-down shirt he'd incongruously paired with a wide purple tie. Garcia was also five or six years older than the photo on his current head sheet.

Tolboth emerged from his office and made quick introductions, then Theodosia said, "Mr. Garcia, I understand you played the Mad Hatter the other night at the Mad Hatter Masquerade."

"Indeed I did," Garcia said with a broad grin. "It was a fun role. Just wander around the party and be amusing." He tucked one hand under his tie and made a fluttering motion.

"And your costume came from right here?" Theodosia asked.

Garcia seemed pleased by her question. "Putting together the perfect outfit is always exciting. For the Mad Hatter role, I wore a pair of baggy pants from an old tuxedo that I've had hanging in my closet for eons. Then Maggie Hart, one of the costumers here at the Westside Theatre, helped me dress it up with pieces from their wardrobe department. We ended up with a ruffled shirt, purple vest, green velvet frock coat, pink silk scarf, enormous floppy bow tie, and an oversized top hat. Kind of steampunk, if you know what that is."

"I do," Theodosia said.

"I don't," Drayton said.

"Well, you might say it's Edwardian meets vintage," Garcia said.

"Okay." Drayton still looked confused.

"So your frock coat was purple?" Theodosia asked. She distinctly remembered that the Mad Hatter in the video wore a black frock coat.

"Purple, yes," Garcia said.

"Okay, what we really want to know is, when did you first become acquainted with Harlan Sadler?" Theodosia said.

"Who?" Garcia gave Theodosia a blank stare.

"Was it at the bank?"

"What bank?" Garcia said.

"Or did you meet Sadler the night of the masquerade party?" Theodosia asked.

Garcia bit his lower lip and shook his head. "I'm afraid I don't know this Sadler person," he said slowly. He looked at Peter Tolboth as if for help. Tolboth just shrugged.

"Excuse me," Drayton said, "but Ms. Browning is referring to the unfortunate fellow who got killed at the masquerade on Sunday night."

Garcia's face suddenly twisted in sadness. "Oh, that. I heard some poor person died. Heart attack, was it?"

"You didn't see the headlines in the newspaper?" Theodosia asked.

"It was on TV as well," Drayton said.

"I never read the newspaper," Garcia said. "Don't watch TV, either." He made a palms-up, what-can-you-do gesture. "It's either bad news or trash."

"And nobody here at the theater mentioned Sadler's name to you?" Theodosia asked. "And the fact that he was murdered?"

"This is the first I've been here since Sunday," Garcia said. "I came in to teach a workshop today and Mr. Tolboth mentioned that some people wanted to talk to me . . . but he didn't say what it was about. So a man was murdered? How awful."

"It certainly was," Theodosia said. "And you didn't by chance run into any other men dressed as the Mad Hatter, did you?"

"No," Garcia said, looking flustered. "Was there another Mad Hatter? I thought it was just me that got hired."

"It was," Tolboth assured him.

"So you didn't see any suspicious characters at the masquerade?" Theodosia asked.

Garcia shrugged. "Not really."

"I think we can safely cross Mr. Garcia off our list," Theodosia said to Drayton.

"Agreed," Drayton said.

"Thank you, Mr. Garcia. I hope we didn't cause you any undue worry," Theodosia said.

Garcia offered a hopeful smile. "I gave up worrying a long time ago. Now I meditate."

"Nice if you can manage it," Drayton said under his breath as Garcia drifted away.

"So, the Red Queen?" Theodosia said to Tolboth.

"That would be Lucinda Harrington. Well, that's her stage name. She's actually Lucy Harris."

"Ms. Harris is here tonight?" Theodosia asked.

"No, but you could probably give Lucy a quick call and maybe drop by her apartment," Tolboth said. "She lives over on Cannon Street in those rehabbed Vanderhorst Square apartments. You know, the brick building with the corner turrets and enclosed courtyard?" He scratched his head. "I can't think of any reason why she wouldn't want to talk to you."

"Thanks," Theodosia said. "You've been a big help."

* * *

Back in Theodosia's Jeep, Drayton said, "If Renee Garcia didn't know the particulars of how Harlan Sadler died, then who was the Mad Hatter we saw running around inside the grist mill? Who was the Mad Hatter you saw on videotape?"

"Good question," Theodosia said.

"So now we know there really were two Mad Hatters."

"A doppelgänger . . . which seems fairly weird." Theodosia started her car and pulled away from the curb.

"Although, there were quite a few people wearing costumes that night," Drayton said slowly.

"There were?" Theodosia frowned. "I guess I hadn't noticed. You mean besides the *Alice in Wonderland* characters?"

"I remember seeing a pirate, two Venetian lords, a cat woman, and a couple of fairy princesses running around the party. There were probably a few more characters all gussied up like that."

"Jeepers. Then a second Mad Hatter might not be meaningful at all."

"We have to remember, it was a masquerade gala. Just because you and I wore conservative black tie with masks doesn't mean others didn't go all out with fancy costumes."

"So maybe the Mad Hatter thing isn't a lead at all," Theodosia said. It bothered her that she hadn't noticed all the costumed guests. Maybe she'd been too busy having fun? Then again, how was she supposed to know there'd be a murder and that she'd be asked to investigate?

They rode along in silence for a few minutes. Cruised down George Street and passed Theodora Park, which Drayton always referred to as Theodosia Park.

"Do you think we should call this Lucy Harris person anyway?" Drayton asked. "Would it be worthwhile to talk to her?"

"Not sure. We're going to drive by her place anyway, so let's think about it for a minute."

Theodosia turned down Anson Street, passed St. Stephen's Episcopal Church and Dob's Barbeque, then hung a right on Society. As she did, she suddenly realized they were within a city block of Sport Luxe.

"That's Sport Luxe over there," she pointed out. "On the corner."

The lights were on inside the dealership, and a canary yellow Corvette and a shiny black Mercedes-AMG SL were clearly visible through a large show window.

"The place looks upscale," Drayton said. "At least for a car dealership."

"Oh, they're upscale alright. The price tags on their cars are astronomical."

"Me, I prefer a classic sports car myself," Drayton said. "One that's *proven* itself. Give me an Aston Martin or a Cord or . . ."

"That's him!" Theodosia suddenly shouted as Wes Lenkov exited the dealership's front door and walked across the street.

"What?"

"That's him! That's Wes Lenkov, the sports car guy I met with today!"

Lenkov crossed in the middle of the street, ambling along as if he didn't have a care in the world. Then headlights flashed on a sleek yellow sports car and he climbed in.

Drayton let loose a low whistle. "Will you look at the car he's driving? It's so sleek and graceful, it looks like it might start purring. What is that anyway?"

"It's a Lambo," Theodosia said.

"A what?"

"Lamborghini."

"Ah. And where do you suppose your Mr. Lenkov is going in

a fancy car like that?" Drayton asked. "Does he always drive a Lamborghini, or do you think he's going somewhere to show off?"

"I don't know," Theodosia said.

There was a throaty roar as Lenkov started his engine. Then he did a hasty check of the road and zipped out into traffic.

Theodosia's hands tightened on her steering wheel. "Maybe," she said. "Maybe we should follow him and find out."

17

"Wait a minute," Drayton cried. "You want to scrub our visit to the Red Queen?"

"We can always check her out later."

Theodosia made a quick U-turn, preparing to follow Lenkov. But when she glanced at Drayton, he still looked dubious.

"Come on, what do you say?" Theodosia had a hunch about Lenkov. Well, maybe a tickle of a hunch, but it was something.

"Well . . . maybe." Drayton wasn't overly thrilled about following Lenkov, but he didn't put up much of an argument against it, so Theodosia floored it and took off after him.

Lenkov drove fast and with authority, accelerating and cutting through traffic like a great white shark on the hunt.

"Watch it," Drayton said. "He's turning. You're going to have to keep up with that beast he's driving."

"I know, I know. But it's tough when the car he's driving can blow the doors off my Jeep."

"Whatever. If we're really going to do this, then hurry up and gun it before you clip this light!"

Theodosia gunned it. And really did do her best as she played cat and mouse with Lenkov. Trying to stay two car lengths behind him, she wove down Bee Street, then merged onto Highway 17 where they crossed the Ashley River. She followed Lenkov through a spaghetti junction of off- and on-ramps and ended up on Folly Road Boulevard.

"Careful now. Traffic is starting to thin out," Drayton said.

"I know, I've got this." Theodosia hung back a bit. She didn't want Lenkov to catch her in his rearview mirror and realize he'd picked up a tail.

They crossed the Stono River onto Johns Island, drove for a good twenty minutes past a scatter of retail, restaurants, and new housing developments, then crossed over onto Wadmalaw Island—another in a chain of South Carolina's tidal and barrier islands.

"He's heading out into the countryside," Drayton said. "I wonder why?"

"Going for a joy ride?" Theodosia said. "Blowing out the carbon? On the way to see a potential customer so they can take a test drive?"

They drove past produce and fishmonger stands. Some were substantial board-and-batten buildings, like Murph's Shrimp and Oysters. Others, like Bill and Begonia Fresh Produce, were just your typical knocked-together roadside stand. No real building, just a weathered sign and a wooden counter. The sky was fading purple to black as they continued on, crossing bridges, twisting and turning through woodlots and open fields.

Ten minutes later, the land turned swampy and wet. Now they drove past vast areas of standing water where bald cypress and tupelo trees stood.

Then it got really dark, as if some omnipotent hand had

dropped a velvet curtain, and Theodosia was forced to crawl a little closer to keep Lenkov's car in sight.

Another mile and the Lambo's brake lights flared red. Then it slowed and turned left, heading down a narrow gravel road.

"Now he's slowed way down," Drayton remarked as they watched the receding lights.

"Because he's turned down a gravel road," Theodosia said. "Lenkov's seriously worried about damaging the paint job."

Theodosia waited a few moments, then snapped off her headlights and turned down the same road. It was bumpy and rough, dark with spindly trees closing in on both sides of the road. Then they dipped unexpectedly, traveling over a narrow, single-lane wooden bridge, the boards rumbling and mumbling beneath their vehicle.

"Oof," Theodosia said. She hadn't seen that bridge coming and worried that she might be overdriving her night vision. But she doggedly stuck with it. After all, Lenkov was still up ahead of her and going somewhere. But where? Very puzzling.

Finally, after another half mile of twists and turns, they began to see a faint glow on the horizon.

"What in heaven's name is going on out here?" Drayton wondered. "Is this some kind of campground?"

"No idea," Theodosia said. "There seem to be lights. And see . . . just through that line of trees over to our left, it looks almost bright enough for a landing strip."

"You think that's it? Small planes are landing here? There's some sort of smuggling operation going on?"

"Don't know."

"Maybe Wes Lenkov is a drug smuggler," Drayton said. "Maybe he gave you a big song and dance about despising Duke Sadler, but they're still hooked up together. Just in a different capacity."

"You could be right. It's not such a stretch to see it all fitting together—high-end cars and people with high-flying lifestyles who have plenty of cash to spend on cocaine."

Another hundred yards brought them to a large grassy area that served as a sort of impromptu parking lot.

"Look at all the cars and pickup trucks," Drayton marveled.

"But mostly older models, not high end at all." Theodosia frowned. "What can be going on?"

Theodosia stopped her Jeep and turned off the motor. Then she rolled down a window. There was a faint drone of crickets and katydids . . . along with something else.

"Listen," Theodosia whispered.

There were a few shouts, then the faint echo of an announcer's voice over a loudspeaker. Then the *briiing* of a bell.

"What *is* that?" Drayton said.

"Not planes landing," Theodosia said. But she suddenly had an inkling as to what might be going on. "If it's what I think it is, we've stumbled onto something highly illegal."

"What are you talking about?"

"Come on. Time to do some serious investigating."

"Easy for you to say, but I don't know what we're investigating," Drayton whispered back.

Theodosia had already climbed out of her Jeep and was tiptoeing between a line of parked cars. Long grass dampened her ankles as she passed an old beater held together with redneck chrome (duct tape), then crept past a pickup truck. Stopping to listen, trying to tune out the crickets, she thought she heard something up ahead. She eased up to one of the SUVs, crouched down, held her breath, and peered in the back window.

There was nothing inside the SUV except a rumpled plaid blanket and two empty metal dog crates.

"Dog crates," Theodosia said as Drayton crept up behind her.

"Say what?" he said. Then, "Oh no, this doesn't have anything to do with dogfighting, does it?"

"I think . . . not. What I'm guessing is this is some kind of
clandestine dog racing operation."

"Dog racing? I thought that was banned."

"It *was* banned. In almost every state except three. If this is
an illegal track, then there's probably illegal betting going on as
well."

Theodosia and Drayton wove their way through the tangle
of trucks and SUVs, getting closer to the track. When they finally popped their heads up from behind a stand of emaciated
poplar trees, they could see the makeshift track. It was a large
bare earth oval enclosed by chicken wire. Dogs and handlers
were milling about near the starting gate, and someone was setting up the mechanical rabbit.

"So this is a problem?" Drayton said.

"Not for us. But it is for everybody here," Theodosia said.

"What are we supposed to do about it? We can't just jump
out at the crowd and yell BOO!"

"There's only one thing I can think of at this point. And
that's put in a call to Detective Burt Tidwell."

"But Tidwell doesn't have jurisdiction out here," Drayton
said.

"I get that. But he's a former FBI agent, so he'll know exactly
what to do and who to call. For all I know, this could be a federal
crime as well as state. Anyway, we'll let the law sort it all out."

They backed away from the racetrack into the darkness and
tangle of vehicles.

"I'd kind of like to see . . . ," Drayton began. Then he suddenly stopped in his tracks. "Oh no, will you look at this?" There
was a note of sadness in his voice.

"What? What have you found?"

Drayton stretched out a hand and pointed. "Look at that poor guy."

"What's there?" Theodosia asked. "I still can't . . ." It was pitch black with wisps of ground fog creeping in. Then her eyes finally focused on what Drayton was pointing to, and with a lump in her throat, said, "Oh, jeez."

Just five feet ahead of them, a dog was tied to a tree by a short leather leash. He was lean, leggy, and looked scared to death. His head was bowed low and he seemed to be shivering.

"Poor thing," Drayton said. He was also a dog lover and owned a rescue dog, Honey Bee, a King Charles spaniel.

Theodosia walked up to the dog, a sable brown greyhound, and let him sniff her hand. The dog stared up at her with sorrowful eyes, then slowly wagged its tail.

Friends?

The dog seemed to read Theodosia's mind and consider the idea for a few moments. Then it licked her hand, his eyes practically pleading with her now.

Theodosia made an instant decision. "We have to take this dog with us."

"You mean steal him?" Drayton was aghast.

"Not steal, *rescue* him."

"Then what are we going to do with the poor thing?"

"We can't leave him here, that's for sure. We'll take him to Loving Paws Animal Shelter—the one Delaine volunteers for. The one she's always hitting us up for support money."

"Are you sure we can do that? Just drop this poor creature off with just a hello-goodbye?"

"Positive. But if it makes you feel any better, I'll call ahead to one of the volunteers and clear it."

They scrambled into Theodosia's Jeep then, all three of them. Theodosia was in the passenger side now, Drayton behind the wheel, and the dog sitting in back. Drayton made a careful turn without benefit of headlights, then drove back down the gravel road while Theodosia got on her phone. Her first call was to Detective Burt Tidwell.

"What?" Tidwell yelped when he came on the line. He was sputtering and angry, making no bones about the fact he was unhappy at being disturbed.

"This is Theodosia," she said. "We . . . that's Drayton and me . . . just discovered an illegal dog racing track off the Maybank Highway. It's . . ."

"Dogs!" Tidwell cried out. "Dogs?"

"Illegal greyhound racing," Theodosia said, enunciating carefully and talking a little louder this time. "Which means there's probably illegal betting going on as well."

The issue of illegal betting calmed Tidwell down a bit, which gave Theodosia a chance to relay as much information as she could about the clandestine track, as well as give exact directions on how to get there.

Tidwell continued to listen, then said, "This racing is going on right now? Even as we speak? You're sure the dog owners are still there?"

"Yes, yes, they're still there," Theodosia said. "We just left the place five minutes ago."

"All the dogs are there, too?"

The sable brown greyhound hung its head over the front seat, looking happy and content, as Theodosia lied through her teeth and said, "Yes, all the dogs are still there as well."

18

Drayton, soft-hearted soul that he was, wanted to name the dog Zeus, but Theodosia told him to hold off for the time being. The poor fellow probably had a name already.

"But we don't want Zeus to go back to his owner," Drayton argued. "We don't want him back in that same dicey situation where they run him after a mechanical rabbit until he has heart failure."

"Of course not. But unless you're prepared to take this dog right now, we have to drop him off at Loving Paws," Theodosia said. "Helen Kirby, one of the volunteers I just spoke to, promised to meet us there and take special care of him."

"Then what?"

"Then it's up to whoever has jurisdiction over all those poor greyhounds."

"But in the meantime?"

"Our boy Zeus will be taken care of properly. He'll be fed, given a bed, vet care if needed, and lots of love. My guess is he'll probably end up going to a volunteer group that specializes in greyhound rehabilitation and then get adopted out as a family pet."

Drayton looked over at Zeus who was now slobbering on the shoulder of his good jacket. Drayton didn't seem to mind.

"That does sound like a best-case scenario," he said.

Once Zeus was dropped off at Loving Paws, Theodosia dropped Drayton at his home.

"You realize we haven't eaten yet," Drayton said as he opened the door and climbed out of the driver's side.

"Is that an invitation?" Theodosia asked. She was tired, but her stomach was rumbling.

"Absolutely it is. Come in and I'll fix us a snack."

"You're on," Theodosia said, knowing Drayton's idea of a snack was often a two- or three-course dinner.

Of course, Honey Bee met them at the back door. She was a girly-girl King Charles spaniel with bright shoe button eyes and a sweet face. Dancing on her back legs, she accepted pets from Drayton and then from Theodosia.

"I see Pepe was here to feed you," Drayton said as he looked around his kitchen.

Pepe was his teenage neighbor from down the block. He was Honey Bee's afternoon dog walker and nanny. When Drayton was going to be late, he could always count on Pepe.

"Now I just have to worry about feeding us."

"Anything is good," Theodosia said. "Please don't go to any trouble."

"Actually, I was thinking of grilled salmon with honey mustard brown sugar crust . . . and maybe a nice side salad."

"That sounds like you're going to a lot of trouble."

"Not really."

Drayton opened his refrigerator and pulled out a head of butter lettuce, a cucumber, and a small bunch of radishes. Then he grabbed an avocado from a bowl of fruit and vegetables that was sitting on the counter.

"Here," he said, shoving the vegetables in Theodosia's direction. "You can make the salad while I grill the salmon."

So that's what they did.

Drayton brushed a thick amount of honey mustard onto two salmon fillets, then dredged them in a plate of brown sugar. Theodosia broke the lettuce into small chunks, diced the cucumber, a couple of radishes, and half an avocado. Working in Drayton's kitchen was always a treat because it was so unusual. His kitchen stove was a six-burner Wolf range, the sink was custom hammered copper, and the cupboards were faced with glass—the better to show off his collection of teapots and Chinese blue-and-white vases. A small indoor herb garden sat on a windowsill, and wouldn't you know it? Drayton was trimming off snippets of fresh parsley right now to top the salad.

It took Drayton all of six minutes to grill his salmon, then he placed the fillets on his favorite Buckingham by Minton plates. The salad was dressed with a lemon vinaigrette that Drayton had in his refrigerator and mounded next to the salmon.

They put their plates on silver trays and carried them into the dining room, settled down on comfortable chairs, and finally relaxed. Until Drayton snapped his fingers and said, "You know what I forgot? The wine."

"Wow," was all Theodosia could say as she took in the silk wallpaper, oil paintings, Chippendale table, and French chandelier dangling overhead.

Drayton came back two minutes later with an uncorked bottle of chardonnay and pulled two crystal wine glasses from a nearby cupboard.

"I'm guessing this Far Niente chardonnay will complement the fish nicely," he said as he poured the wine.

Theodosia took a sip and slowly savored the taste. It was crisp and delicious. "Drayton, this wine is so good you could serve it with a grilled carburetor."

"A toast, then," Drayton said, lifting his glass.

"A toast," Theodosia echoed back.

Dinner was lovely and Theodosia was hard pressed to leave. But she finally did, arriving home around nine thirty that night. Earl Grey hadn't been out since Mrs. Barry, his dog walker, had taken him for his afternoon stroll, so he was eager for a chance to stretch his legs.

That was fine with Theodosia. Still keyed up from the discovery of the illegal dog racing track, she changed clothes quickly and was out the door with her dog some ten minutes later.

The evening was dark and cool. Moon shadows lit the alley as they raced along, then turned down Legare Street. Theodosia loved running past the grand old homes that stood like proud sentinels. Some she'd visited when the Heritage Society sponsored its autumn Lamplighter Tour. Others she just imagined what they might be like. Floating staircases, enormous fireplaces you could roast an entire hog in, secret back staircases that led to third-floor garrets . . . she grinned thinking of all the old Charleston families with their many skeletons still hidden in attics.

As Theodosia and Earl Grey stepped off the curb, heading for Church Street, a dark car seemed to come out of nowhere. Sleek and slung low to the ground, the car roared down the street heading directly at her. Frozen for a few seconds, Theodosia stepped back as the car braked and swerved at the very last second, then spun away.

"What was that?" Theodosia shouted as anger boiled up inside her. Could that have been Wes Lenkov? Had he somehow escaped Tidwell's raid on the illegal dog track and followed her home? Was that even possible? This car had been dark and sleek, unlike his Lamborghini, but he could have easily switched cars.

Or could it have been Ethan Stacks? Or even Duke Sadler? Both of them knew that she and Drayton had been sniffing around, asking questions. Had one of them been trying to throw a scare into her? Or had it been a lousy, distracted driver who'd been jabbering away on his phone?

Theodosia made it home without any other incidents. And, as she was walking in her back door, received a text message from Detective Tidwell. It was short and sweet and said "ALL ROUNDED UP."

She grinned, did a fist pump, and said, "Yes!" At which point her phone rang.

Tidwell? No, it's probably Pete Riley calling.

"Hey there," Theodosia said as she bent down and unclipped Earl Grey's leash. "How are you doing?"

"Staying out of trouble," Riley said. "You?"

"Um." Theodosia wasn't sure how much to tell him.

"Never mind, I know all about it," Riley said.

"All about what?"

"The fact that you tailed Wes Lenkov, discovered an illegal dog racing track, and then called in the cavalry. Tidwell called me. So I guess your little escapade beats sitting home at night."

"Speaking of which, when are *you* coming home?"

"Nice try at changing the subject, sweetheart."

"I had to give it a shot," Theodosia said.

"You'd better be a lot more careful or you *will* get shot. Whoever murdered Harlan Sadler has probably figured out by now that you're poking around where you shouldn't be."

"You think so?"

"I think you're in someone's crosshairs now."

"You're just trying to scare me," Theodosia said. "And you should know by now that I don't scare easily."

"You *should* be scared. Sadler's murder may have started out as an investigative lark for you, but now everything's turned dead serious. My advice to you is to bow out while you still can."

"I hear you," Theodosia said, knowing full well she was going to keep pushing ahead.

"No," Riley said. "That's the problem. You *don't* hear me."

19

The Indigo Tea Shop was awash with sunlight this morning. The day had dawned pink and gold with a butter yellow orb suspended in a robin's-egg blue sky. Sunbeams danced across tables and chairs, tea kettles chirped, and tea aromas mingled with that of scones baking in the oven. All should be right with the world, except for the fact that Theodosia was worried about her talk with Pete Riley last night. Riley wanted her to drop her private investigation—practically begged her to let it go. She'd hemmed and hawed about it, making excuses, fooling neither one of them. Now Theodosia knew she had only a few days to make something happen—to pull a suspect out of thin air—before Riley returned and really laid down the law.

She sighed, set down the teacup and saucer she'd been gripping for the last five minutes, and turned toward the front door as she heard the latch click open. In wandered Bill Glass, looking disheveled and cranky.

"What's wrong, Glass?" Theodosia asked. "You look like you

lost your best friend." Glass was dressed in ripped blue jeans and a schlumpy gray hoodie, no doubt trying to look younger and hipper than he really was.

"It's worse than that," Glass said. "Last night somebody broke into my office and stole a couple of cameras."

"Another break-in," Theodosia murmured. She wondered if it might be the same person who broke into her shop on Tuesday night. Then she immediately dismissed it, because her break-in had seemed more like intimidation, while Glass's break-in had been an actual robbery.

Although . . . if someone had seen Glass shooting footage at Harlan Sadler's funeral yesterday, perhaps they figured he also shot footage at the Mad Hatter Masquerade. So . . . was Glass now in danger as well?

"Did they steal your still camera or your video camera?" Theodosia asked.

"One of each, actually. I borrowed a Panasonic professional camcorder from Bill Boyet's Camera Shop—you know, the guy just down the block from you? I thought I'd fiddle around with it . . . well, you saw me at the funeral yesterday . . . to see if I maybe wanted to invest in one for myself."

"And the gear was stolen from your office?" Theodosia asked.

"My office, the *Shooting Star* office. I mean, the camera was there, sitting on a shelf, and then it *wasn't* there."

"You're sure it's gone?"

"Yes, I'm sure it's gone." Now Glass looked even crankier. "Some dirtbag jammed a screwdriver into my lock and popped the whole darn thing." He shook his head. "It's my bad luck that now I'll have to *pay* for that video camera!"

"Maybe your insurance will cover it," Theodosia said.

Bill Glass thought about that for a moment, then his face

brightened. "Doggone, girl, that just might work." He tapped a finger against the side of his head. "Did anybody ever tell you you've got a brilliant scheming mind?"

"It's not a scheme, Glass. That's how insurance works."

"Still, it's a great idea." He grinned as he warmed up to the idea. "Yeah, I can file a claim on *both* cameras, then collect the insurance money and buy new cameras, better cameras."

"Right," Theodosia said as she packed two scones in a bag for him. Drayton poured English breakfast tea into a take-out cup and snapped on a lid. "Now kindly accept our tea and scones and be on your merry way posthaste. We're having our Book Lovers Tea today, and I need to get the tea shop ready."

"Oh, I . . ." Glass blinked in surprise, saw the serious look on Theodosia's face, and capitulated. "Okay. Bye."

"What's his problem?" Drayton asked, once Glass had left the tea shop.

"He had a break-in, lost a couple of cameras."

"Another break-in," Drayton said. "You think it means anything?"

"Besides the fact that crime is on the rise? I'm not sure."

The tea shop was busy this Thursday morning, and Theodosia was glad to have Miss Dimple and Beth Ann helping out. Haley had outdone herself with chocolate chip scones and banana muffins, and Drayton had broken out a tin of Chinese Osmanthus oolong tea and brewed up a pot so they could give their regular customers—who often stuck with their regular orders—a taste of something a trifle more exotic.

By eleven fifteen, with only two tables of customers left sipping and munching, Theodosia decided it was time to get ready for their Book Lovers Tea.

"I'm thinking we should break out the Ladore by Haviland china," Theodosia told Miss Dimple.

"Oh, I adore that pattern," Miss Dimple said. "The scalloped edges and the wispy gold flowers."

Theodosia pulled out a stack of plates, then looked around. "Wait. Where's Beth Ann?"

"She ran down to Antiquarian Books to pick up a few more cartons," Miss Dimple said.

"More books?"

"We thought we'd turn up the volume," Miss Dimple said. Then she giggled and said, "That's a book joke. You know, volumes?"

"Cute," Theodosia said as she dug into the silverware drawer. "Oh, and let's use the pink crystal water glasses."

They had most of the tables set and looking lovely by the time Beth Ann and Lois came trooping in, laden with boxes of books.

"Man, these books weigh a ton," Beth Ann groaned.

"Try working full-time in a bookstore," Lois said. "That'll get your muscles in tip-top shape."

"Probably better than a membership at a pricey health club," Beth Ann said. She set two boxes down on the front counter with a resounding THUNK.

"Let's see what you've got here," Theodosia said. She flipped open the box and pulled out an oversized book. "Art books. No wonder you were struggling so hard. Are these all art books?"

"In that box, yes," Miss Dimple said. "They're big sellers at my shop. Most people are fond of art books, and decorators adore coffee-table books, so I thought they'd be just as popular here."

"Let's stack them on our tables and find out," Theodosia said.

They finished setting the tables, then placed two or three stacks of books in the center of each table. As they were working, Haley wandered out to see what was going on.

"Look how cool this is," Haley said as she perused a stack of books. "I see books by Poe, Dickens, J. K. Rowling, Mary Higgins Clark, John Sandford, and Terrie Farley Moran."

"That's just the fiction stack," Beth Ann said. "Over here are books on art, poetry, music, and home decorating."

"This is so wonderful," Miss Dimple cooed. "It's like we've created a grand literary salon."

"What else do you need?" Beth Ann asked Theodosia.

Theodosia pushed a tangle of curly auburn hair off her forehead. It was getting close to noon and her guests would be arriving soon. Time to kick it into high gear. "Let's see. The flowers from yesterday's tea still look good, so they can go back on the tables. We'll need a few candles in . . . let's use the white tapers in pewter candleholders. And I've got bunches of pens with feathers on them to set out as favors."

"Are the books already priced?" Miss Dimple asked. "How are we going to handle that?"

"They're priced," Lois said. "So you could . . ."

"Not to worry," Drayton called from across the room. "We'll just ring the books up with the luncheon tickets. I'll make note of the amounts and then settle up with you later."

"Perfect," Lois said.

The guests spilled in all at once. Holly Burns and her new assistant, Erica Pratt, from the Imago Gallery. A dozen guests from the Lit Girls Book Club. A few women who'd been on the Chocolate Stroll and vowed to come back. And Judi Cooper, a friend of Theodosia's who'd driven up from Savannah with two of her girlfriends.

"I heard about your Book Lovers Tea and couldn't resist,"

Judi told Theodosia. Then she looked around the tea shop and said, "I'm guessing you have books on art? And antiques?"

"Lots of books on antiques," Theodosia said.

"Good," Judi said. "Since my husband's an antique dealer, he can never have enough books on English sideboards and mantel clocks."

Theodosia greeted the rest of her guests and got them seated. A couple of extra people had shown up, so Miss Dimple and Beth Ann had to scramble for more place settings and chairs, but finally everyone was situated. Then Theodosia strolled to the center of the room to formally welcome her guests and announce the menu.

"Welcome to our Book Lovers Tea," Theodosia said. There was an extra twinkle in her eye because she and Haley had come up with some fun names for their food courses. "Since we're doing a salute to authors and their wonderful books, we're going to start your luncheon off with what we call Game of Scones—in other words, a choice of apple scones or cherry-walnut scones."

That brought peals of laughter and some good-hearted applause.

"Your soup du jour will be clam chowder à la *Moby Dick*, and your tea sandwiches today are *Joy Luck Club* sandwiches that feature fresh tomatoes, bacon, sliced turkey, and sweet Bibb lettuce. For dessert, we'll be serving *James and the Giant Peach* cobbler."

"I love it," one woman cried. "So bookish and creative!"

"And what about the tea?" another guest asked.

Theodosia nodded to her audience, then looked over at Drayton. "And for our tea, Drayton?"

Drayton stepped to the center of the room and stood next to Theodosia. With a sly grin on his face, he said, "Today I've brewed three marvelous teas for you—a Charles Dickens black tea blend from Simpson and Vail's Literary Tea Line, Mr. Darcy oolong and black tea from Bingley's Teas, and Reading Nook Blend by Plum Deluxe. Just tell our servers which tea you'd like to start with," Drayton said.

As conversation rose in an excited hum, Miss Dimple and Beth Ann circled the tables, pouring tea. Minutes later, Theodosia and Haley brought out the fresh-baked scones and placed one (and sometimes two) on all the guest's plates.

"There's Devonshire cream, lemon curd, and strawberry jam on the table," Theodosia told her guests. Feel free to dip and spoon to complement your scones, or use all three if you want to experiment."

"What about all these books on the table?" one woman asked. "Are they for reading or for show?"

"They're actually for sale," Theodosia said. "Our dear friend Lois Chamberlain from Antiquarian Books brought them from her shop."

"They're for sale?" a woman said excitedly, which produced an exuberant litany of comments . . .

"Here's a book on poetry."

"Pass me that book on Charleston ghosts, will you?"

"You see any children's books?"

"Oh my gosh, here's a classic by Alexandre Dumas."

And it went on and on like that. Their guests enjoying their tea luncheon, exclaiming over books, and piling up personal stacks of books for purchase.

"Our tea party is going smashingly well, don't you think?" Drayton said to Theodosia. They were both standing behind the front counter, happy their guests were enjoying the soup and tea sandwiches.

"They're loving the menu and the books," Theodosia said. "I have a good feeling that Lois is going to rack up quite a few sales." She reached over to turn up the background music. Their sound system was playing "Rolling in the Deep" by Adele, when, suddenly, the front door flew open with an explosive BANG!

What? was Theodosia's single, confused thought.

Then she looked over and saw . . .

20

❧

"*Emily Bates,*" *Theodosia* murmured. Flustered, she stared at the woman who wore a sensible blue suit and a tight-jawed grimace. Then Emily advanced on Theodosia, looking as if she were about to spit forth a toxic mixture of fire and brimstone. That's when Theodosia realized this wasn't exactly a social call.

"Theodosia!" Emily shrilled, her voice rising high and loud, practically rattling the glass in the chandelier. "I just found out you've been asking questions about me!"

"Excuse me?" Theodosia was suddenly at a loss for words. For one thing, every one of her guests had turned to stare at her, wondering what on earth was going on. For another, she had no idea who told Emily she'd been asking questions about her. Then her mind clicked over into clear analytic mode and she thought, *Oh poop, could it have been Delaine?*

Before Theodosia could lodge any sort of protest, Emily Bates bared her teeth and completely let loose.

"Are you hearing me?" Emily shouted. Her face had flushed

an ugly bright red, her thin lips twisted into a harsh grimace, and she was darn near spitting. "I'm sick and tired of people whispering behind my back about this Sadler thing. I'm warning you, back off now. Leave me alone and tend to your . . ." Emily flung out an arm, gesturing wildly at the guests in the tea shop. "Your stupid tea thing!" she shouted.

That was the point at which Drayton stepped in to intervene. The stern look on his face said he'd had enough of Emily's outrageous behavior.

"Excuse me, miss, but you're being exceedingly rude," Drayton said to Emily as he came around the counter, bearing down on her with a purposeful stride.

"You haven't *seen* rude," Emily snarled back, barely giving him a cursory glance. "I'm furious and I'm here to say my piece!"

"I really must ask you to step outside," Drayton said. His voice was calm but determined.

Emily turned toward him, eyes blazing. "Get lost, bozo. I'll leave when I'm good and ready."

"I'd say you're ready now," Drayton said. He grasped Emily's upper arm, guided her into a firm but gently controlled spin, and began moving her in the direction of the front door. In other words, exit stage right.

"How dare you!" Emily sputtered as she struggled to break free. "Let go of me, I'm not done!" But Drayton was taller and outweighed Emily, so she remained pretty much his prisoner.

"Madam, you *are* done. You're so done we could stick a fork in you," Drayton said with pleasant determination. He kicked open the front door and led a still-protesting Emily out onto the sidewalk. When they were safely away from the door, he released her quickly, as if he'd been handling a poisonous reptile. Then, darting back inside, Drayton turned the lock and heaved a sigh.

"Whoa," Theodosia said to Drayton. "My hero. I can't believe how well you handled her. I mean, that wasn't just a hissy fit. That woman went totally nuclear."

"Anyone that disruptive simply has to go," Drayton said as he straightened his bow tie then touched a hand to his heart. "This is a tea shop after all. Decorum must be maintained." He glanced at their guests, who'd all gone back to talking and enjoying their luncheon, and heaved a second sigh of relief. Then he lowered his voice and said, "Exactly *how* did Emily Bates know that you've been asking questions about her?"

"I might have an idea about that," Theodosia said.

"Delaine?" Drayton asked. "She *is* a little loose in the hinges."

"Loose with her tongue as well."

Once the guests had finished with dessert and began to gather around Lois to talk books, Theodosia slid into her office and picked up the phone.

"You blabbed," Theodosia said once she had Delaine on the line.

"I did nothing of the sort!" Delaine cried. Then, in a slightly quavering voice, said, "Um, what exactly are we talking about here?"

"You told Emily Bates that I was asking questions about her, didn't you?"

The silence on the other end of the line was deafening.

"Delaine? I'm waiting for your answer."

"Well . . ."

"So you did tell her."

"I *might* have let a few things slip when Emily stopped in for a fitting," Delaine squeaked.

"Which led to Emily Bates going nuclear and having a complete and total meltdown."

"What'd she do?" Delaine asked.

"Stomped into my tea shop, smack-dab in the middle of our Book Lovers Tea, and started screaming at me!"

"Emily did that?" Delaine said.

"All because *you* spilled the beans."

"Theo, I'm sorry, really," Delaine whined. "But you know me, I'm a cray-cray little chatterbox, talking all the time. I mean, who doesn't love to hear all the news plus a hot dose of gossip?"

"Don't try to change the subject."

Without missing a beat, Delaine said, "And, truth be told, when it comes to helping Cricket, I'm just so darned *proud* that you're smart and able to ferret out clues to solve crimes and stuff . . ."

"Flattery will get you nowhere," Theodosia said.

"Nothing's working, huh?"

"Not even close."

"Then I . . . well, I guess I apologize," Delaine said.

Theodosia was working to pull her anger back from DEF-CON 3 to DEFCON 1. Once she got her emotions under control and digested Delaine's words, she said, "Apology accepted."

"Really and truly?" Delaine squealed. "You won't hold this against me? Still besties? Pinky swear?"

"Sure," Theodosia said. "Why not."

"And you're still coming to the silent auction and cocktail party tonight?"

"Delaine, best not to push it."

"But you will come, won't you? Pretty please? You said you would."

"I'll be there." Theodosia decided she'd go for Cricket's sake and not Delaine's.

"Oh," Delaine said. "On another matter. Bettina will be dropping by your tea shop later this afternoon. There's something important she wants to ask you."

"What's that?"

"I'm sure Bettina will tell you when she gets there," Delaine said. And promptly hung up.

"Well?" Drayton said when Theodosia returned.

"It was Delaine. She claimed she was in one of her talky phases."

Drayton shook his head. "I'd say Delaine has more phases than the moon."

Just at the tail end of the luncheon, Detective Burt Tidwell strolled in. He glanced around, looking like the proverbial bull in a china shop, seemingly confused by the clusters of women. Then he spotted Theodosia behind the front counter. Walking over to her, he said, without preamble, "You did the right thing last night."

"I did?" Theodosia was amazed that Tidwell actually had a positive word for her. His usual modus operandi was to shoo her away from any and all police business.

"We dispatched an entire army out there to round up as many people as we could. A few wily ones slipped away from us, but we managed to arrest most of the dog owners and organizers."

"Good. What happened to the dogs?"

"They were transported to the Charleston County Humane Society for safekeeping."

"Please tell me they won't go back to their owners."

"A judge has to rule on that. But between you and me? Doubtful. We've already spoken with two rescue groups who want to foster the dogs and then place them in good homes."

"Those poor dogs deserve forever homes and a normal life,"

Theodosia said. Then, because she was feeling kindly toward Tidwell, said, "Would you like to stay for lunch?"

Tidwell's lips twitched into a mousy smile. "I thought you'd never ask."

Theodosia stepped around the counter and led him to a clean table near the fireplace. "This should do." Then she hurried into the kitchen and made up a luncheon plate—a scone, cup of chowder, and three tea sandwiches—and carried it back out to him. Drayton, meanwhile, had set a small pot of tea on Tidwell's table.

"Here you go," Theodosia said. "I had to give you Devonshire cream and lemon curd for your scones. Apologies, but we're clean out of strawberry jam."

Tidwell pursed his lips and said, "Sit for a moment, will you?"

This was an unprecedented invitation on Tidwell's part, so Theodosia sat down.

Tidwell poured a cup of tea, took a noisy slurp, swallowed, and said, "I have news."

Theodosia leaned forward, feeling a tickle of excitement. This had to be it. "You caught Sadler's killer!"

"No. Not yet, I'm afraid."

"Then what . . . ?"

"You can stop harassing young Mr. Ethan Stacks for the time being, because we've managed to locate his father."

Theodosia practically fell off her chair. "What? Jeb Stacks is *alive*?"

"Apparently he is *compos mentis* since the man is working . . . *has* been working as a trainer at Ruidoso Downs for the past several years."

"I've heard of it . . ."

"A racetrack in New Mexico."

"So why was Ethan Stacks so mysterious about where his father disappeared to?" Theodosia wondered. "Why did he let people believe he was dead?"

"I don't know. Maybe to keep pressure on Harlan Sadler? To make him look guilty as sin and ruin his reputation? You tell me."

Theodosia shook her head. "I have no clue."

"No clue," Tidwell repeated. "That does seem to be the watchword of the day."

"That's it," Theodosia said to Drayton. "Jeb Stacks is alive and well and living in New Mexico."

Drayton gave her a startled look. "He's not dead?"

"Not if he's still training horses."

"So Ethan Stacks is no longer a suspect?"

"I don't think so. Unless there was something between Ethan Stacks and Sadler that we don't know about."

"What are you going to do now?"

Theodosia shrugged. "Clean the tables?"

"No, I mean . . ."

"I know what you mean and I'm not sure what to do about anything right now. Gotta think for a while."

Theodosia went to work, cleaning tables and chatting with the last of her guests. She mulled over Sadler's murder and her sort-of list of suspects, then realized she still hadn't talked to Lucy Harris.

Maybe give her a call?

After all, Lucy had played the role of Red Queen at the masquerade, so maybe she had some insight to toss into the mix.

But after a couple minutes of conversation, Lucy Harris didn't seem to know much of anything.

"I heard about the murder," Lucy told Theodosia, speaking with precise diction as if she were onstage. "The news spread like wildfire the night of the masquerade, but then we were all told to go home." She hesitated. "I wasn't acquainted with the victim, though I have met Cricket Sadler. She's one of our theater's benefactors. I'm guessing her husband was an important man?"

"Harlan Sadler was a banker and Cricket was the chairperson for the Mad Hatter Masquerade."

"Oh no, I didn't realize that. How awful."

"So you didn't see anything suspicious going on?"

"Not really," Lucy said. "Well . . . that whole evening was a little surreal."

Theodosia perked up. "How so?"

"All the partygoers—the black-tie people—seemed super jacked up, as if they hardly ever got a chance to let loose and have fun. But they certainly were celebrating that night."

"Anything they did or said stand out to you?" Theodosia asked.

"The croquet players acted a little crazy."

"In what way?"

"You know how men get when they drink. The particular guys I noticed were acting all macho and pretending to smash things with their mallets," Lucy said.

Theodosia winced. "Did anything actually get smashed?"

"Some cocktail glasses, I guess," Lucy said. "At least I saw one of the waiters on his hands and knees scooping up shards of glass."

"But nothing else?"

"Not that I can think of."

"Do you remember who these guys were?" Theodosia asked.

"No, I'd never seen them before."

"Thanks, Lucy, you've been a big help," Theodosia said. Even though she really hadn't.

Theodosia walked out of her office, checked the tea room—six tables were occupied—and went to the front counter.

"Lucy Harris didn't have anything new to add," she told Drayton.

"The Red Queen?" Drayton said. "Pity." He remained quiet for a few moments, then cleared his throat and said, "What you said about Cricket the other night . . ."

"Remind me. What did I say?" Theodosia said.

"That you were ninety-nine percent sure she didn't have her own husband murdered. Are you still that sure?"

"None of my suspects seem to be panning out. So, no, I'm not completely sure about Cricket. I mean, she seems utterly overwhelmed with sadness, but who knows? There is that one percent unknown that it could be an act."

"Peter Tolboth mentioned that Cricket and her husband were big supporters of the Westside Theatre," Drayton said. "You don't suppose . . ."

"That Cricket took one of their acting classes and learned how to fake her distress? That seems like an enormous stretch."

"Remember, truth can be stranger than fiction," Drayton said.

"You think I should call Tolboth and ask him?"

"You said it yourself, none of your suspects are panning out."

"Something to think about."

So Theodosia did think about it. While she stacked bottles of green tea moisturizer and chamomile calming lotion onto the shelves of her highboy, she let the idea percolate in her brain.

Cricket. Taking acting lessons? To make her distress seem all the more real? Should I call the theater? Not call the theater?

Theodosia called the theater. And asked to be put through to Peter Tolboth.

"I hope we were able to help you the other night," Tolboth said to Theodosia, once they'd exchanged initial pleasantries.

"You did. And it was really fun for Drayton and I to peek into the backstage workings of what you do," Theodosia said.

"Come back anytime. Take a tour, see a show, take a class."

"You give classes to amateurs?"

"Oh sure," Tolboth said. "We have a lot of businesspeople who take our improv classes just so they can learn how to sharpen their presentation skills. You know, learn to think fast on their feet."

"That sounds like a fairly smart idea. And you have acting classes as well?"

"At all levels," Tolboth said. "We teach acting techniques, scene study, cold reading, commercial acting, body and movement, you name it."

"I know Cricket Sadler was impressed by your repertoire of classes," Theodosia said. It was a little white lie that she hoped Tolboth would pick up on.

Luckily, he did.

"That's kind of her to say. Believe it or not, Cricket actually took our acting techniques class a few months ago. Said she wanted to build her confidence when it came to public speaking and such."

"Well, it certainly worked for her," Theodosia said. "Anyway, I just wanted to touch base with you and thank you again for passing along the head sheets."

"I hope I was able to help," Tolboth said.

"I think maybe you did," Theodosia said.

Back in the tea room, Theodosia said, "You were right. Cricket *did* take an acting class at the Westside Theatre."

"Sometimes I hate it when I'm right," Drayton said.

"But that doesn't mean Cricket is guilty. Or that she's been overacting."

"Of course not."

"On the other hand . . ."

"You think Cricket will show up for the silent auction tonight?" Theodosia asked.

"I don't know," Drayton said. "Why don't we go and find out?"

"I thought that was the plan all along," Theodosia said. She grabbed a gray plastic tub from behind the counter, cleaned off two tables, then carried the dirty dishes into the kitchen.

Haley had just set two pans of croissants on the counter to proof.

"Those look good," Theodosia said.

"For tomorrow," Haley said. She washed her hands, dried them on her apron, and said, "That bank lady who came in and yelled at you before? I have a friend who works at that bank. Well . . . she used to work there."

"At Unity One? What happened to your friend? Did the dragon lady fire her?"

Haley shook her head. "She quit to take a job at Parasol, that cute little gift shop over on Queen Street. Izzy, that's my friend's name, said it was a whole lot more fun. Claimed working at the bank was toxic."

Interested now, Theodosia said, "Do you think your friend would talk to me? About her experience at the bank, I mean?"

"I dunno. Maybe. I could give her a call."

"Do that, will you?" Theodosia said.

21

Just as Delaine had said they would, Bettina and her fiancé, Jamie Wilkes, showed up at the Indigo Tea Shop some twenty minutes later. Bettina was dressed in a hot pink twin set and jeans. Jamie wore a white T-shirt and jeans. Together they looked like Barbie and Ken dolls.

As Theodosia greeted them warmly, Bettina said, "You remember Jamie, don't you?"

"Indeed, I do," Theodosia said, shaking Jamie's hand. "When we first met, you were playing bartender at Delaine's boutique. Dispensing champagne to a bunch of crazed fashionistas."

"Delaine likes to shanghai anybody and everybody," Jamie said.

"She does indeed," Theodosia said. "And now Delaine tells me that the two of you have moved up the date of your wedding?"

"That's right," Jamie said, ducking his head shyly as he clutched Bettina's hand. He was tall and broad-shouldered, with longish light brown hair that gave him a sort of surfer dude look.

If Theodosia had been ten years younger, she would have considered Jamie a serious hunk.

Theodosia led Bettina and Jamie to a table, sat them down, and said, "I understand you have something you want to ask me?"

At which point Bettina dimpled prettily and said, "We have a catering job we'd like you to consider."

"Oh my gosh," Theodosia said, touching a hand to her mouth in surprise. "This is about your wedding, isn't it?"

Bettina reached over and clutched Jamie's hand again. Then she winked at Theodosia and said, "It sure is."

"Was this Delaine's idea?" Theodosia asked.

"Are you kidding?" Bettina feigned utter shock. "If Aunt Delaine was planning my wedding, she'd have me dressed up like a Disney princess with at least a dozen bridesmaids. The wedding would be in a church, there'd be a white dove release, and we'd be serving caviar and lobster at our reception."

"And riding in a horse-drawn carriage," Jamie added.

Bettina wrinkled her nose. "I think we're going to have to learn to live with the horse and carriage, sweetie. But we can still keep things simple." She smiled at Jamie. "Just like we both want."

"I'm thrilled you thought of me," Theodosia said. "So tell me what you're thinking. And when you're planning to tie the knot."

Fairly bubbling with enthusiasm, Bettina pulled a notebook out of her purse and opened it. "Actually, we want you to cater two *different* events—a rehearsal breakfast and our wedding reception."

"And these would happen when?" Theodosia asked.

"We're going to be married next month," Bettina said. "The third Saturday in October."

"And you've already reserved a wedding venue?" Theodosia asked.

"We're going to do it at Foxtail Flower Farm just south of Fenwick Hills," Bettina said. "They have the most gorgeous greenhouse there filled with all sorts of green plants and hanging flower baskets. We thought we'd set up tables inside the greenhouse and decorate them with candles, white pumpkins, and apples on a runner of green moss. Everything very eco-friendly. That tea will be held right after our wedding rehearsal on Friday morning. The next day, Saturday, is our actual wedding day. We'll hold the service outside in their garden."

"Unless it rains," Jamie said. "Then I suppose we'll have to move the wedding into the greenhouse."

"A contingency plan," Theodosia said. "Always a smart idea."

"But I really have my heart set on the out-of-doors. So we can stand under an arch of pampas grass, dark red maple leaves, and red bittersweet," Bettina said.

"She wants all the colors to be autumn jewel tones," Jamie said, gazing at Bettina with love.

"Oh, and the cool thing is, Foxtail Flower Farm has a small kitchen where you'll be able to prepare and stage the food," Bettina said. "The kitchen's all nice and modern and is housed in a cute little white cottage that sits next to two other cottages."

"So one cottage will be reserved exclusively for the bride and her bridesmaids," Jamie said.

"And the other cottage is for my groom and groomsmen," Bettina said as they gazed at each other with tenderness.

"Two events, two different menus," Theodosia said. "One for your rehearsal tea, the other for your wedding reception. Why don't I work up some ideas and get back to you in a few days?" She paused. "Is there anything important I should know about the wedding? Something to keep in mind?"

"Just that we're trying to keep everything very natural and

organic and outdoorsy. And we don't want anything too fussy," Bettina said.

"Tell Theodosia about your dress," Jamie said.

"Aunt Delaine is probably going to strangle me," Bettina said, "but I plan to wear a vintage linen dress from the sixties. It's very free-flowing and boho, kind of low-cut with lots of lace."

Theodosia grinned. "You're right, Delaine is going to kill you."

"She's been pitching me on a blingy fishtail dress with a thirty-foot train and froufrou veil," Bettina said, giving a mock shudder.

"And you want none of that," Theodosia said.

"I want simple and romantic," Bettina said, batting her eyes at Jamie. "We both do."

"So you roped us into catering a wedding?" Drayton asked, once Bettina and Jamie had walked out the door, hand in hand, of course. He pushed a cup of tea across the counter to Theodosia. "Try this. Something new in the repertoire."

"Not roped in. Just a catering job, which is something we're pretty good at," Theodosia said. "And it's going to be particularly easy since they're planning a small ceremony at a casual venue."

"Which is?"

Theodosia took a sip of tea, then said, "A place called Foxtail Flower Farm. Out on Highway 700."

"I saw an article in *Charleston Today* about that place," Drayton said. "They raise flowers for commercial florists, but the public can also go there and pick their own bouquets."

"I love that idea. Maybe I'll take a run out there next week and check the place out. Take a look at their greenhouse and kitchen." Theodosia took another sip of tea. "Gosh, this is delicious. What is it?"

"An Oothu Estate Nilgiri," Drayton said. "So we'd be catering Bettina's wedding reception?"

"And a tea party the day before. A morning rehearsal tea instead of a rehearsal dinner. I think it's smart they're not spending a gazillion dollars on an overblown wedding and decided to keep things simple."

"Just you wait until Delaine sticks her fingers in the pot," Drayton warned. "Then you won't be so upbeat about this wedding."

"I suppose that's bound to happen. As soon as Delaine gets wind that the wedding venue is at a flower farm, she's going to have a major freak-out."

"Or claim a major case of hay fever," Drayton said.

At five o'clock, Theodosia was the last one left at the tea shop. She did a final tidying up, then locked the doors and went home.

Earl Grey was ready and waiting for her at the back door.

"It'll have to be a short walk for now," Theodosia told him. "Then I need to come back here and get all glammed up."

Earl Grey tilted his head and stared at her. "Rowwr?"

"You're exactly right, it's black tie."

Theodosia and Earl Grey did a quick foxtrot around the block, stretching their legs, then came home. Theodosia gave Earl Grey his kibbles and fresh water, then hurried upstairs to change.

When Theodosia first moved into her little cottage (which had the adorable name of Hazelhurst), she spent a little money converting the entire upstairs into a bedroom / bathroom / reading room. She covered the walls in Laura Ashley wallpaper and bought the matching comforter for her four-poster bed. Her reading room had a sagging-with-books bookcase and a plump, chintz-covered chair and footstool. And her mother's dresser and antique vanity sat against one wall in the bedroom.

Right now, the vanity held a scatter of jewelry, perfume bottles—Miss Dior, Chanel No. 5, and Creed's Fleurissimo—a Jo Malone candle, and a sweetgrass basket that contained stacks of colorful bangles and strands of beads. A pair of Chinese ginger jar lamps lent soft illumination to what was a cozy, slightly kitschy space.

Stepping into the shower, Theodosia dialed it up hot and let the spray hit her with needle-like intensity. When she emerged, fresh, clean, and wrapped in a thick, terry cloth robe, she found that Earl Grey had come upstairs and was curled on his over-priced L.L.Bean dog bed, watching her.

"What do you think I should wear tonight?" Theodosia asked him. Then, "Oh right, it's black tie. So maybe . . ." She padded over to her walk-in closet, peered inside, and said, "Hmm." She spotted a black cocktail dress with a fitted bodice, slightly flared skirt, and hot pink sash—a dress she'd always thought of as her tulip dress. She grabbed the dress, held it up to her in front of a mirror, and said, "Yes, I think this will work just fine."

Her makeup was a snap. She wasn't a fussy person, so she didn't fuss too much with makeup. Just a dab of foundation, a touch of mascara, and some brow gel. Her hair, on the other hand, was a little tricky. Heat and humidity from the shower had caused her hair to expand into an auburn halo that encircled her head. And while it did give the impression of an ethereal subject from a Pre-Raphaelite painting, her hair was a handful to work with.

Tonight, Theodosia brushed it into a massive, loose, and

slightly messy bun, and secured it with a large gold clip that had belonged to her mother.

There. That should hold it. For a while, anyway.

Her earrings went on next. A pair of blue sapphire studs that perfectly matched the color of her eyes.

What else?

She grabbed a black sequin evening bag from her top drawer, then put on a pair of strappy black heels. She slid her phone into the purse, then immediately pulled it back out when she heard its musical chime.

"Hello?"

It was Riley, calling from Savannah where he was *still* tied up. Theodosia grinned and switched over to FaceTime.

"Wow," Riley said when he saw her. "You're all dolled up. Where are you going looking like that? You got a hot date?"

"No, silly, I'm going to a cocktail party and silent auction that benefits the Opera Society."

"Speaking of which, how goes the sleuthing? Have you disregarded my warning and fingered Harlan Sadler's killer yet?"

"Not yet, but I'm still working on it."

"Please promise me you'll be careful."

"You know I will," Theodosia said.

"No, I don't know that. You look up the word *trouble* in *Webster's Dictionary* and there's a little picture of *you* there."

"Say now . . ."

"And trouble *will* find you if you continue bugging Duke Sadler and Ethan Stacks to death."

"Stacks didn't pan out," Theodosia said. "Because his father . . ."

"Is alive. Yeah, I know," Riley said. "I'm fairly sure that rules him out."

"So you're *always* in the loop? Tidwell tells you *everything*?"

"Not everything. I'm sure there are a few things we don't

know about since you've been prowling the city, overstepping your boundaries, and getting into trouble."

"Getting into trouble?" Theodosia said. "Me? *That's* not going to happen."

Riley was suddenly so convulsed with laughter he could barely say goodbye.

22

"You look like a million bucks in that tuxedo," Theodosia said as Drayton climbed into her Jeep.

"Brioni," Drayton said as he pulled his seat belt across and buckled it. "Which almost *did* set me back a million bucks."

"So once again we're on our way to a black-tie party," Theodosia said as she pulled away from the curb. "Hopefully this one will go off without a hitch."

"You mean without a murder?" Drayton said.

"Well, sure. I mean, I hope so."

"As do I."

They cruised down Meeting Street, passing the Circular Congregational Church and Gibbes Museum of Art. Lights blazed from the windows of the museum as a dozen or so people streamed in.

"What's going on in there?" Theodosia asked.

"I think an exhibition by local artists opens tonight," Drayton said.

"Always lots going on in Charleston."

"Because it's a society town," Drayton said. "We have museums, theaters, great restaurants, even sporting events. People love gadding about, to see and be seen."

"Speaking of which . . . do you think Cricket will show up for the silent auction tonight?"

"Cricket? No," Drayton said. "Probably not, since Delaine offered to take it over. But I do think a lot of folks will come out to swan around. It's a cocktail party, which always brings out the old money crowd as well as the nouveau riche, cocktail-swilling yuppies. Plus, there's the silent auction with lots of fancy-schmancy items to bid on."

"The auction is for a good cause."

"And a run-up event to the big Opera in the Park on Saturday night," Drayton said.

"In Petigru Park?"

"Yes, and it's downright perfect with that natural grassy bowl that can function as an amphitheater. They're probably setting up chairs and the stage right now."

"I've been so busy, I don't even know which opera is being performed," Theodosia said.

"*Aida* by Verdi, one of my absolute favorites."

"Ah, that is lovely," Theodosia said as she pulled into the circular drive that led to the Lady Goodwood Inn.

The cobblestone drive was lined with stately palmetto trees that swayed gently in the night breeze. Strung with tiny white lights around their trunks, they gave the impression of an ethereal fairy world. Luminaries in glass orbs lit a path to the inn's double doors where young valets, resplendent in red-and-gold livery, hopped to as they greeted guests and parked cars.

Theodosia jumped out of her Jeep—carefully, she didn't want to break a heel—and entered the Lady Goodwood Inn with Drayton. The lobby was an elegant affair, featuring original

Georgian paneling, a fireplace with white marble facing, two French Empire card tables, and cozy furniture upholstered in a deep apricot fabric. Throngs of people buzzed everywhere, all dressed to the nines and heading in the same direction—to the Sandpiper Ballroom where the silent auction was being held.

"Crowded already," Drayton said as they walked into the ballroom. It was wall-to-wall people, everyone smiling, air kissing, laughing loudly, shrieking at friends, and hurriedly grabbing drinks.

"And look at all the auction items," Theodosia said. "There has to be—what? A dozen tables?"

"At least."

Theodosia and Drayton pushed through the crowd, greeting a few people they knew, nodding to a few people they sort of knew.

"Folks are lined up at the bar ten-deep," Theodosia said. "Should we maybe take a look at the auction items first?"

"If you insist," Drayton said.

"You're really not into this, are you?"

Drayton shrugged. "Too early to tell."

"Let's at least have a look."

They strolled along, looking at the items up for bid. There was a gift certificate for dinner at Poogan's Porch, a Panasonic video camera, a diamond ring from Charles Kerrison, a set of Baccarat wine glasses from Britain's of Charleston, a pair of tickets to the Charleston Ballet's production of *Swan Lake*, a goose-down comforter from Palais Royal, a sterling silver necklace-and-bracelet set from Hearts Desire, and about a hundred more seriously luxe items.

"There's so much good stuff here," Theodosia said. "Makes it difficult to choose what to bid on."

"We're fairly early, so you can bid on whatever you feel like,"

Drayton said. Then added, "After all, somebody's bound to come along two minutes after you write down your bid and up it by twenty dollars."

"And that will go on all night," Theodosia said. "So maybe it's smart to wait until the end? After everyone's placed their bids?"

"Then you can come in for the kill," Drayton said. "Probably an excellent strategy."

"Which means we probably should relax for a while and enjoy a couple of cocktails."

Drayton brightened. "Yes. And the bar is where again?"

"Over against that wall." Theodosia raised herself up on tiptoes. "And thank goodness it looks a little less crowded now."

On the way to the bar, they passed Ethan Stacks. He was talking to an older couple, looking fairly animated as he described an Irish crystal chandelier that he'd just acquired.

"Stacks," Theodosia said to Drayton. "The antique dealer." She noted that tonight Ethan Stacks wore an ill-fitting navy blue suit with a gray shirt, and had slicked his hair back with some kind of shiny gel. He still had a scruffy goatee and wore his wire-rimmed Trotsky glasses.

Drayton looked back at Stacks, looked back a second time, and said, "Mr. Stacks?" in a pleasant tone.

Stacks turned toward Drayton with a practiced smile. "Yes?" he said. Then he saw Theodosia standing next to Drayton and his smile turned sour.

"I was wondering if you ever got in that pair of yellow glazed tea bowls you mentioned," Drayton said. "If you recall, I bought a pair of oyster plates from you at the Fall Antique Fair."

"No," Stacks said, still fixing his hostile gaze on Theodosia as his glasses slid halfway down his nose. "I don't have any tea bowls for sale." And with that, Stacks pushed up his glasses, turned, and hurried away.

"How rude," Theodosia said.

"But kind of amusing, too," Drayton said with a crooked grin. "Your visit must have really upset him. Maybe Ethan Stacks *is* the guilty party."

"No," Theodosia said. "I don't think so. And neither do the police."

"They're quite sure about that?"

"Since his father was found alive and well, the police don't believe Ethan Stacks is connected to Sadler's murder in any way."

"At least there's one person you can cross off your list," Drayton said as they pushed their way to the bar that was only two-deep with customers. "What shall we have? How about a glass of champagne?"

"Perfect."

They stood behind a small woman wearing a tight black cocktail dress with a high ruffled collar. She'd ordered a glass of red wine from one of the busy waiters, taken a taste of it, and was unhappy.

"Don't you have anything better?" the woman asked. "Perhaps a nice cabernet?"

"That's our house pour," the bartender said politely. "I'm afraid it's the best we can do, ma'am."

"Well, it *won't* do for me," the woman said in a belligerent tone. She shoved the wine back across the counter, slopping most of it on the bar, then turned quickly and almost collided with Theodosia. "Could you possibly crowd me any closer?" the woman said in a nasty voice. Then her eyes went big as saucers as she recognized Theodosia. "You again!" the woman cried.

It was Emily Bates.

"Emily Bates?" Theodosia squeaked. She was just as surprised as Emily was. Maybe more so. Then she gathered her wits about her and said, "Apologies, Ms. Bates, if we . . ."

"Will you two get *out* of my way," Emily cried before Theodosia could finish her sentence. She stuck out a boney arm and elbowed her way between Theodosia and Drayton, practically stepping on their toes.

"Nice to see you, too," Theodosia said to a retreating Emily.

Drayton shook his head. "With that ruffled collar and vile expression on her face, she reminded me of one of those nasty spitting lizards." He paused. "Did you know Emily was going to be here tonight?"

"No. And I'm truly sorry she is. Emily Bates seems to spread unhappiness wherever she goes."

"Do you still think she could have murdered Harlan Sadler?"

"Without a doubt, but I don't know what more I can do to investigate her," Theodosia said. "I've asked around and the woman has no friends to speak of."

"You need to grab a broom and fly after her to her lair," Drayton said.

"Ding dong, the witch is dead," Theodosia said. "I wish."

They got glasses of champagne—the house pour, which turned out to be quite nice—and headed back to peruse the auction items.

"Maybe we should keep our distance tonight," Drayton said. "Since we seem to have ruffled a few feathers."

"Agreed," Theodosia said. "Say, here's a golf weekend for two at Hilton Head. That could be fun."

"Maybe for you," Drayton said, "but I don't golf. Chasing a little white ball around a pastoral setting is not my idea of cerebral amusement."

"There must be something here that appeals to you, something you can bid on. It is for a good cause."

They studied the auction items again.

"How about a fishing trip with Blue Boy Sportfishing Charters? Or here's a gift certificate for a leather-bound set of Shakespeare," Theodosia said.

"Pass. I already own a set. *Vintage.*"

"There's a nice bottle of wine . . ." Theodosia pointed to a bottle of red wine, then peered at its description page. "Says here it's a 2016 bottle of Château Angélus Saint-Emilion."

"Now you're talking. Emily Bates would probably approve of this wine. What's the most recent bid?"

"Um . . . fifty-five dollars. Looks like people are bidding in five-dollar increments."

"Then I'll go seventy-five," Drayton said. "If I can get a bottle of Château Angélus for that price, it's an absolute steal."

"Here's a gift certificate for a pair of shoes at Robertson's."

"Dancing shoes?" Drayton did a quick, light-hearted imitation of a soft-shoe dance.

"I suppose if you want. But . . . oh no." Theodosia stopped dead in her tracks.

"What?" Drayton said.

Theodosia pointed at a shiny wooden croquet set that was perched on the table. "A croquet set?" she said, her brows pulled together in dismay. "Is this someone's idea of a bad joke?"

"It does seem in rather poor taste. Are there any bids on it?"

Theodosia scanned the sheet. "No."

"Good," Drayton said. "Let's hope it stays that way."

"Is this somebody's idea of a joke?" Ray Crispin asked. He'd suddenly joined Theodosia and Drayton and was staring angrily at the croquet set.

"That's exactly what we were wondering," Theodosia said. "Mr. Crispin, this is Drayton Conneley, my tea sommelier. Drayton, this is Ray Crispin, Harlan Sadler's former partner."

"Hello," Drayton said. "Sorry for your loss."

"Thank you," Crispy said as they shook hands. "And pleased to finally meet you." He gestured at the croquet set. "A bizarre item for the silent auction, wouldn't you say?"

"At least nobody's bid on it," Theodosia said.

"It's offensive," Crispy said. "I think it should be removed." He glanced around, saw a waiter collecting dirty cocktail glasses, and said, "Young man? Excuse me, young man?"

The waiter came over to him. "Yes sir?"

"When you get a chance, would you kindly remove this croquet set?" Crispy asked. "It isn't supposed to be here. There's been a mistake."

"Of course, sir, I'll take care of it right away."

Crispy pulled a wad of cash from his pocket, peeled off a twenty for the waiter, and said, "Good man." He gave a two-fingered salute to Theodosia and Drayton and was on his way.

Theodosia and Drayton watched as the waiter grabbed the croquet set, hefted it off the table, and hauled it away.

"Well, that was strange," Drayton said. "Almost like a direct taunt."

"That's what I was thinking. Somebody's sick joke."

"But whose?" Drayton said. Then, "Hopefully we're not in for any more weird surprises."

Theodosia nudged Drayton and said, "Want to bet? Take a look at what's happening over there."

"What?" Drayton spun around to see what she was looking at.

"You're not going to believe this," Theodosia said. "But Duke Sadler and Wes Lenkov just faced off. And they look like they're ready to kill each other!"

23

Duke and Lenkov were squared off against each other, both posturing like WWE fighters who were ready to do serious battle. Fists curled, shoulders hunched forward, and heads down, they kept their weight balanced on the balls of their feet as if they were on a hair trigger, ready to attack.

"Sweet dogs," Drayton exclaimed. "This is awful. Hopefully they'll only exchange words."

"Looks to me like they're ready to exchange blows," Theodosia said. "Maybe we should . . . get a little closer? See what's really going on?"

They elbowed their way through the crowd, closing in on the two men who'd actually begun to taunt each other.

"What are you doing here?" Duke Sadler demanded of Wes Lenkov. "This isn't your scene."

"Get out of my face, you worthless punk," Lenkov spat back. "Or I'll shove my fist in your face and flatten you."

"Still the sad little poser, aren't you?" Duke said with an angry snarl.

"*You're* the poser," Lenkov said. His voice had risen above conversation level, causing a restless stir around him. "Acting like a bigshot, but cheating people out of their money. You should be *ashamed* of yourself. You're a *moshennik,* a crook!"

A number of curious guests now circled the two men, watching with fascination as Sadler took a step forward, putting his face inches from Lenkov's. "You want to take this outside?" Sadler asked.

At which point Ned Grady, Delaine's new boyfriend, came huffing up to them, stuck an arm between the two men and said, "Come on, guys. This is a social event, not WrestleMania."

"Get lost," Duke said.

"I'm not gonna do that," Grady said. "In fact, I'm going to insist that you two gentlemen stop this silliness immediately."

"He started it," Lenkov said.

"Whatever," Grady said. "Just shake hands. Walk away and call it a night, okay?"

Duke and Lenkov had no intention of shaking hands, but they did exchange dirty looks as they grudgingly parted.

"Well, they're no fun," Theodosia said.

Drayton, who looked relieved that blood wasn't about to be spilled, took a sip of champagne and said, "You once mentioned something to me about the possibility of Lenkov still doing deals with Duke?"

"I did say that, didn't I?" Theodosia said.

"Did that little scenario convince you otherwise?"

"Those two men clearly despise each other. So, no, I guess there's no way they'd ever be working together."

As the crowd around them broke up, Drayton said, "You know what we need in order to restore *bonhomme* to the evening?"

"Another glass of champagne?"

"Right. You ready for another?"

"Always," Theodosia said as Drayton turned and headed for the bar.

Delaine was suddenly at Theodosia's elbow, looking cute and shimmery in a short, gold sequined dress. "Did you see how Ned handled that?" she cooed. "Isn't he a sweetheart? Don't you just adore his quiet calm and finesse?"

"I'm impressed that he was able to defuse that fight before it became a barroom brawl."

Delaine took a step closer to Theodosia and said, "You'll never in a million years guess where Ned took me last night."

"You're right, I'd never guess."

"We flew down to Nassau. In a private jet."

"For real?" Theodosia said. "Wow." This relationship was looking more and more serious. "But you've only known the man for, like, a few weeks."

Delaine waved a hand. "Doesn't matter. Ned and I are completely homed in on the same wavelength. We both love fashion, art, and fine wine." She squinted at one of the auction items, picked up a pen, frowned, then bid two hundred dollars for a day of beauty at Nicola's Garden Spa.

"You're telling me that you and Ned Grady are compatible," Theodosia said.

Delaine stopped writing and looked up with a faraway gleam in her eyes. "Last night . . . was like a fabulous dream. We ate grilled lobster on a moonlit patio overlooking the Caribbean, then gambled the night away in a fancy casino. I mean, have you ever played baccarat? It's so *glam*, like something out of a James Bond movie." Delaine hunched her shoulders forward and yawned. "I still feel fuzzy from all the champagne and late hours."

"Wow, Delaine. Moonlight, champagne, and a private jet—it sounds like you're living the high life."

"I think I finally found a man I could fall in love with."

"I'm happy for you," Theodosia said. And she meant it. Delaine had endured more than her share of goofballs, gadabouts, and cads. At this point in her life, she deserved a man who could treat her like the princess she imagined she was.

"By the way," Delaine said, "I found my cell phone."

"So it wasn't stolen?"

"No. Funny thing, though. It's like it suddenly materialized out of thin air. Very mysterious." She giggled again, then said, "Goodness me, there's Bunny Badelia over there." Delaine raised a hand and shouted, "Bunny, dear! It's me, Delaine!" She clutched Theodosia's arm and whispered, "Bunny is one of my absolute primo clients." Then Delaine was gone, running as fast as her four-inch stilettos could carry her.

Theodosia started to look for Drayton and suddenly found a young woman blocking her path, giving her a strange, enigmatic smile. The woman was late twenties with long dark hair, green eyes, a gold nose ring, and trendy Oliver Peoples glasses. She wore a silky black slip-dress paired with a pair of lug-sole shoes. Theodosia decided she was definitely a Gen Z type.

"Hello," Theodosia said pleasantly while her brain scrambled to place her.

Should I know this woman? Is she a tea shop customer?

"You're Theodosia Browning, right?" the woman said. "The tea shop lady?"

"That's right," Theodosia said.

The woman touched a hand to her chest. "I'm Charlie Skipstead. I host a mystery and true crime podcast. Maybe you've heard of it? *Charleston Shivers*?"

"Heard of it, but I'm afraid I haven't had a chance to listen yet."

"I also cover local hauntings, supernatural phenomena, and unexplained mysteries," Charlie said.

"*Okaaay*," Theodosia said. She had a pretty good idea where this conversation might be headed.

"Lately I've been venturing more and more into true crime," Charlie said. "And I've heard—through the unofficial grapevine, of course—that you're a fairly talented amateur sleuth."

"Oh, not really," Theodosia said.

Charlie was undeterred by Theodosia's modesty. "That's not what people tell me."

"What people?"

Charlie ignored Theodosia's question and said, "Like right now, I know you're trying to figure out who killed that fat cat at the Mad Hatter Masquerade."

"A lot of us are concerned about Harlan Sadler's murder," Theodosia said.

"Yeah, but you're the one who's been running around town asking questions."

"Well . . ."

"Maybe even getting a hop, skip, and a jump ahead of the police?"

"I wouldn't go that far."

"You're too modest," Charlie said.

"Not really." Theodosia was finding this conversation more and more disconcerting.

"Listen, I'd love to have you come on my podcast some time. You just say when."

"Probably not right now," Theodosia said.

"I get it. You're hot and heavy into your investigation," Charlie said. "So afterwards then, once this murder mystery is solved and put to bed. Then you can come on and discuss all the ins and outs. My listeners would be keenly interested in hearing how you go about running a shadow investigation."

"They're not really . . . I'll talk to you later, okay?" With a smile and a wave, Theodosia managed to slip away from Charlie Skipstead. She took a deep breath, let it out, and looked around. Wondered where Drayton had run off to. Then she noticed that Wes Lenkov was still here. He was glad-handing a circle of men, all well-groomed, well-to-do thirty-somethings who looked as if they shopped at Charleston's best men's shops—either Granger Owings or Berlin's Clothing. They were probably trust fund guys, no doubt the perfect demographic for an overpriced European sports car.

Lenkov slapped hands with one of the men, then broke away from the group and headed for the door. Theodosia hurried after him.

"Mr. Lenkov," she called. "Do you have a minute? Can we talk?"

Lenkov glanced back over his shoulder, recognized Theodosia, but didn't stop walking. "Not now, doll. Gotta run. I have a guy coming in to look at a pearl gray Maserati."

"But this will only take a moment."

The word, "Sorry," floated back to her.

Theodosia found Drayton talking to Bertrand Hill, one of the curators at the Heritage Society. He was late fifties, with a white beard and bushy eyebrows. A professorial type.

When Drayton saw Theodosia he said, "Apologies, Theo. I ran into Bertrand and we got caught up in talking about our upcoming Swamp Fox exhibition."

"Hello," Hill said, giving Theodosia a shy wave.

Theodosia waved back.

"I totally forgot about your champagne," Drayton suddenly blurted out, touching a hand to his forehead. "I'll fetch it immediately."

"That's okay," Theodosia said. "I think I'm ready to leave."

"So soon?" Hill said.

"No, she's right. I should be getting home, too," Drayton said. He clapped Hill on the shoulder and said, "Good to see you, Bertie."

"Did you ever run into Cricket?" Theodosia asked as they threaded their way through the lobby, heading for the front door.

"No, she never showed up," Drayton said. "Then again, I didn't expect her to."

"It's probably too soon," Theodosia said as she handed her parking ticket to one of the valets. "I'm sure she still feels awful."

"Poor dear," Drayton said.

They waited five minutes for Theodosia's car to be brought around, enjoying the night, the cool breeze, the stars sparkling in the blue-black sky. Then the car arrived, and Drayton slipped the valet a tip while Theodosia thought some more about Wes Lenkov. The anger and hostility he'd demonstrated tonight could be an indication of an erratic, highly impulsive personality.

So what to do? The ball was in her court, and she didn't want to just let it fly past her.

Theodosia thought for a few moments, and decided that maybe, just maybe, she'd pay a visit to Lenkov tonight. After all, she did have a few more questions for him.

24

Theodosia dropped Drayton off at his home, turned down his offer of a nightcap, then drove through the darkened streets, heading for Sport Luxe. All the while she kept asking herself, *Should I do this? Should I do this?*

The answer always came back *Yes*. She had a strange itch about speaking to Lenkov.

When she pulled in front of Sport Luxe, the street was deserted, except for a gray striped cat prowling down the sidewalk.

So, still a good idea? Theodosia asked herself as she climbed out of her Jeep. Yes, she thought so.

Theodosia walked to the dealership's front door and knocked on the glass. When nothing happened, when nobody responded, she pressed her nose against the glass and peered in. There were no people inside, no lights burning.

No, that wasn't quite true. There was a shaft of yellow light spilling out of Lenkov's office. So maybe he was still there? Had he sold that Maserati and was staying late to finish up the paperwork?

Theodosia knocked on the door again. Harder this time, rattling the glass.

Still, nobody came to let her in.

Curious now, wondering if there was another entrance, Theodosia walked along the front of the building, looking into the partially lit showroom. When she came to the corner of the building, she turned and found herself in a wide alley. Signs posted on the brick walls said HONK FOR ADMITTANCE and AFTER HOURS LEAVE KEYS HERE. Next to the sign was a metal box with a slot for depositing keys.

But the really interesting thing was that one of the garage doors was halfway up.

So Lenkov is here. I mean, nobody would leave this door open with so many valuable sports cars parked inside.

Theodosia ducked under the door and found herself in the repair shop.

"Mr. Lenkov," she called out. "Are you there? It's me again, Theodosia. Theodosia Browning."

Her voice echoed hollowly in the dark garage.

"That's funny," she said out loud. "Lenkov said he was coming here." It was a kind of whistling-in-the-dark statement because she wasn't sure what she was about to find.

She walked past a red Corvette that was up on a lift. Other sports cars were parked in bays, waiting to be worked on. Some had their hoods up; a few were up on jacks waiting for new, wide tires. Streetlights shone through the garage windows, reflecting off chrome, tools, and wheel rims, casting an abundance of shadows.

Kind of spooky.

Just past the last bay, Theodosia found the customer service area. It was dark and empty now, with small humps that indicated desk chairs and monitors. Past customer service was a room that had a soda machine, coffee maker, and a bunch of merchandise stacked on glass shelves. Hats and T-shirts with Porsche and Ferrari logos on them. A red leather jacket with a Lamborghini logo. Visors embroidered with the Maserati logo.

Theodosia walked down a hallway and into the showroom proper. All around her were sinewy-looking cars, crouched in the dark and looking ready to pounce.

All these expensive cars and a door was left open? Something's not quite right here.

Theodosia hesitated again, her senses on full alert. She was looking for something, anything, that would tell her where Wes Lenkov was—or if he was still here. Maybe he'd ducked out for a few minutes to grab a coffee? There was a Starbucks down the street . . .

As Theodosia stood there, she was gradually aware of a faint noise—some kind of sound.

A radio?

As she walked past a Ferrari, Theodosia trailed her hand along its sleek front fender and headed for the yellow crack of light that still streamed from the half-closed door to Lenkov's office. It was like a tractor beam pulling her in.

He's probably on a phone call.

Theodosia continued toward his office, making sure her footsteps rang out purposely. She didn't want to frighten Lenkov by popping in on him abruptly.

"Mr. Lenkov?" Theodosia called out as she knocked on the doorframe.

No answer. But sound. Some kind of music. A little louder now. Theodosia put her hand against the door and slowly pushed it open.

"Mr. Lenkov, are you in there?"

Lenkov was in there alright. Only he was dead.

Sprawled in his thousand-dollar Herman Miller chair, Lenkov was missing a good portion of his skull.

What? He's been shot?

Theodosia's brain stuttered out weird impulses to the rest of her body.

Run. Get away. Go now.

She shook her head to try to dismiss these warnings, then blinked and forced herself to take a more measured second look.

What she saw freaked her out.

Besides being shot in the head, Wes Lenkov had some kind of rubber tubing stretched around his neck.

None of this is making sense to me.

She stared some more. Lenkov's left eye was shattered and part of his skull was definitely missing. He looked like he'd died hard.

What. Just. Happened? Somebody tried to strangle him, then shot him in the head? Why? Who?

But no. There was a pistol lying on his desk.

Did he do this to himself?

Repulsed as Theodosia was by this bizarre notion, the glow of Lenkov's laptop computer drew her closer.

Was there an explanation here? Had Lenkov been in the middle of sending an e-mail? Calling for help? Or was something else going on?

She stepped closer. His laptop computer was fired up and open, the cursor pulsing, and a few words typed against a white screen.

Theodosia tiptoed closer to Lenkov, studiously avoiding the blood, and peered at the screen.

The words she saw chilled her.

They read: *I deeply regret taking the life of Harlan Sadler. It was a terrible mistake that caused pain and suffering to innocent people. I can no longer live with myself.*

Theodosia backed up so fast she almost tripped and fell down. Then she shivered, a deep visceral vibration that seemed to run the full length of her spine.

It looked like a confession of sorts, but there were no details, no reasons, no rationale. Just boom—I'm sorry, goodbye.

Could this message be legitimate? Why would Lenkov have killed Harlan Sadler? Had he really mistaken him for Duke? Or was this a dastardly clever cover-up?

Theodosia's hands trembled as she dialed 911.

One minute Sport Luxe had been dark and spooky, like a moonless All Hallows' Eve. Then it seemed as if someone pulled a lever and every light in the house popped on. And now the dealership wasn't just dazzlingly bright; it was teeming with almost a dozen first responders.

Theodosia was questioned by two uniformed police officers who'd arrived first on the scene. She told her story in bits and pieces, finally managing to get it all out. Ten minutes later, she was questioned again by another officer who came rushing in. Finally, after three separate go-rounds of telling her story—of standing there, looking a little ragged and forlorn—one of the uniformed officers took pity on her and found her a folding chair so she could sit out in the showroom.

And as EMTs and uniformed officers shuffled around, trying to piece together the events that led up to this, Theodosia was puzzling around her own theories. Could this be a legitimate suicide? Or had Lenkov been murdered and set up to take the fall for Harlan Sadler's murder? If that was the case, then who was the mastermind?

Was this Duke Sadler's dirty work so he could point the finger at Lenkov and hand his stepfather's killer to the police on a silver platter? And then take over his stepfather's businesses?

Could Emily Bates have somehow engineered this? She'd been adamant about her bank not merging with Sadler's bank. So maybe she'd murdered Sadler, then decided the police were looking at her a little too hard? So she killed Lenkov to make it look like he was the killer? But was Emily tough enough, flinty enough to kill someone? Theodosia thought about that for a minute. Yes, maybe she was.

And what about Ethan Stacks? He'd been floating around the silent auction this evening. Had he followed Lenkov here and set this up? Had Stacks been the mysterious person who was supposedly interested in buying the pearl gray Maserati? But if he hadn't killed Harlan Sadler, then why would he kill Wes Lenkov?

Theodosia stood up from her chair, stretched and wiggled her shoulders, trying to release some of the tension that had built up. Then she sat back down as another thought came crashing at her.

Was Ray Crispin not the mild-mannered ex-partner he pretended to be? Had he killed Harlan Sadler, then worried that the police might look in his direction? Had Crispin killed Lenkov for insurance purposes? Then typed a fake confession on Lenkov's computer and went on his merry way? Crispin was a smart guy. He could have easily engineered this setup.

Theodosia's mind was in turmoil. Any one of her suspects could have done this . . . or none of them. They all could be innocent. Maybe there was an unknown person out there who was laughing their head off because they had the police—and everyone involved—running in circles.

There's too much to think about. I need to go home. Hug my dog and crawl in bed.

But no, now another investigator wanted to talk to her. Thank goodness they were calm, respectful, and seemed to believe her story.

That all changed in an instant.

Because when Detective Burt Tidwell arrived on scene, all hell broke loose.

"Now what did you do?" Tidwell thundered when he saw Theodosia sitting there on her folding chair.

"Don't blame this on me!" Theodosia cried in protest as Tidwell stormed past her, all the officers jumping out of his way like errant bowling pins flying from a strike. "I'm the innocent party. I came here looking to have a chat with Wes Lenkov and found him exactly as you see him."

"And that is . . . ?" Tidwell turned abruptly and headed into Lenkov's office.

Theodosia jumped up and followed Tidwell into the office where one of the uniformed officers had been posted to guard the body until he arrived.

Tidwell took one look at Lenkov, spun toward Theodosia, and said, "*That's* how you found him? Shot with . . . what's that wrapped around his neck? A fan belt?"

"I think it's an oil pan gasket," the uniformed officer volunteered.

"Shut up!" Tidwell shouted. Then he took a deep breath and circled Lenkov's mangled body, trying to take in the circumstances and oddities of his death.

"He tried to strangle himself first?" Tidwell said to the officer.

"It's possible," the officer answered.

Tidwell's beady eyes continued to study the bizarre crime scene. "And when that wasn't enough, Mr. Lenkov shot himself? Execution-style?"

"It could have happened that way," the officer said, his voice practically quavering now. "There's gunpowder residue and some stippling on one side of his head. Looks as if the bullet went straight into his brain."

"Not much brain matter left," Tidwell grunted. "In Mr. Lenkov or in this room." He whirled in the direction of the officer and said, "It did *not* happen that way. Do you see that pistol?"

The officer swallowed hard. "Yes."

"You think this man shot himself to death and then casually set down his pistol?" Tidwell asked.

One officer leaned in the door and called, "The Crime Scene techs just pulled up in their van."

"Goody," Tidwell said.

The uniformed officer, desperate to save face, said, "Um, you probably noticed there's a bag of weed sitting in that open desk drawer?"

"Do you think that's relevant to the murder?" Tidwell snapped.

"Uh, maybe not."

"Then kindly get out and send in those Crime Scene techs, will you?"

"Yes sir," said the officer. By this time, he was desperate to make his escape.

When two Crime Scene techs came in, carrying lights, camera gear, and a black case full of equipment, Tidwell said, "Take a look here. Would you say this man died instantly? From a gunshot wound?"

One of the techs, an older guy with gray hair and a bristly mustache, did a cursory inspection of Lenkov and said, "That would be my initial guess. Not a particularly large wound. Maybe a 9mm?" He turned to the other tech and said, "Let's process the scene, photograph everything in situ, diagram the blood spatter, then transport the victim to the morgue for testing and autopsy. Maybe ask the ME to check for possible petechial hemorrhaging behind the victim's eyes."

Theodosia crept forward. "Which would indicate what?" she asked.

"That our victim was still alive when he was strangled with that . . . whatever it is," the tech said. "And when that didn't do the trick, someone shot him."

Tidwell glared at Theodosia. "Happy now? Now that you know all the grisly particulars?"

"Not really," Theodosia said. But her brain was cranking out ideas. If someone had tried to strangle Lenkov first, it meant his assailant had gotten close to him. Probably someone he knew.

Whoa. So Lenkov knew *his killer?*

Theodosia thought for a moment, then said, "Detective Tidwell, what if someone . . ."

But that was as far as she got, because outside in the showroom voices were suddenly raised. Then came the distinct sound of a scuffle.

Tidwell frowned, shook his head, and stepped out to see what was going on. Once again, Theodosia stayed right on his heels.

Bobby, the reporter from Channel Eight, was trying to shove his way past one of the uniformed officers. Trevor was right behind him, aiming a camera, probably rolling film the whole time.

"I'm a reporter," Bobby shouted. "I need to know what happened here. We've got First Amendment rights!"

"Young man, you do not," Tidwell shouted back.

Bobby saw Tidwell's rage and immediately decided to regroup and take another run at it. A more tactful run.

"My police radio's been blowing up like crazy," Bobby said in a more neutral tone. "I mean . . ." He threw up his hands in a wild gesture. "You've got everybody who's anybody here—officers, detectives, Crime Scene, even the meat wagon." He glanced in Theodosia's direction and gave a quick nod. "This has to be a major news story. Something big must have gone down and I'd like to know what it was!"

"You'll have to wait until morning," Tidwell said. "We need to process the scene, transport the victim, and determine cause of death. Tomorrow we'll know more and be able to call a press conference."

"By morning everybody will have this," Bobby wheedled. "The other channels, especially that shark, Ken Lotter, from W-BAM, even the print guys. C'mon, man, just give us a hint. It was that car guy, wasn't it? He got axed, right? Was it a car theft gone bad? A gang killing?"

But Tidwell was adamant. He kicked Bobby and Trevor out, stormed around some more, terrorized a few more officers, and pestered the Crime Scene techs as they set up work lights, diligently took photos, and examined the body.

Then he remembered Theodosia and kicked her out, too.

At that point she was happy to go home.

25

Friday morning and Theodosia slouched across the table from Drayton. He'd brewed them a pot of Russian Caravan blend, expecting to start the day on a high note. What he hadn't counted on was listening to Theodosia's blow-by-blow description of Wes Lenkov's murder.

"Sounds like you walked into a fairly hideous situation," Drayton said.

"You have no idea," Theodosia said.

She'd been awake half the night with the image of Lenkov's head blown off and that weird thing stretched around his neck. It still bothered her.

"So why kill Lenkov?" Theodosia said as she tapped a finger against her teacup. "I mean, it makes no sense at all."

"Unless, as you said before, Sadler's killer was trying to set Lenkov up by writing that confessional note. To conveniently take the heat off him."

"But he botched it. Maybe the killer got Lenkov to write the note, tried to hang him, and it all went—kapow—off the rails. So then he was forced to shoot him."

"So it's definitely possible that last night's mysterious killer figures into Harlan Sadler's murder."

"It *feels* like it does, but I just don't know how." Theodosia took a sip of tea and continued. "I tell you, Drayton, I'm stumped. Maybe . . . maybe there are two different killers. Two different motives I can't quite figure out."

"You've done your best so far," Drayton said. "Maybe it's time to defer to the police and their professional expertise."

"Tidwell would like that for sure. But last I heard the police were still questioning board members."

"That sounds like a dead end, no pun intended," Drayton said. He touched two fingers to his bow tie, put on his most serious look, and said, "I understand you not wanting to let this go." When Theodosia didn't reply, he said, "Why don't we try looking at these crimes from a different angle? What did the two victims have in common? Or, rather, *who* did they have in common?"

"Well, Duke Sadler wasn't all that crazy about his stepfather," Theodosia said. "And we know Duke was also scornful of Lenkov. And Emily Bates . . . well, I don't know how Emily fits in. Or if she even does anymore." Theodosia took another sip of tea and looked at her watch. "And then we have a couple of outliers."

"Those being . . ."

"Ethan Stacks and I guess Ray Crispin."

"It's possible either of them could be a cold-blooded killer," Drayton said.

"Or maybe all our suspects just have serious personality disorders," Theodosia said. "Which makes them difficult to deal with, but doesn't necessarily mean they're cold-blooded killers."

"So what do you want to do?" Drayton asked.

Theodosia scrunched up her face. "Give up?"

Drayton's face creased in a wan smile. "Doesn't sound like you."

"Maybe put it on the back burner for a while?"

"There you go," Drayton said. "Give your brain cells a well-deserved hiatus from this investigation."

"And then?"

"We pick it up fresh at a later date."

"You mean like this afternoon?"

"No," Drayton said as he pushed back his chair and stood up. "I was thinking more like next week."

Drayton may have been content to let the two murders go for a while, but Theodosia wasn't engineered that way. When something was bothering her—or when someone was counting on her, like Cricket surely was—she couldn't help pushing ahead. She was like a dog with a bone.

Or maybe I'm more like a shark. Never sleep, just keep moving forward.

She shrugged at the analogy as she began setting the tables for morning tea. No, that wasn't quite right, she told herself. Not a shark—more like the dolphins that swam off the prow of a boat. They were always a leap ahead, plunging forward even as fifty thousand tons of steel bore down upon them.

Yikes. Is that what I'm doing?

The notion unnerved her. So much so that Theodosia was actually glad when Bobby and Trevor walked into the tea shop.

"Good morning," Bobby said with a friendly wave. "Sorry we didn't get a chance to talk to you last night before we got the bum's rush. You any worse for wear?"

"Nothing a little caffeine won't fix," Theodosia said. "How about you guys?"

"Aw, Trevor and I hung around outside for a couple more hours. After the big guy—Tidwell—is that his name?"

Theodosia nodded.

"After Tidwell left, we talked to a couple of friendly uniforms. They weren't as tight-lipped as Tidwell was."

"So you know what happened?"

"Only that somebody offed the sports car guy," Bobby said. "In a fairly bizarre manner. But we shot some footage of police cars outside Sport Luxe, and we pieced together an okay story. They ran it this morning on the seven AM and will probably have it on again at noon."

"So you got your story," Theodosia said. "And Lenkov's murder was on the news."

Bobby nodded. "Yeah."

"Did you happen to mention my name?" Theodosia asked.

"Nope," said Bobby.

Trevor edged forward. "So you really were the one who found him? The murdered car guy?"

"Afraid so," Theodosia said.

"Any idea who killed him?" Bobby asked.

"Not offhand," Theodosia said.

"Do you think it might be related to that bank guy's murder?" Bobby asked. "What's his name—Sadler?"

"I don't know what to think anymore," Theodosia said. She gazed at Bobby. His hair stuck up in odd places and he looked a little frazzled, as if he'd had only three hours' sleep. "So was there a press conference this morning?"

"No, we called media relations downtown and they had nothing on the docket," Bobby said. "Tidwell was just blowing smoke at us."

"Sorry to hear that," Theodosia said. "Would you guys like to stay for tea and scones?"

"We'd love to," Trevor said.

"But we can't," Bobby said. "We've got a couple assignments, so we got to keep moving."

· "Takeout, then?" Theodosia asked.

"That'd be great!" Trevor said.

Theodosia packed up takeaway scones and tea for the two reporters, then welcomed guests and helped serve the Indigo Tea Shop's usual morning cream tea. This morning, Haley had baked cherry-almond streusel scones and lavender-infused tea bread, while Drayton had outdone himself by brewing pots of orchid plum and jasmine tea.

When there was a slight lull, Theodosia went into her office and called Tidwell. He came on the phone with a gruff, "Hello. What?"

"It's Theodosia. I wanted to see if anything was happening."

"Nothing. Not much going on at all, thank you very much."

"Are your investigators looking at Duke Sadler? Or . . . or Emily Bates?" Theodosia wasn't sure how Emily would fit in, but decided to throw her name out just the same.

"We've *been* looking at both of them."

"Really? Then another quick question," Theodosia said, trying to ignore his impatience.

"What?" Tidwell barked.

"Do you think Harlan Sadler's killer also murdered Wes Lenkov?"

There was a long hesitation, then Tidwell said, "We're looking at these two cases from a number of angles, and the only connection we've found so far is something one of our forensic accountants uncovered."

"Which is?"

"Sport Luxe had a line of credit at Elysian Bank—the bank

where Sadler was CEO—but that could just be a standard business practice. These two murders seem far more *personal*."

"In what way?"

"They're both highly violent in nature, as if our killer experienced a psychotic break."

"That's not good," Theodosia said.

"No, it's not," Tidwell said, which was followed by a distinct CLICK. He'd hung up on her.

Beth Ann was off today, but at ten o'clock Miss Dimple came bouncing into the tea shop—the dear lady bringing her usual high note of cheer. But as she stood next to Theodosia at the front counter, waiting for Drayton to fill tea orders, Miss Dimple studied Theodosia and said, "Are you okay, honey? You look a little off today."

"I'm fine," Theodosia assured her. "Really. I just have a lot on my mind." Theodosia didn't want to mention Lenkov's murder because it would probably upset and worry Miss Dimple. As it was, she was worrying enough for the both of them.

"This pot of Indian spiced is ready," Drayton said, sliding a blue-and-white teapot across the counter to Miss Dimple. "And, Theo, I have your Puerh tea for table six. But please inform them it must steep another minute or so. Some of these teas take their own sweet time for their full flavor and body to develop."

"Got it," Theodosia said.

She delivered the tea, bustled about the tea shop, chatted with a few guests, then dipped into the kitchen to check on Haley.

"Are you all set for our Silk Road Tea?" Theodosia asked.

"I'm not only on top of it, I've got a surprise for you," Haley said. "Well, really, for all of us."

"Something to do with your menu? Which I totally adore, by the way."

"This is something else."

Haley reached down and grabbed a large plastic bag from underneath her butcher-block counter. "Take a look," she said as she handed the bag to Theodosia. "Something I borrowed from Ben."

Theodosia opened the bag and pulled out a bright red kimono. "Whoa. This is gorgeous. You say it's from Ben?" There was a note of puzzlement in her voice.

"You may not know this, 'cause Ben's kind of a biker guy, but he's also into theater."

"Theater," Theodosia repeated. She was having trouble associating Haley's leather-clad biker boyfriend with the theater. Any theater.

"Oh yeah, the theater group he's in, the Cooper Community Players, just got done putting on Gilbert and Sullivan's *The Mikado.*"

"Thus the kimonos," Theodosia said, pulling out three more kimonos. Two were floral kimonos; one was a black kimono jacket.

"I thought it'd be fun if we wore them. You know, since we're doing a Silk Road Tea? I mean, our menu is a little bit Chinese as well as Japanese."

"Sure, why not?"

"The black one's for Drayton," Haley said. "But do you think he'll wear it?"

"Only one way to find out. Let's go ask him."

But when Haley showed Drayton the black kimono jacket, he was intrigued.

"This is a Japanese *haori* jacket, yes? Done in silk?"

"I think so," Haley said.

"And look at the brushstroke character on back, it's really quite compelling," Drayton said.

"The thing is, will you wear it?" Haley asked. But Drayton was already slipping off his summer-weight tweed jacket and reaching for the black *haori* jacket.

"I guess that answers your question," Theodosia said.

"Oh," said Haley. "I talked to my friend Izzy last night."

When Theodosia gave her a blank stare, Haley said, "Isabelle Tod. Izzy. The woman who used to work at Unity One Bank."

"Izzy. Right."

"She agreed to talk to you."

"When?" Theodosia asked.

"Dunno. Guess you gotta call her up. I'll stick a note with her cell number on it on your desk."

"Thanks."

Theodosia busied herself then, setting the tables with their blue-and-white china, adding silverware and pairs of chopsticks, and putting out small ceramic teacups without handles.

Miss Dimple was already floating around in her kimono, a vision in pink silk with purple chrysanthemum motifs all over it.

"This is so much fun," Miss Dimple exclaimed. "And such a clever idea. A Silk Road Tea. Where do you people come up with these ideas?"

"Pretty much out of necessity," Theodosia said with all honesty. "We want to intrigue our customers and keep them coming back for more fun events."

"Well, it's working. Drayton tells me we'll have almost a full house today." Miss Dimple cast a careful eye at the tables and said, "What else?"

"Flowers," Theodosia said. "A single stem of hibiscus in a small vase."

Miss Dimple beamed. "Like the tea. How lovely."

26

❧

The tea room filled up as if by magic today. Customers streamed in, grabbed seats, saved adjacent seats for friends, and exclaimed over the elegant table settings.

Theodosia, wearing her red kimono, greeted guests, seated guests, and ducked into the kitchen to make sure Haley had all of her multiple courses ready to go. Then she walked to the center of the room and, as graciously as possible, welcomed her guests to the Silk Road Tea. Then, because she'd studied up on the Silk Road (actually, she'd read a Wikipedia entry), decided to give them a brief history.

"As you probably know, the Silk Road was a network of Eurasian trade routes," Theodosia said. "It spanned more than four thousand miles and lasted over fifteen centuries. The Silk Road brought silk, tea, horses, camels, honey, and wine from Asia to the Middle East and Europe. It also facilitated an exchange of ideas on economics, religion, philosophy, and even scientific discoveries." She paused as a spatter of applause broke out, as well as several exclamations of "Wow" and "Fascinating."

"To pay tribute to this intricate web of land and sea routes, we've put together a special Silk Road menu for you," Theodosia said. "It combines foods and tastes from both China and Japan, and begins with our first course of fresh-baked ginger scones and bowls of miso soup. For your second course, we'll be serving a plated assortment of shrimp toast, grilled teriyaki salmon, and small noodle salad. If you can make it through all of that, we still have dessert—because the Indigo Tea Shop *always* serves dessert." On top of more laughter, she continued. "Today we're offering green tea cheesecake, lychee ice cream, and almond cookies." Theodosia stopped and took a breath. "As for tea . . ." She looked over at Drayton who was wearing his *haori* jacket and looking rather Zen.

"We won't be serving all the tea in China," Drayton began, which prompted a slew of giggles. "But we will be serving *almost* all the tea. For your sipping pleasure, I've brewed pots of Sencha green tea, Empire Keemun, and Yunnan tea."

Theodosia and Drayton circled the tables then, pouring out streams of fresh, hot tea, while Haley and Miss Dimple brought out the food. Each course seemed to be a hit, and Drayton was getting pulled in a million directions with guests peppering him with questions about tea and tea etiquette.

"When I brew tea, how much tea should I use?" one woman asked him.

"Here's the rule of thumb," Drayton said. "Use one heaping teaspoon of loose tea to five ounces of water per person."

"What's the best way to store tea?" another woman asked.

"Always store your tea in an opaque, airtight container in a dark, dry space," Drayton said. He lifted a finger. "And remember, heat, humidity, and light are the enemies of tea."

"But we're in Charleston," a woman laughed. "We're all about heat and humidity."

"Which means you need to be all the more resourceful," Drayton said.

As Theodosia was grabbing another pot of Empire Keemun, the front door flapped open. Turning with a smile on her face, expecting to greet a late-arriving guest, Theodosia found herself staring at Charlie Skipstead, the podcast lady. Today Charlie was dressed in jeans and a tight purple T-shirt that barely stretched down to her waist.

"Please don't freak out on me, okay?" Charlie pleaded. "And don't say no."

"No," Theodosia said.

Charlie wasn't one bit deterred. "Come on, Theodosia, just consent to doing *one* simple little podcast. I promise, you'll love it."

"No, I won't."

"Okay, how about this? Will you at least *think* about it? Just as a wild, free-spirited, fun thing to do?"

"Just think about it? I could probably do that," Theodosia said.

"Good. Great. Alright." Charlie did a fist pump. "I'll catch you later, okay?"

"Sure," Theodosia said.

"By the way, love your red kimono," Charlie said, then left as quickly as she'd arrived.

Smiling to herself, Theodosia figured that by agreeing to think about the podcast, that might be the last of it. Hopefully, anyway.

As Theodosia helped serve lychee ice cream, she noticed that Drayton had once again been drawn into a discussion. This time it was about the actual Silk Road.

Well, why not? Drayton's a well-read history buff, so he probably knows a thing or two.

As the Silk Road Tea wound down, Theodosia thanked

guests, cleared dishes, and packed to-go orders of tea and scones. Finally, by one thirty, she was able to duck into her office and call Haley's friend Izzy.

Izzy answered her phone on the third ring, listened to Theodosia's pitch to talk about her time at Unity One Bank, and said, "Yeah, I'll talk to you."

"Great. When?"

"Haley said you're in a hurry, so I could see you today. But it's gotta be a fast conversation because I'm meeting some friends at five to drive down to Hilton Head for the weekend."

"What time do you get off work?"

"Today? Four."

"How about I meet you at your shop exactly at four?" Theodosia said.

"See you then."

Theodosia and Miss Dimple cleaned the last of the tables, then reset them for afternoon tea. Good thing, because Delaine and Ned Grady came wandering in soon after.

"This place is so dang cute," Grady said as he looked around the tea shop. He waved at Drayton, then grinned and said, "Look at that, a chandelier. Plus, Oriental carpets, fancy teapots, and . . . I love your little fireplace." Then he focused on Theodosia and said, "You make a *living* doing this?"

"She makes a very good living," Delaine said. Grabbing Grady's arm, she steered him to a table, and said, "Now will you please sit down?"

Once they were seated, Theodosia said, "What can I bring you folks? Can I interest you in a full luncheon or will it be afternoon tea and scones?"

"I'm starving," Grady said.

"No, you're not," Delaine said. She tapped a red enameled fingernail hard against the table and said, "We'll have tea and scones, Theo. Cardamom tea and please make my scone low-carb."

"Sure thing," Theodosia said. Whenever Delaine dropped by, they went through this low-carb discussion. Of course, Haley *never* made low-carb scones and wasn't about to start. Deep down, Delaine probably knew this, but still, it was the game they played.

Theodosia brought them a pot of cardamom and two plates arranged with cream scones, strawberry jam, and Devonshire cream.

Grady poked a finger at the small glass container. "Is that whipped cream?"

"Devonshire cream," Theodosia said. "You slice your scone lengthwise, dab on a little jam, and top it with Devonshire cream."

"Okay," Grady said as he got to work, putting far more jam and Devonshire cream on his scone than was needed. He popped a gooey bite into his mouth, nodded, and said, "This is delicious."

"Told you so," Delaine said with a smirk. "Try the tea."

Grady took a small sip of tea. "Good."

"You see?" Delaine said. "We'll make a real gent of you yet."

"So what's the deal with the murder last night?" Grady asked Theodosia. "You were there, huh?"

"How do you know that?" Theodosia asked. "I don't believe my name was mentioned in this morning's paper or on TV."

Grady pointed at Delaine and, with his mouth full, said, "She got the inside scoop."

"How?" Theodosia asked Delaine.

"My friend Gloria Papalle owns Papalle's Deli just down the block from Sport Luxe," Delaine said. "She managed to scrape together a lot of the dirt. Apparently, Gloria went in super early for a delivery and saw the Crime Scene van still parked there and a few police officers hanging around. Then a reporter who asked her for a quote mentioned that you'd been there."

"So now all sorts of people know I was there?" Theodosia cried. "That I was the one who discovered Lenkov's dead body?"

"Compliments of Miss Blabby Pants here," Grady said, indicating Delaine. "Now you know what I have to deal with on a daily basis."

"Rats," Theodosia said. So a few people would know about her grisly discovery even though she'd managed to avoid the news. Well, she'd have to live with that. She had no choice.

Grady popped another bite of scone into his mouth. "I wonder what's going to happen to all those fabulous cars?"

"They'll probably all get trucked back to the manufacturers," Theodosia said. "I doubt Lenkov owned any of them outright."

"Or the bank will be stuck with them," Delaine said.

Theodosia was about to turn away from their table when she heard Delaine's words. And her ears perked up as she suddenly remembered Tidwell mentioning that Lenkov had a line of credit with Elysian Bank.

"This is kind of strange," Theodosia said. "But I just learned that Lenkov had a line of credit at Elysian Bank."

"He did?" Grady said.

"Isn't that Harlan Sadler's bank?" Delaine said.

"It sure is," Grady said. "Interesting coincidence. Or is it?" He squinted at Theodosia. "If you're investigating these murders—and it sure seems like you are—maybe you should call somebody at that bank. See what's going on. See if there's some kind of link."

"Maybe I'll do that," Theodosia said.

*   *   *

Twenty minutes later, Theodosia was on the line with Ron Dowdle, one of the vice presidents at Elysian Bank.

"Excuse me, you're working on the Lenkov case that was just on the news? You're one of the investigators?" Dowdle asked.

"I've been working closely with Detective Burt Tidwell, the lead detective on the case," Theodosia said. If Dowdle thought she was doing follow-up phone work for the police, so much the better.

"We don't generally deal with car dealerships when it comes to financing their inventory," Dowdle told her. "We're a commercial bank that puts more of an emphasis on loans to local manufacturing, medical, and tech companies."

"We were under the impression Wes Lenkov had a line of credit with you," Theodosia said.

"I see. And you're thinking there might be a connection between Harlan Sadler's murder and that of the car dealer last night?" Dowdle said.

"We think it's possible," she said, keeping up the ruse.

"Well, I can divulge that Mr. Lenkov enjoyed a *personal* line of credit with us, but did not have one for his dealership."

"Was that arranged through Harlan Sadler?"

"No, that would be Mrs. Hegseth in our consumer loan department."

"Sorry to bother you," Theodosia said. Then, hoping to get a little more mileage out of her phone call, said, "It must be strange not to have Mr. Sadler around the bank anymore."

"You don't know the half of it," Dowdle said. "Harlan really was our guide star. We all looked up to him."

"I'd like to ask you a business question if you don't mind."

"Sure."

"What about the acquisition of Unity One Bank that Mr. Sadler was trying to negotiate? Is that off?"

"No, it'll probably go through," Dowdle said.

Theodosia was surprised to hear this. "Really? Even though Emily Bates is opposed to it?"

"Ms. Bates is only one person. The board of directors at Unity is slowly warming up to the idea. In today's banking climate, smaller banks are often perceived as being on shaky ground, so a buyout or a merger to consolidate assets is highly desirable."

"Thank you," Theodosia said. "Thank you very much."

27

~❦~

Four o'clock couldn't come soon enough for Theodosia. As she walked into Parasol, she was fizzing with nervous energy, anxious to talk to Izzy and hopeful she might learn something new about Emily Bates.

Parasol turned out to be a cute, funky little gift shop, the kind you could get lost in for an hour or so. It was jam-packed with Kit-Cat Klocks, slogan T-shirts, contemporary puzzles, trivia games, crystals, geodes, jewelry, homemade fudge, colorful nylon purses and backpacks, and unique kitchen items. There was a pillow with a dog image on it and the words, "Every snack you make, every meal you bake, I'll be watching you."

Izzy spotted Theodosia immediately and said, "Theodosia, right? We can talk in back. There's a break room with a table and chairs."

They wound their way through displays and racks of merchandise to a small room that was painted bright pink and held a round table, four mismatched chairs, and a small refrigerator with a microwave sitting on top.

"Thanks for seeing me," Theodosia said to Izzy. Izzy had a halo of frizzy dark hair, a square jaw, earnest face, and wore trendy, purple-framed glasses. She was dressed in a khaki jumpsuit and wore Birkenstock sandals.

"How can I help you?" Izzy asked.

"I'll get right to the point. I'm interested in working up a kind of profile on Emily Bates. Haley mentioned that you'd worked at Unity One Bank and found the work environment there to be toxic?"

"It was awful," Izzy said, nodding vigorously. "All the tellers and loan officers were scared to death of Ms. Bates. If you made a single mistake, no matter how teeny-tiny it was, you'd feel the full force of her wrath. Believe me, it wasn't fun."

"Sounds stressful," Theodosia said. "So Emily was basically horrible to everyone? Even customers?"

"She didn't much deal with customers," Izzy said. "Too far below her pay grade, I guess, even though Unity handled a lot more consumer accounts than commercial accounts."

"So Emily was the one who dealt with Unity's commercial accounts?"

"Not really, but it's funny you should mention that, because . . . well, I probably shouldn't be telling you this, but every few weeks a group of business guys would come in. I only remember this because they were kind of strange, not like our usual business customers. Anyway, there were always three of them. Ms. Bates would be sweet as pie, whisk them into her office, and close the door."

"For a business meeting?"

"That's what I always figured. But Tessa Jean, one of the tellers, told me she checked the records once and those guys didn't appear to have traditional bank accounts with us. Only a safe-deposit box."

"Weird," Theodosia said. "Um, could you describe these men?"

"They were big guys, kind of tough-looking. They all dressed alike in cheap leather jackets and jeans. You know the kind of leather that squeaks when you move? And when you'd hear them talk, they all had accents."

"What kind of accents?" Theodosia asked.

Izzy shrugged as she checked her watch. "I'm no linguistics expert, but it kind of sounded like they were Eastern European. Like maybe from Romania or Bulgaria."

"Interesting," Theodosia said. *Is it ever.*

Izzy pushed her chair back and popped up. "And now I've got to run since I haven't even started to pack." She gave Theodosia a perfunctory smile and said, "Whatever you're trying to figure out, I hope I was some help."

"I think maybe you were," Theodosia said.

Back at the Indigo Tea Shop, Drayton was just finishing up.

"I was wondering if you'd be back," he said. "I was about to lock up and head home."

"You need to hear this," Theodosia said. "I just met with a friend of Haley's who used to work at Unity One Bank."

Drayton's brows rose in twin arcs. "Emily Bates's bank? So you're still investigating."

"Right. Anyway, Haley's friend, Izzy, told me that Emily Bates was nasty to everyone at the bank except this gang of Eastern European guys who came in every once in a while. When they showed up, Emily was all hearts and unicorns."

"Pardon?"

"Emily was friendly, bordering on vivacious."

"Huh. That doesn't sound like the Emily Bates we know and love."

"No, it doesn't," Theodosia said. "But what really piqued my interest was the fact that these guys had accents. Kind of Eastern European, like Wes Lenkov."

"Sweet Fanny Adams, do you think those were the guys who murdered Lenkov? That there was some kind of disagreement or problem and they killed him?"

"I don't know," Theodosia said. "And I'm sorry to keep saying that, but I really don't know."

"You don't have to apologize," Drayton said. "As far as I can see, you've managed to unearth a good number of disparate clues. And you certainly had a successful fact-finding mission with this Izzy person. Now we just have to figure out what to do with all this information."

"I know one thing we can do," Theodosia said.

Drayton stared at her. "What?"

Theodosia stared back at him.

"Oh no," Drayton said slowly. "You're not thinking of . . . no, I want no part of your scheme."

"Come on, Drayton. You're just as invested in these two cases as I am."

"Yes, and I can see you're determined to solve them both and tie everything up nice and neat with a big red bow," Drayton said.

"No, I just want to . . ."

Drayton took a step backward. "Don't say it!"

"Do a little reconnaissance." There, she'd said it.

Drayton was shaking his head vigorously. "I know what you want. You want to sneak into Emily's house, don't you? Well, don't expect me to be a part of it! I mean, it's completely illegal and . . . and . . . what if she's home and catches us?"

"If Emily's home we won't do it," Theodosia said.

"You're certifiably crazy, you know."

Theodosia lifted a shoulder. "I'm curious."

"What you're proposing is completely bonkers."

"But it might solve a crime," Theodosia said.

"I can't go. I won't go." Drayton folded his arms across his chest in a show of stern denial.

But in the end, after Theodosia laid out her plan and twisted Drayton's arm a little bit, she got him to capitulate. Which is why they were in Charleston's Radcliffeborough neighborhood, cruising Warren Street in the dark and squinting at house numbers. They were trying to pinpoint exactly which house belonged to Emily Bates.

"How did you find her address?" Drayton asked.

"Internet," Theodosia said.

"Is nothing sacred?" Drayton asked. "Is *everything* just hovering there like a soul in purgatory waiting to be plucked out of cyberspace?"

"Pretty much," Theodosia said as she slowed her Jeep to a crawl. "I think it's that one." She was referring to a white Charleston single house that was set almost smack-dab up against the sidewalk with no front yard at all. It was a narrow, two-story house with a black wrought iron gate and matching wrought iron fence stretching around the sides of it.

"For heaven's sake, don't stop or slow down," Drayton warned. "We don't want to look like we're casing the place."

"Even though we are."

"Yes, but not to rob her blind. Just . . . just keep moving and we'll park around the block."

They parked under a sweeping oak tree and sat in the Jeep for a few minutes, trying to formulate a plan of attack.

"We go up to the front door and knock politely?" Drayton said. "Hoping to be invited in?"

"Why don't we slide around the back instead?"

"That sounds dangerous and underhanded."

"Because that's what it's going to be," Theodosia said. "Look, Drayton, maybe I did twist your arm a little too much. If you really don't want to do this, I can for sure go in alone."

"So you're saying it's ride or die?"

"That sounds a trifle dramatic."

"Not really," Drayton said. Then he heaved a reluctant sigh and said, "No, I'm in. You know I'm in. But if something goes horribly wrong, I pray that my cooler, saner head will prevail."

"Which is why I trust you implicitly," Theodosia said.

They climbed out of the Jeep, found the narrow alley that snaked behind Emily's house as well as the neighboring houses, and turned in. A combination of packed gravel and crushed shells crunched beneath each footstep, forcing them to step more gingerly so as not to announce their presence. The alley was also pitch dark with heavy foliage meeting overhead to create a kind of tunnel. Up ahead, a black cat stared at them, then disappeared behind a trash can.

Walking softly, Theodosia and Drayton peered into a few of the backyards and found them surprisingly large for Charleston.

"Kind of interesting back here," Drayton said. "Lots more trees and foliage than in front."

"This entire block of houses is set almost on the street, but they all have decent-sized backyards," Theodosia said.

"Because they're classic Charleston single homes. I think it was a tax thing, back when homes were taxed according to their frontage on the street. So the less frontage you owned, the lower your taxes."

They arrived at Emily's back gate and stood there for a few moments, taking stock of her house. From this view, her home looked far more ramshackle than it had from the street. A window screen hung awry, the back steps had a broken railing, and paint peeled from the wood in long strips.

"A definite fixer-upper," Drayton said.

"You think Emily Bates is handy with paint and a nail gun? That she has a Home Depot charge card?"

"Offhand, I'd have to say no." Then, "You think Emily's home?"

"I haven't seen a single light shining from any of her windows," Theodosia said.

"Maybe Emily's got the shades pulled down."

"Maybe she's not home."

The gate creaked horribly as they opened it, like hinges on an old casket. And when Theodosia and Drayton stepped into the backyard, they saw that the grass hadn't been mowed for a while, flowers had withered and died, and weeds sprouted everywhere.

"Emily's not a gardener either," Theodosia said as they crept along a path of broken concrete up to the back door. She climbed two rickety wooden steps to a small back porch and pulled open the screen door. Then she put an ear to the inner door and listened. There was complete silence. "I'm pretty sure Emily's not home."

"We have to be positive," Drayton said.

So Theodosia knocked on the back door and called out Emily's name. "Nobody answers," she said finally.

"Now what?" Drayton asked.

Theodosia pulled a screwdriver out of her pocket and said, "Let's take a look-see inside."

"You're going to pry open the door?" Drayton sounded terrified.

"Actually, I'd rather try forcing one of the windows. That way Emily might not notice."

They stepped off the tiny back steps, felt their way along the back of the house, and found the window with the old-fashioned screen hanging from it.

"You're taller than I am, Drayton. Take a peek in there and tell me what you see."

Drayton stood on tiptoes and peered in. "It's dark, but there's a small light on—like an appliance light in her kitchen."

"Is this the window over her sink?"

"I think so."

Theodosia glanced around the yard. "Now I just need something to stand on." Her eyes landed on a rusty wheelbarrow. "That should do the trick."

Together they pushed the wheelbarrow over to the house and positioned it right below the window.

"It's a little tippy," Drayton warned.

"But it'll work," Theodosia said. She stepped up into the wheelbarrow, balanced herself carefully, and said, "Perfect." Then she swung the broken screen away from the window and ran her screwdriver up the side of the window. When she came to an old metal latch, she shoved it in hard and levered it sideways. The thing popped like a cheap cork in a bottle of Chianti.

Startled, Drayton said, "What was that?"

"A lucky break," Theodosia whispered as she tucked the screwdriver back into her pocket. Then she slid the window all the way up, stuck one leg in, and gave a sort of hop. The wheelbarrow teetered for a split second, then Theodosia was crawling through the open window and into darkness.

28

Theodosia banged the top of her head as she clambered in, but managed to land on all fours in Emily's sink.

"Are you okay?" Drayton called from outside.

Theodosia squirmed around until she was seated on the edge of the sink, legs dangling, then hopped down. The kitchen smelled like fried eggs, coffee, and wet dishcloths. She looked around, taking in the outmoded appliances and cracked linoleum, and said, "Yeah, I'm good. Can you boost yourself up?"

"You want *me* to come in there?"

"You're the calmer, cooler head, remember?"

Drayton climbed into the wheelbarrow and muttered, "Here goes nothing." With the window slid all the way up, it was fairly easy for him to hang one leg over the sill and slowly ease himself inside.

"Careful with those long legs of yours," Theodosia cautioned as his second leg bumped through the opening and immediately kicked over a plastic holder that held a dish scrubber and sponge.

Drayton was huffing and grunting as he struggled awk-

wardly to bring his head and shoulders through. "I think I've . . .
got it." The rest of him finally squeezed in and he ended up
crouched in the sink.

"Okay, be careful now. Here, take my hand and jump down."

Drayton did a few contortions, and, seconds later, was standing next to Theodosia.

"I feel like a criminal," Drayton whispered.

"Tuck that feeling away for now," Theodosia whispered back.
"And help me look."

"What are we looking for?"

"A pistol would be good. Especially a 9mm."

"Why that caliber?"

"Because the police think that's what killed Wes Lenkov,"
Theodosia said. She figured there might have been two pistols—
one left as a clue, the other owned by the killer.

"Okay."

They poked around the kitchen, opening drawers, looking in
cupboards. Drayton found a flashlight in a utility drawer. The
batteries were low, but they flashed it around anyway as they
searched high and low.

"What about inside her freezer?" Theodosia asked.

Drayton pulled open the freezer drawer. "Not much here.
Lots of ice crystals, a half-eaten carton of frozen yogurt, and a
desiccated-looking chicken that's past its 'use by' date."

"Emily must eat out a lot," Theodosia said. "Or maybe she
hardly eats at all." She'd known women like that—women who
barely consumed any food in order to maintain their svelte figures. In her mind that wasn't a good way to live.

"Nothing here," Drayton said. "Maybe we should leave?" He
sounded hopeful.

"We can't bug out yet," Theodosia said. "We haven't checked
the living room. Or maybe she's got a home office."

Theodosia took the flashlight from Drayton and shone it into the next room. The dining room. There was a dining table with six chairs and a built-in cabinet with a glass front that held a set of dishes and a dozen wine glasses. Above the table, bare wires dangled from the ceiling where a chandelier must have once hung.

"I guess Emily doesn't do a lot of entertaining," Drayton said.

"At least not at home," Theodosia said as she searched the built-in cabinet and found nothing of interest.

The dining room led directly into a living room which was also sparsely furnished. A lumpy sofa with a cocktail table in front of it, two club chairs, a TV set on a stand, floor lamps . . .

"This whole place looks kind of mismatched," Drayton said. "As if she's only living here part-time."

"It is a little strange," Theodosia said. "Though maybe Emily bought this place as a fixer-upper." She flashed the light around, didn't see anything worth investigating, then focused on the staircase that led upstairs.

Drayton saw her looking and said, "Do we dare?"

"Let's take a quick peek," Theodosia said as she started up the stairs.

At the top of the stairs, they found a hallway with three rooms off of it. The first two were bedrooms, which looked fairly austere. The room at the end of the hall was Emily's home office.

"Bingo," Theodosia said. "If we're going to discover anything at all, I'd bet it's in there."

They walked into Emily's office and looked around. There was a clunky old wooden desk with a computer on it and a contemporary-looking desk chair. One wall was floor-to-ceiling bookshelves stuffed with books, stacks of file folders, photos in frames, and a few knickknacks.

Theodosia immediately sat down at the desk and tried the computer. It was turned on but password protected.

"We're not going to get anything from her computer," Theodosia said. "Unless we can pull her password out of thin air."

"Try 'Emily,'" Drayton said.

Theodosia typed in the word *Emily*. "Nada," she said.

"How about the word 'Unity?' For her bank."

That one didn't work, either.

"Okay, I'm stumped," Drayton said. Then he shifted his gaze to the bookshelves. "And we can't sift through all that stuff. It would take hours."

"Agreed."

"So it's a bust. We can go home now?"

"Give me a minute." Theodosia hunted through the desk drawers but found nothing out of the ordinary. Just envelopes, pens, a roll of stamps, and a staple puller.

"Now can we go?"

"No, wait, there's a file drawer, too."

"Is it locked?"

Theodosia reached down and gave the drawer a tug. It slid open with a protesting squeak. "Got it. But there's not much in here, only a few folders."

"Pertaining to what?"

"Mostly household bills. Looks like Emily is fairly organized when it comes to paperwork and bills." Theodosia was about to close the drawer when she saw a file labeled HOME. She pulled it out and opened it, searching quickly through the few papers. "Holy cats, Drayton, Emily owns a second home."

"What do you mean? Like a rental property?"

"I don't know, it's . . ." Theodosia was scanning the paperwork. "Looks like Emily has a home on Hilton Head. A rather large home that she owns free and clear. And she paid . . . let's see . . . one million seven hundred thousand dollars for it. Yikes!"

"She must pull down a fairly high salary at the bank," Drayton said.

"I guess." Theodosia replaced the file folder. "We came here looking for something incriminating, but I'm not sure we found anything. I have to say I'm somewhat disappointed."

"Maybe Emily Bates is a completely innocent person. Good at real estate, lousy when it comes to decorating, but still innocent."

"You could be right," Theodosia said. She stood up, moved to the bookshelves, and ran her fingers over the tops of a few books.

"Don't touch anything," Drayton said suddenly. "You don't want to leave any fingerprints. You know, just in case."

Theodosia frowned. "I touched the mouse. On the computer. And the handles on the desk drawers."

"Easily taken care of." Drayton pulled a white hanky from his jacket pocket, sat down at the desk, and wiped the mouse and handles clean. "You see? Like it never happened."

"Thanks."

"What I'd call a clean getaway." Drayton slowly swiveled the chair back around, then stopped mid-swivel. He blinked hard and frowned.

"What?" Theodosia said.

"I hit something. With my foot."

"What is it?"

"Probably a wastepaper basket." Drayton leaned sideways to peer under the desk while Theodosia flashed the light back there.

But there was no wastebasket. Only a brown leather suitcase.

"Only a suitcase," Drayton said.

"Maybe it's Emily's go bag," Theodosia said. "You know, just in case she is involved in something weird. Pull it out. Let's see what's inside."

Drayton reached down and under and slid the suitcase out. "It's surprisingly heavy."

"Can you lift it up onto the desk?"

Drayton grunted as he swung the suitcase onto the desk.

"Now let's take a look," Theodosia said.

"Is it locked?"

"No," Theodosia said as her fingers worked the two latches. Then she opened the suitcase and gaped at what she saw inside.

Money. Cash. Lots of it.

"It's a suitcase full of money," Drayton said in amazement.

"Why would Emily have all this money?" Theodosia wondered.

"Because she stole it from her bank?"

"I think pilfering this much cash would be difficult to pull off, even for a bank president. Although . . ." Theodosia recalled that someone she'd talked to recently had referred to bankers as "banksters." Was that what Emily Bates was? A banker gangster?

"Now what?" Drayton asked as he tugged at his bow tie nervously. He'd edged into fight-or-flight mode. In his case, flight.

"Look at this money," Theodosia said. "What do you see?"

"Um, paper money, kind of worn-looking. Mostly twenties and fifties."

"Right. No large bills. Twenties and fifties are easy to pass, easy to spend."

"You're saying they're counterfeit?" Drayton asked.

"Not at all. But what if . . . and I know this sounds preposterous . . . what if Emily Bates is laundering money?"

"I thought only the mob laundered their money," Drayton said. "At least that's what you see on TV."

"Drayton, maybe those European guys Izzy told me about *are* the mob?"

Drayton inhaled sharply, giving Theodosia a shocked, bug-eyed look. "And maybe they're dangerous killers. So *our* lives are in danger as well."

"Okay, I hear you. We've got to leave this money and get the heck out of here. But we've also got to alert the authorities."

"And say what? Tell the police that we broke into Emily's house and just happened to discover a huge stash of cash? Not on your life!" Drayton cried.

"We have to tell them something. To have this much money is . . . suspicious."

"What about an anonymous call to the police?" Drayton said.

"Too easy to trace."

"Then we go somewhere off the beaten path and make our call. Maybe a place like Birdsong, that bar over on Bee Street. I think they still have an old pay phone in the back hallway."

"Might work," Theodosia said. "But you'd for sure have to disguise your voice."

"Me?" Drayton gave her a look of terror as his voice rose three octaves.

"Sure, you can do it," Theodosia said with encouragement. "You *have* to do it. I just spoke to Tidwell this morning. He knows my voice. He'd recognize me in a heartbeat. So it's all up to you."

Drayton considered this for a few moments. "But we don't take the money with us."

"No, because it's evidence."

"What if Emily moves the money before the police show up?"

"We tell the police to keep a keen eye on her, stake out this house if needed. Until they figure out a way to get a search warrant."

"Do you think they'll do it?" Drayton latched the suitcase and placed it back where he'd found it.

"There's big money involved and a woman who's already under suspicion," Theodosia said. "They have to do it."

29

❧

Back downstairs, Theodosia and Drayton grabbed a dish towel and wiped everything that they'd touched—the banister, the cupboard in the dining room, everything in the kitchen.

"That's it, right?" Drayton said. "We got it all?"

"I think so," Theodosia said. "I hope so."

"What about the window we crawled through? It looks a little wonky."

Theodosia thought for a minute. "Why don't we close it from the inside and lock it. Then exit through the back door. It's got one of those locks you punch on the door handle. We shut it behind us and—presto—it's locked."

"And we fix the screen when we get outside."

"And stow away the wheelbarrow."

"Sounds like a plan," Drayton said.

They hustled out of the house and banged the window screen back in place. Just as they were pushing the wheelbarrow across the back lawn, a flash of light splashed across them.

"There's a car coming down the alley!" Drayton said.

"Duck!" Theodosia cried.

They both crouched down in the weedy lawn just as a car rolled to a stop at Emily's back gate.

"Now what?" Drayton whispered, half-panicked.

Theodosia looked around and spotted a sad-looking stand of palmettos in the corner of the yard.

"This way," she said. She was half crawling, half walking as she made a beeline for the palmettos. Drayton scurried after her, directly on her heels.

By the time Emily Bates came through the back gate, Theodosia and Drayton were snuggled behind the palmettos, hopefully enveloped in a little pocket of darkness.

They both stiffened as Emily's steps rang out as she walked up the back sidewalk. Then they peeked out as she inserted her key in the door. The door swung open, a kitchen light was turned on, and Theodosia and Drayton heaved a sigh of relief.

"That was a close one," Drayton whispered. "Let's go."

"Wait one," Theodosia whispered back. Emily was still in the kitchen because she could see the woman's shadow moving around. Then, moments later, the light went off. "I think maybe she moved into the living room."

"You think Emily suspects anything?"

"She's such a lousy housekeeper that I can't imagine she'd notice if something was out of place," Theodosia said.

They gave it another three minutes and then they were out of there. Taking care with the squeaky gate, fast walking down the alley, and jumping into Theodosia's Jeep.

The Birdsong Club on Bee Street was buzzing tonight. Patrons crowded the front of the club, sitting on barstools and at small

tables along the length of the bar. The interior was fairly dark
with the usual array of neon beer signs that included local brew-
eries like Edmund's Oast and Holy City Brewing. The place
smelled of beer, burgers, and onions, and the occasional scent of
a bootleg cigarette wafting out from the kitchen.

As Theodosia and Drayton shouldered their way through,
one of the bartenders—a big, burly guy with a shaved head and
single hoop earring—nodded at Drayton and said, "Lindsay's
about to begin her set. You might want to stick around and
catch it."

Drayton nodded back as they continued toward the back of
the club.

"They know you here," Theodosia said.

"Because I patronize this club," Drayton said. "I happen to
like jazz."

"I thought you were more of a Shostakovich kind of guy."

"Surprised you, did I?"

"Drayton, you never fail to surprise me." Then Theodosia
looked around and said, "Okay, where's this anonymous phone?"

Drayton led her through another room crowded with tables
and down a narrow hallway past a door that said MANAGER'S
OFFICE and one that said KITCHEN STAFF ONLY to an old-
fashioned black wall phone.

"This has to be the last public phone in the history of the
world," Theodosia said.

Drayton smiled faintly and said, "Got a quarter?"

Theodosia dug into her bag, found a quarter, and gave it to
Drayton. "Are you nervous?"

"Not as much as I was when we broke into Emily Bates's
home." Drayton shoved the quarter in the slot and said, "Go
ahead, dial the number."

Theodosia dialed Tidwell's private number—the one he'd given her years ago and had probably forgotten about.

When Tidwell came on the line, sounding annoyed at having his evening interrupted, Drayton said, "There's a suitcase full of money in Emily Bates's home office. We suspect it's money that's about to be or was laundered illegally." Then he slammed the phone down on the hook.

"Short and sweet," Theodosia said. "Right to the point. You did good."

"It didn't *feel* good. It felt shaky and unsettled."

"Do you want to go home?"

"I'd rather sit down and have a drink," Drayton said.

So that's exactly what they did. Theodosia had an amber ale called "Brain Storm" from South Carolina's own Rock Hill Brewing, and Drayton had scotch on the rocks while they watched Lindsay's set. Lindsay Lovell was a Black woman in her mid-fifties, a highly trained jazz vocalist, who was accompanied by a trio of fine musicians who seemed to key off her finesse and energy. She breezed through "Round Midnight," "Cry Me a River," and a few more songs, then ended her set with a bluesy rendition of "Feeling Good."

"She's terrific," Theodosia said as she joined in the applause.

"One of the best," Drayton said.

"Seems like you feel better now."

"I'll feel better when I know that Tidwell took my call seriously."

Theodosia thought for a minute. "So will I."

Fifteen minutes later, Theodosia dropped Drayton off at his home, then drove the few blocks to her own place.

When she opened the back door, the lights were on but there was no Earl Grey waiting to greet her.

"That's strange," she said as the hairs on the back of her neck started to tickle.

But when she crept through her kitchen and into her dining room, she got the surprise of her life.

Pete Riley was sitting in her living room, drinking a glass of wine and reading a copy of *Southern Living.* Earl Grey was snoozing at his feet.

"What are you doing here?" Theodosia cried.

Riley jumped up abruptly, letting the magazine slide off his lap. It landed on Earl Grey who jumped as if he'd been shot from a cannon.

"Waiting for you," Riley said. He set his wine down on the coffee table and moved toward her, sounding casual, looking relaxed.

"How did you get in?" Theodosia asked him.

"You once told me there was a spare key hidden beneath that bumpy gray rock in your garden," Riley said. "So, like a good detective, I lifted the rock and found the key." He tilted his head. "Why? What's wrong? Where have you been?"

"Just . . . hanging out with Drayton." Theodosia shook her head to clear away the nervous cobwebs. Then she stepped into his open arms and pressed herself up against him. "Am I ever glad to see you."

Riley hugged her tight as he lifted a single brow. "Why? Are you in some kind of trouble?"

"No! Not at all."

"You seem a little unsure about that, which leads me to believe you've been up to something."

"Not really."

"Are you quite positive?"

Theodosia mustered a smile. "I think so." Then she looked over at his glass.

"You've got wine."

"I brought along a bottle of High Tide. It's a light-bodied red wine from our local Deep Water Vineyard. I think you'll like it. Want me to pour you a glass?"

"Maybe half a glass."

"*In vino veritas*," Riley said.

"Excuse me?"

"It's Latin for 'in wine there's truth.' Maybe after you sip a little wine, you'll tell me what's really going on."

"Oh, I don't know about that."

But fifteen minutes later, after Theodosia had sipped a half glass of wine, she did spill her guts—told Riley exactly what was going on. What *had* been going on. About the creepy-crawl that she and Drayton had gone on tonight, and finding the suitcase of money.

Riley listened thoughtfully and (*thank goodness!*) nonjudgmentally—if that was a real word—until she'd finished completely.

Then he said, "Wow. When you set out to investigate something you really go for broke." There was a hint of admiration in his voice.

"But do you think Tidwell will figure it out?" Theodosia asked. "That Drayton and I were the ones who snuck into Emily Bates's house and discovered the money? And that Drayton was the one who tried to alert him with a phone call?"

"I don't know," Riley said. "I guess you'll have to wait and see."

"Okay, but even if Tidwell does guess correctly, will he take our call seriously? Will he believe that Emily Bates is sitting on a suitcase full of cash?"

"With Bates being a sort of suspect in Harlan Sadler's murder, Tidwell *has* to take it seriously. If you ask me, he's probably got an unmarked car parked on her street already."

"That'd be good," Theodosia said. "Real good."

30

❧

Theodosia was on pins and needles this Saturday morning, scurrying around the Indigo Tea Shop, almost dropping a pot of tea, as she wondered if she'd hear from Tidwell.

"I'm the one who made the anonymous call last night, but you're the one who's got the jitters today," Drayton said.

"I feel like a cat in a room full of rocking chairs," Theodosia said.

"Maybe you should call Detective Tidwell. Fess up and see if he took our warning about Emily Bates seriously."

"My guess is he probably did," Theodosia said. Then she checked her watch and said, "But you're right, I'd like to talk to him, but it might be too early to call. I'll wait until ten."

"You have to be prepared to face repercussions."

"I know, I've got this," Theodosia said. She was resolved that she'd make Tidwell believe her about Emily Bates and the suitcase full of money. And maybe even prompt him to connect the money to the Eastern European guys Izzy told her about. If

Tidwell doubted her, she'd try to get Riley to talk some sense into him.

But when ten thirty rolled around and Tidwell still hadn't called, Theodosia couldn't wait any longer. She called his office, but only got as far as Glen Humphries, his assistant.

"I'm sorry, Detective Tidwell isn't in this morning," Humphries told her.

"When do you think he'll be in? Or, rather, *is* he going to come in?"

"Hard to say. But I'll certainly relay your message, should you have one."

Theodosia wasn't sure if she detected a note of satisfaction in Humphrey's voice or not, so she said, "No, just tell him I called. That Theodosia called."

"Tidwell's not in yet," Theodosia told Drayton when she went to grab a pot of tea.

"Maybe he's busy arresting Emily Bates," Drayton said. "Reading Emily her rights."

"Don't I wish." Theodosia fiddled for a minute, then said, "I'm going to check in with Haley about lunch."

Saturday luncheons at the Indigo Tea Shop always consisted of two different prix fixe choices. And, thus far, Haley had always come up with winners.

Today was no different.

"Orange blossom scones, citrus salad with oranges, grapefruit, and pomegranate, and a slice of mushroom and cheese quiche," Haley said.

"And for our second prix fixe option?" Theodosia asked.

"Cream scones, mushroom bisque, and a grilled tuna sandwich oozing with melted Swiss cheese."

"You must have bought a ton of mushrooms from your greengrocer."

"You have no idea. I'm thinking ahead to Monday's lunch. Maybe mushroom pâté on crostini?"

"Sounds delish."

"Oh, and you can take that plate of goodies out to the counter," Haley said, pointing to a tasty array of scones and slices of banana bread. "You know we always get a lot of takeaway orders on Saturday."

Theodosia grabbed the plate, went back into the tea room, and carefully stacked the scones and banana bread in their glass cake saver. As she was putting the cover back on, the bell over the door *da-ding*ed and Cricket Sadler walked in. She was wearing dark glasses and a short black shift dress, and carrying a pink Gucci bag. She looked like she was still in mourning, but a stylish form of mourning.

"Cricket!" Theodosia cried. "I was just thinking about you. How are you doing?"

"Hanging in there," Cricket said. "It's been tough, but . . . well, I guess life goes on."

"You poor dear, you've been so strong."

"Trying to be anyway," Cricket said as she slid off her sunglasses.

"I hope you can stay for lunch?"

"Well . . . maybe."

Theodosia led Cricket to a small table and said, "Here you go." But Cricket hesitated, then grabbed Theodosia's hand, squeezed it, and said, "The real reason I'm here is to thank you for everything you've done."

"I'm not sure I've done all that much," Theodosia said.

"That's not what Delaine tells me." Cricket lowered her voice and said, "Thursday night? At Sport Luxe? You discovered that man's body."

"I wish Delaine wasn't so free with her tongue."

"It wasn't just Delaine. The police talked to me about it, too. Told me they found a confession on that man's computer. That he confessed to killing my husband." Cricket wiped away a tear, pursed her lips, and said, "They also told me they thought it was fake. That the man, Lenkov, had been set up."

"That's what I think, too."

"Then who . . . ?" Cricket was suddenly choked up, almost unable to talk.

"I don't know, honey." Theodosia put an arm around Cricket and eased her into a chair. "There are still lots of balls in the air. I'm still working on things. Detective Tidwell is, too."

"Having an answer would give me great comfort."

"Of course it would," Theodosia said. She glanced at Drayton and gave him a meaningful look. He immediately grabbed a pot of tea and hurried over.

"Here's a nice pot of peppermint tea for you," Drayton said as he poured a golden stream into Cricket's teacup. "Good for relaxing the nerves and calming any errant thoughts."

"Thank you," Cricket said.

"Now I hope you plan to stay for lunch," Drayton said.

Cricket nodded as Theodosia said, "Let me run in the kitchen and put together something special for you."

"You're too kind," Cricket said.

"Nonsense," Theodosia said. "It's what we do here at the Indigo Tea Shop, right, Drayton?"

"That's right," Drayton said. "We always take care of our own."

A busy lunchtime at the tea shop kept Theodosia hopping. Good thing there were only two choices. And, interestingly enough, their customers seemed to love the put-together prix fixe luncheons.

"Because they don't have to think so hard," Haley told Theodosia. "We've done the matching and pairing for them."

"And Drayton always brews the perfect tea to accompany your luncheon plates," Theodosia said.

Haley stuck a hand on her hip, cocked her head sideways, and said, "Ain't we the clever ones?"

Theodosia served lunches and poured tea, always keeping a watchful eye on Cricket. When Cricket finished her lunch and headed for the front counter to pay her bill, Drayton held up a hand and said, "No need. It's on the house."

"Are you sure?" Cricket asked.

"We're sure," Theodosia said as she came up behind her.

"You two are such dears," Cricket said. "You've shown me such kindness." She gave a faint smile and said, "I hope you're planning to attend Opera in the Park tonight."

"We'll be there with bells on," Drayton said. Then, in a more respectful tone, said, "Will *you* be in attendance?"

"I wasn't planning to go," Cricket said. "But I realized I have to show my face in public sooner or later. So I'm going. After all, it's for a good cause."

"The very best," Drayton assured her.

"And any rain is supposed to hold off until after midnight," Cricket said.

"Fingers crossed," Theodosia said as she walked Cricket to the door and gave her a hug. Then she walked back to the front counter where Drayton was brewing a pot of hibiscus tea.

"You know, I'm supposed to attend this lovely Opera in the Park tonight and I don't even have a ticket," Theodosia said. "I don't know how I'm supposed to get in or find a seat."

"Not to worry," Drayton said. "Timothy Neville has reserved box seats. We'll sit with him."

"Just like that?"

"No, just like this," Drayton said as he pulled two tickets from his jacket pocket and held them up.

"Those are for us?"

"And there's more where these came from. I have tickets for Haley and Ben as well. And for Pete Riley, if he's inclined to attend."

"I mentioned the opera to Riley, but he said he couldn't make it. I don't know if he didn't want to spiff up in black tie or if he was really truly busy with police business."

"Maybe he's helping Tidwell make an arrest."

Theodosia sighed. "I don't know about that. We can only hope." Then she brightened and said, "But at least we've got tickets."

Drayton lifted an eyebrow. "Not only that, my dear. Our ticket stubs entitle each of us to a complimentary glass of champagne."

"Free champs," Theodosia said. "Now it's a party."

31

❧

Getting ready for the opera turned out to be a pleasant ritual for Theodosia. Even though she hadn't heard from Tidwell all day, she was bound and determined not to let that one thing spoil her evening. No, tonight she was going to forget about murder and mayhem and simply have fun. Go with an open, happy heart and enjoy the excitement of opera under the stars.

Theodosia did her makeup, giving her eyeliner an extra swoosh at the outer corners. She used NARS cream blush to highlight her cheeks, then lined her lips and filled them in with pale peach Chanel lip gloss.

She fiddled with her hair, trying it up, then pulled to one side with a clip. Finally, she decided to let her auburn locks go *au naturel*. If she poufed a bit from the evening's humidity, then so what?

Some women would kill to have big, bouncy hair, right? Right?

She walked into her closet and studied the rack where she kept her fancier pieces. Looked at a black cocktail dress, decided no. Maybe the long silver skirt with . . . no, that wasn't striking a chord, either.

Instead, Theodosia opted for a long black shantung silk skirt with a slit up the side and a black boucle jacket. The jacket was carefully tailored with an oyster collar, French cuffs, and jeweled buttons down the front.

She put everything on, then looked down at her feet and said, "Shoes."

Scurrying back to her closet, Theodosia pulled out a shoebox and removed the cover. There, nestled in their own little cloth bags, was a pair of black leather Yves Saint Laurent stilettos. They'd been horribly expensive, and the only reason she'd bought them was because she'd been goaded into it by Delaine. But they were gorgeous, surprisingly comfortable, and the four-inch heels took her to new heights.

A black beaded bag held her phone, lipstick, tissues, two twenty-dollar bills, and her car keys.

Oops, better call Drayton.

She dialed his number as she walked downstairs, taking care not to trip on her skirt or Earl Grey, who was following close behind.

"Are you ready?" she asked when Drayton answered.

"With bells on. You're picking me up, right?"

"Five minutes."

"I'll be waiting on the curb."

Drayton was waiting as promised and looked spectacular in his tuxedo. He'd paired it with a white pleated shirt, slightly floppy bow tie, cummerbund, and highly polished shoes.

"Those look like tap shoes," Theodosia said as he climbed in her Jeep.

"They are," Drayton said with a straight face. "I've been invited to do a dance number during intermission."

"No, you haven't," Theodosia laughed as she pulled away from the curb. "Although I'd for sure pay to see you do it."

"Then I'd have to pay someone to do it for me." He leaned back and said, "I'm looking forward to this."

"Me, too. I've decided I just want to have fun tonight. Drink a little champagne, get swept up in the majesty of *Aida*."

"And so we shall."

They cruised down Archdale Street and hooked a right on Morton. As they approached Petigru Park, where the opera was being held, they saw beams from searchlights piercing the night sky.

"Looks like they're making a big deal out of this," Drayton said.

"Because it *is* a big deal," Theodosia said as she joined a long line of cars. Up ahead she could see red-jacketed valets helping people out of cars, then handing the vehicles off to car parkers.

"I suspect they've got a red carpet," Theodosia said.

"Good Lord," Drayton said. "Do we have to walk a red carpet?" He wasn't enthused at the prospect.

"Where's your sense of style? Of fun?"

"Back home in my sock drawer."

When Theodosia reached the head of the line, she was helped out of her Jeep by a valet and directed toward the entrance.

"Oh, it's a step and repeat," she said to Drayton.

"A what?"

"You know how it works. We walk along a red carpet with a big banner behind us that lists all the opera's sponsors. All the while, photographers are snapping our pictures."

"Ye gads."

But Drayton proved to be a fairly decent sport. He stepped

smartly along, guiding Theodosia by the elbow. Looking dignified in his tuxedo, he nodded and blinked as photogs bombarded them with flashing lights.

"That was awful," Drayton said as they finally walked through an archway of flowers and twisty vines into the cordoned-off park area.

"It was all of six seconds," Theodosia said. "You practically dragged me along that step and repeat. I could barely keep up." She smoothed her hair, looked around, and said, "Oh my," because Petigru Park had been transformed into an amazing-looking outdoor opera house.

Set in an amphitheater-like bowl of parkland, an enormous stage and backdrop had been constructed, along with elaborate wings on either side where the cast no doubt changed costumes and had their hair and makeup done. Directly in front of the stage were chairs and music stands for the orchestra. Then there was a wide aisle flanked by flaming torches, and, to either side, hundreds of chairs to accommodate the audience.

"I say," Drayton said. "This does look magnificent."

"Aren't we glad the weather decided to cooperate," Theodosia said. The night sky was a chiaroscuro painting of clouds and moonlight with a gentle breeze floating in off the Atlantic that brought a hint of salt.

The flaming torches lent a flickering moody atmosphere as they wandered through the black-tie crowd, greeting friends and exclaiming over the lovely evening.

"You can feel the undercurrent of excitement," Theodosia said.

"Absolutely," Drayton said. "And everyone who's anyone is here tonight."

"Including Haley and Ben. Look." Theodosia pointed as Haley and her boyfriend, Ben, strolled toward them. Haley was wearing a long sea green dress that set off her blond hair to perfection. Ben wore a suit with a bow tie and, as far as Theodosia could tell, black motorcycle boots. Oh well.

"This is so cool," Haley exclaimed. "So elegant and grown-up!"

"Thanks for the invite," Ben said.

"You're welcome," Theodosia replied. "Have you two seen Timothy yet?" Timothy Neville was the octogenarian executive director of Drayton's beloved Heritage Society. He was also descended from French Huguenots who'd fled to Charleston in the early seventeenth century to escape religious persecution. Timothy's ancestors had prospered, and now he resided in a spectacular mansion on Archdale Street that he shared with his beloved Siamese cat, Chairman Meow.

"Timothy's sitting right behind the orchestra," Haley said. "There are six private seating areas all enclosed by velvet ropes, and Timothy's got the best one with, like, ten chairs in it. I guess the private areas are where all the big-buck people sit."

"Supporters and donors," Drayton said, quietly correcting her.

"Well, yeah," Haley said.

"You have drinks," Theodosia said, noticing the glasses in Haley's and Ben's hands.

"Champagne. The bar's set up right over there," Haley said, lifting a hand and pointing. "And I'm pretty sure there's an hors d'oeuvres table, too, though we haven't hit it yet."

"Shall we get something to drink?" Theodosia asked Drayton, who nodded in response.

On the way to the bar, they ran into Delaine and Ned Grady. Delaine was in a silver dress trimmed with white marabou feathers, Grady in a tuxedo.

"Isn't this *fantastic*?" Delaine cried, giving an excited little shiver. "It's like an outdoor venue that you'd find in *Europe*. Like in Paris or Vienna or Rome." She leaned forward on tippy silver shoes and said, "And wasn't that step and repeat crazy fun? All those flashes going off. Honestly, I felt like I was at a Hollywood premiere!"

"Glad you got off on it, honey," Grady said with a sardonic smile.

Delaine stuck out her bottom lip. "Well, I did. Say it wasn't fun. Theo, it was fun, right?"

"It was a blast," Theodosia said.

Drayton gestured at Grady's drink—amber liquid in a heavy glass. "Is that by any chance scotch?"

"Glenlivet," Grady said.

"That's what I'm looking for," Drayton said. "Come on, Theo, we'd better hurry. The opera's going to start in something like ten minutes."

Theodosia and Drayton elbowed their way toward the bar. It was slow going since they kept running into people they knew, and social niceties dictated they exchange greetings and sometimes even air-kisses. Before they reached the bar, they'd said hello to Ray Crispin, Susan Monday, Brooke Carter Crocket, and Lois Chamberlain.

Charlie Skipstead, the podcast lady, gave Theodosia a little finger wave and mouthed, "Are you still thinking about it?" Theodosia pretended not to notice.

On their way back, drinks in hand, Theodosia saw Ethan Stacks, the antique dealer, chatting with two older men. Luckily, Stacks didn't see her and make a fuss.

They located Timothy's box seats—which wasn't a box *per se*, more like ten chairs enclosed by a velvet rope—and said their hellos. Timothy welcomed them eagerly and indicated their seats, even as he glad-handed scores of influential people around him.

"Never let it be said that Timothy passed up an opportunity

to cater to well-heeled donors," Drayton whispered to Theodosia. "Even if it's at another organization's fundraiser."

"Timothy's a smart old fox," Theodosia replied. "Whether he's running a business or a nonprofit." She took a sip of champagne, turned in her seat to see who was sitting nearby, and noticed Cricket sitting in the next box over with her son, Duke.

"Cricket and Duke are here," Theodosia said to Drayton as she watched the musicians file in and take their places.

"It's good that Cricket came tonight," Drayton said. "Probably therapeutic for her."

Theodosia twisted around in her seat to see who else was there. For a moment, her eyes lit on a small woman that she thought might be Emily Bates. But then the woman leaned forward, and she could tell by her profile that she wasn't Emily.

Good. I guess.

But thinking about Emily caused a frisson of worry to intrude on her thoughts.

No, I'm here to have a good time. I need to shake off any thoughts of murder or suspects.

She swished a hand in front of her face as if she possessed superpowers to banish such thinking.

Didn't work.

Thoughts of a murdered Harlan Sadler and Wes Lenkov were suddenly capering through her brain like divisive evil spirits.

No. Not here. Not tonight. I need to focus on something positive and free my mind.

The lights had dimmed and the orchestra was warming up, so Theodosia focused her mind on those dulcet sounds. The hum of the strings, the deep thrum of the viola, a gentle twitter from the wind section.

Lovely. Thrilling, really.

And that's when it all went to hell.

Bright lights suddenly splashed across the audience, and the scream of sirens drowned out the orchestra's efforts. Off to the left, racing down a gentle hill, were three police cruisers heading straight for them. Red and blue lights strobed crazily, high-intensity searchlights scanned the audience, and a voice on a bullhorn shouted, "This is the Charleston Police Department. You are asked to remain in your seats! Please, remain seated!"

Of course, no one did.

The audience jumped to their feet en masse and looked around, craning their necks, trying to figure out what was going on. A few women screamed. Some men started shouting.

And then the real shouting began as Detective Burt Tidwell, flanked by six uniformed officers, rushed down the center aisle. There was a brief scuffle, and then a bright light was shone into the tenth or eleventh row of chairs behind Theodosia.

Shocked beyond belief, Theodosia turned to see that Emily Bates was the target of this bizarre raid.

So Emily was here after all.

But not for long.

Theodosia watched in utter amazement as two officers plucked Emily Bates out of her chair, as if she were a spring chicken destined for Sunday's dinner table.

"Help!" Emily cried as she struggled against the officers. "Help me, somebody! Please!"

Nobody helped.

32

꧁❦꧂

"*They're arresting Emily* Bates," Theodosia said to Drayton as an excited buzz rose up all around them. It sounded like cicadas on a summer day. Then she was on her feet and pushing her way up the aisle and through the frenzied crowd. She spotted Detective Burt Tidwell as he hastily read Emily her rights. And, all the while, Emily moaned pitifully and shook her head.

"They've got her," Theodosia said out loud to herself.

"Got who?" a man standing next to her asked.

"Emily Bates. From Unity One Bank," Theodosia said.

Now a wave of whispers swept through the crowd like wildfire. "*Emily Bates. The bank lady. She's being arrested.*"

Emily was already in handcuffs and looking scared to death by the time Theodosia made her way to Tidwell.

"You got her," she said.

Tidwell gave a sideways glance, recognized Theodosia, and gave a quick nod of his head.

"Was it money laundering?" Theodosia asked.

But Tidwell ignored her as his officers hurriedly cleared a path so they could lead Emily away.

Theodosia touched a hand to her chest to try and still her beating heart. "Oh my gosh."

Then someone poked her shoulder. She jumped slightly at the intrusion, then turned and found a frightened, doe-eyed Delaine staring at her.

"What just happened?" Delaine demanded.

"Emily Bates was arrested," Theodosia said.

"Who?" Ned Grady was suddenly beside Delaine, a quizzical look on his face.

"The president of Unity One Bank," Theodosia said.

"Oh, her," Grady said as all around them people continued to talk and mill about, wondering what exactly had happened. Wondering if something else was about to go wrong.

Delaine, suddenly frantic at the uproar, put her hands on top of her head and screamed, "Somebody *do* something! This event is turning into a complete and utter fiasco!"

Ned Grady grunted, then turned and bounded toward the stage. He climbed a set of stairs, two at a time, strode to the center of the stage, and raised his hands.

"People. Please," he shouted in a booming voice. "There's been a slight disturbance, but nothing to worry about. Please, I ask you to please take your seats immediately." He looked behind him where a stage manager was signaling to him. Grady took a step back, had a whispered conversation, then walked to the front of the stage.

"Ladies and gentlemen," Grady said in a calm voice. "The opera is slated to begin in exactly five minutes, so kindly take your seats." He smiled out at the audience. "That's right, everything's under control. There's nothing to worry about."

A nervous hush fell over the crowd, then a spatter of applause broke out as people began to relax and take their seats.

"Wow," Theodosia said. She was impressed by Grady's quick command of both the situation and the audience.

"Heroically handled," Drayton said.

From then on, the evening was truly divine. The singers burst into their opening song, the orchestra soared, and the audience clapped wildly. *Aida* was a magnificent opera, complete with colorful costumes and possessing a fairy-tale quality. Enormous images of Egyptian tombs were projected on a large backdrop, and the stately production was replete with a large cast, rousing marches, and lusty choruses.

"This is amazing," Theodosia whispered to Drayton.

"As good as the Met," he responded.

Near the end of act two, when the battle scene took place, two live horses made their triumphant entrance onto the stage, causing the crowd to stand up and cheer wildly.

It was just a tick before intermission when Theodosia saw Ned Grady ghost by her and head around the back of the stage. She put a hand on Drayton's arm and whispered, "I'll be right back." Then she slipped out of her chair and ran lightly down the aisle. Because the second act hadn't quite concluded, it was still pitch dark and Theodosia was having trouble finding her way. Really, all she wanted to do was thank Grady for bravely saving the day.

Passing the bar, where a few lights glinted off glassware, Theodosia saw Grady's outline some twenty feet ahead of her. She put a little more hustle into her steps until, suddenly, the heel of her right shoe sank into the earth, completely throwing her off-balance.

Theodosia barely caught herself as she started to go down. She fluttered her arms like a large bird, trying to regain her balance, then grabbed hold of a nearby tree.

She was okay, but her heel was stuck tight. And the more she tried to free it, the deeper it seemed to dig into the turf.

Dang it.

There was only one answer. Theodosia stepped out of her shoe, bent down, and wrenched it from the mud.

Now I've got a dirty shoe. An expensive dirty shoe, at that.

She dug a tissue out of her bag and tried to wipe off the sticky mud. It worked some, but the results weren't great. She hopped along on one foot until she was on *terra firma*, then put on her muddy shoe.

Okay. What was I doing? Oh, right. Grady.

She was directly behind the stage now where it was dark as a coal mine. And as she looked around, saw hunks of soon-to-be-used scenery scattered everywhere—pillars, a large sphinx, some painted flats. Finally, she saw Grady, standing some thirty feet ahead of her, conversing with two men. One of them lit a cigarette, illuminating their faces for a split second, and giving the scene a surreal feel. Slowly, gingerly, Theodosia crept toward them until she was ten feet away, hidden in the shadows. Something about the way they were huddled together made her hesitant to interrupt.

And that's when Theodosia saw one man dig into his pocket, pull out a wad of cash, and hand it to Ned Grady. Grady accepted the cash eagerly and quickly jammed it into his jacket pocket.

What?

Shielded by a piece of scenery, Theodosia crept even closer.

"You'll owe thirty points on that," the man said. His voice was harsh and guttural. "Collectible in one week."

"Got it," Grady said.

"Just so you know, we're not fooling around on this," the other man warned Grady.

"I'm good for it," Grady promised, though he didn't sound particularly sure of himself.

"You better be," the man who'd given him the cash growled. "You oughta pray that Lady Luck swoops down and puckers up on you."

"No problem," Grady said.

Startled, Theodosia spun away from the men just as the backstage lights came up and Petigru Park was rocked with applause and multiple shouts of "Bravo." It was intermission.

Like a salmon swimming upstream, Theodosia fought her way back through the tide of people heading for the bar. Five minutes later, she found Delaine and grabbed her by the arm, spinning her around.

"Ouch," Delaine said. "What do you think you're *do*ing?"

"Delaine, when you jetted down to Nassau with Ned Grady, what kind of plane did you fly on?"

Delaine frowned as she looked around at the throngs of people. In her silver dress with fluffed-up feathers around the neck and hem, she'd been busy preening, checking to see how many eyes were focused on her.

"Delaine?" Theodosia said again.

"It was a private jet, silly. The upscale kind with cream-colored leather seats and a fully stocked bar. Why are you asking? Jealous?"

"No. But please just . . . indulge me. Was there a name or company logo painted on the outside of the plane?"

Delaine lifted a shoulder. "I really don't remember."

"Think hard. It's important."

Delaine squeezed her eyes shut, managing a good imitation of concentration. "Okay, I think it might have said 'Lucky Calypso.'"

"And was that also the name of the casino you went to?"

Delaine touched a finger to her lower lip and gave a faint smile. "The Lucky Calypso. I guess it was. Isn't that a fun coincidence?"

Theodosia knew darn well that casinos sent private jets to pick up habitual gamblers for one reason only . . . to entice those high rollers back to their casino where they'd win—or better yet, lose— big bucks. Yes, by offering free transportation, they made it as seamless as possible to lure in their pigeons. So, the question was— was Ned Grady a high roller, or a big loser? Could Grady be in debt up to his eyeballs? And if so . . . what exactly did that mean?

Theodosia looked around and saw Cricket and Duke chatting with a group of people. She thought about Cricket— thought about Cricket's husband being murdered. Then her thoughts began whirling like a centrifuge.

Harlan Sadler had been a banker, and not just any banker. A bank president. A veritable big shot at the bank. A guy who had access to money. So what if . . . what if Ned Grady had tapped his old pal Harlan Sadler for a whopper of a loan? And maybe . . . what? Maybe it had been off the books? And Grady, losing big and unable to pay Sadler back, had killed him? Had to resort to murder to resolve his debts?

Click.

The click felt both audible and tangible, as if a final piece of the puzzle had dropped into place.

"Theo," Delaine said in a petulant tone. "Let go of me. I want to go talk to June and Jeffrey McDonald over there."

Theodosia released her hold on Delaine's arm and stood there as happy opera fans continued to swirl around her.

"But what if I'm wrong?" she whispered to herself. To accuse someone of murder without hard evidence was . . . well, difficult at best. No one would believe her.

"So I've got to talk to Grady myself. Question him carefully. See what I can find out."

Theodosia spun in her tracks and ran back toward the bar and backstage area.

She found Grady standing at the bar, joking with one of the bartenders. With her eyes focused directly on him, Theodosia eased her way through the crowd, moving ever closer to Grady. And just when she was within three feet of him, she saw Grady reach up and scratch the back of his neck, his jacket sleeve riding up to reveal his wrist.

Theodosia blinked hard and caught her breath. Because just for a few seconds, she'd seen a Breitling Chronomat circling his wrist.

The exact same watch Wes Lenkov had worn when I first met him.

Wait a minute, it *looked* like the watch Wes Lenkov had worn. But was it the same watch? When she'd discovered Lenkov's murdered body, had he still been wearing his watch? Theodosia couldn't remember.

What to do? Got to figure this out.

Had Grady murdered Lenkov, too? Had he set Lenkov up with a phony confession so Lenkov would take the fall for killing Harlan Sadler? She'd guessed that Lenkov had been set up, but now she had to be sure.

Theodosia watched, feeling helpless, as Grady tossed a twenty-dollar bill on the bar, grabbed his drink, and sauntered toward the backstage area. What should she do? Grab Drayton? Call Pete Riley? Or follow Grady and see what was up?

Theodosia spent five minutes hunting around the backstage area but couldn't find Grady. Where had he disappeared to? Had he gone back to sit with Delaine? Theodosia ran back to the front of the stage where Delaine was now talking to Rita Dale, owner of a children's clothing shop.

Nope. Now what?

She looked over and saw Drayton laughing with Haley and Timothy Neville. Should she interrupt them? Get Drayton to help her corner Grady?

No, that could put him in danger.

Theodosia spun around and hurried back, knowing she was running out of time. Intermission would be over in a few minutes and, once everything went dark, it would be almost impossible to locate Grady.

There were panel trucks and dozens of large trucks parked behind the stage. They'd been used to haul in costumes, lighting, stage materials, and elaborate sets and scenery. Maybe Grady was somewhere among those vehicles doing who knows what?

Just as Theodosia darted around a white panel truck that had the words ALHAMBRA LIGHTING on it, the whole place went pitch black. Music swelled as the orchestra began playing again and the actors sang their arias.

Now what?

It was so dark, Theodosia could barely see her hand in front of her face. The moon, which had been most obliging up until now, had slid behind a bubble of dark clouds, robbing her of even faint moon shadows. Touching the side of the truck to guide her, Theodosia walked deeper into the backstage area.

All of a sudden, an arm snaked around her neck and grabbed hard, almost pulling her over backward.

"What are you doing back here?" Ned Grady snarled. "Spying on me?"

33

Even with Grady's arm bent tight around her neck, Theodosia gasped out the first thing that came to mind. "I was looking for you."

"And why is that?" Grady asked in a low voice.

"I . . . I wanted to thank you," Theodosia said, trying to pry his arm from her neck. "For keeping everyone so calm, getting them back in their seats."

"You little weasel, why do I not believe you?" he said.

"The third act's started. We should . . ."

"Shut up!" Grady cried.

Theodosia decided to play it straight. Maybe that would disarm him.

"You killed Harlan Sadler," she said in a cold voice. "Over a loan he made to you."

"What if I did?"

Oh my Lord, he isn't denying it!

"And you killed Wes Lenkov, too," Theodosia said.

"Smart girl. And now I'm going to kill you."

Theodosia lost it then. She squirmed wildly in his grasp, trying with all her might to escape. She fought hard, stomping her heel down on his instep, kicking him, twisting around to try and bite his arm. Nothing seemed to work. She tried to bend forward, then whip her body backward, but Grady was so strong she couldn't put enough force behind it.

And all the while Grady kept his arm pressed around her throat, choking off her airway with every passing second.

"You want to fight me?" he said in a low voice. "Maybe this will change your mind."

The cold, hard barrel of a pistol was suddenly pressed into the small of Theodosia's back.

Fear shot through Theodosia's brain. "You can't . . ." Theodosia choked on her words and let loose a harsh cough. Grady's arm was still bent tight around her, cutting off her oxygen, making her feel faint. Sparks flashed before her eyes and she feared she was about to pass out . . . and die.

"Can't what?" Grady taunted, as off to the left there was a crunching sound. Someone approaching.

Then a man appeared from around the front of the truck— *one of the lighting guys?*—and shouted, "What's going on back here?"

Grady loosened his grip and dipped his gun momentarily, giving Theodosia a split second to escape. Quick as a fox, she dropped to all fours and rolled under the lighting truck.

"Hey!" Grady shouted.

Theodosia kept rolling. She spun out from under the lighting truck and rolled under a much larger truck that was parked right next to it.

She lay on her back, holding her breath, wondering if Grady had caught on to her escape route. But as she listened, she heard heavy grunts and groans. Now Grady was struggling with the lighting guy!

Please don't let Grady shoot him.

Pondering her next move, Theodosia heard a muffled stomp directly overhead. Then another stomp.

Horses. I must have rolled under the horse trailer.

Carefully, and ever so quietly, Theodosia crawled out from beneath the truck and ducked around to the back. She caught a quick glimpse of Grady and the lighting guy still struggling with each other. Grady held his gun in one hand, but the lighting guy had a death grip on that hand. Moving fast, Theodosia hopped into the truck and squeezed between the two big horses.

Maybe I'm safe. But what about that poor lighting guy? Grady could still overpower him and shoot him.

Theodosia, no stranger to horses, looked around and discovered a bridle hanging on a peg. Working fast, she slipped it onto the large brown horse and buckled the chin strap. Creeping to the back of the trailer, she kicked off her shoes and ripped her skirt up the side to give herself more freedom of movement. Then she dropped the tailgate and gave a good tug on the reins. Obligingly, the big horse backed out.

Five seconds later, Theodosia was on top of the horse, tightening up on the reins. He was a good animal, a spirited animal, and when she gave him a firm kick with her heels, he spun around the side of the horse trailer and, under her guidance, headed right for the still-struggling men.

They heard pounding hooves as the enormous horse flew directly at them. Startled, Grady tried to raise his arm to shoot, but the lighting guy struck him hard.

Theodosia reined hard, sending the horse into a tight, almost out-of-control spin. Theodosia gripped the horse's mane and hung on for dear life. Once she had him under control again, she drove the horse straight toward Grady. The horse side swiped Grady's shoulder and delivered a bone-rattling *whomp* that sent him sprawling in the dirt. The gun flew out of his hand, causing him to swear loudly.

"Get his gun!" Theodosia shouted at the lighting guy. "Grab the gun!"

"Where is it?" the man cried frantically. "I don't see it!"

Grady was slumped on the ground, fighting to recover from the hit, and pawing the ground around him trying to locate his gun.

Clouds shifted overhead and a rare slice of moonlight shone down—unlucky moonlight that glinted off the gun, revealing its exact location.

"Ha!" Grady barked as he scrabbled wildly in the dirt. His fingers brushed against the gun, and then, seconds later, he had it! An evil grin crossed his face as he stumbled to his feet, the gun clenched tightly in his right hand.

That's when Theodosia went for the knockout blow. She jerked the reins and spun her big horse directly at Grady again. Just as Grady lifted his gun, the horse's right shoulder slammed into Grady's head with the catastrophic force of a sledgehammer. Grady's head whipped back sharply and he let out an agonized moan. The gun dropped from his hand as he sank to his knees. Then he slumped forward, moving almost in slow motion.

With a grim expression on her face, Theodosia watched Grady crumple like a cheap card table and land flat on his face.

34

❦

So of course 911 was called and the police came charging in again, followed by an ambulance. But this time their vehicles took a more judicious route, coming in behind the stage. With slightly less fanfare, the audience and performers barely realized there'd been any trouble at all.

"No," Theodosia said when she saw Detective Tidwell jump out of a shiny black Suburban with tinted windows and an oversized front bumper. "No," she said again when Pete Riley jumped out the other side. She touched a hand to her head. "What are you two doing here?" she asked somewhat breathlessly.

"We came to save you," Tidwell said as he sauntered toward her. Because Theodosia was still holding the horse, he was careful to give them both a wide berth. "But it looks as though you've managed to work things out on your own."

"Ned Grady killed Harlan Sadler and, I think, Wes Lenkov," Theodosia said.

"I believe you may be right," Tidwell said. He stared down

at a still-knocked-out-cold Grady. Then he looked at the two EMTs who were approaching and gave a nod.

"No, Grady really killed them," Theodosia said. "He told me he did. Just before he threatened to kill me." Theodosia pointed to the lighting guy who was standing a few feet away. He'd since introduced himself to her as Jake Crowley. "Then Jake came along and helped save the day."

"But you did some mighty fancy riding," Jake said to Theodosia. "Knocked that old boy clean off his stride."

"Theodosia can ride a horse, that's for sure," Riley said. He walked over to Theodosia, put his arms around her, and pulled her close. When he finally released her, he gave the horse a good pat, too.

"Now you guys need to tell me about Emily Bates," Theodosia said. "Why was she arrested?"

Tidwell screwed up his face and said, "I hate to say this, but you were right about Ms. Bates. She was in fact laundering money."

"Out of Unity One Bank?" Theodosia asked.

"It's a bit more complicated than that," Riley said.

"You remember the illegal dog races?" Tidwell said.

Theodosia nodded. "Well, yeah."

"Emily Bates was laundering money for the organizers," Tidwell said. "Obviously the dog race people dealt strictly in cash."

"Those were the guys Emily was working with?" Theodosia shook her head. "Jeez, she really was a piece of work."

Tidwell looked at his watch, an ordinary Timex. "One of the dog race organizers we had in custody started talking his head off a few hours ago. Gave up his partner and the entire operation. Emily Bates, too."

"So when you took Emily Bates into custody she admitted

her role?" Theodosia asked. She felt a sense of poetic justice along with a good deal of relief.

"The lady all but sang an aria for her supper," Tidwell said.

"Wow," Theodosia said. "I thought maybe . . ." She stopped abruptly. Drayton had just emerged from the dark. He looked confused and upset when he saw all of them together.

"What's going on?" Drayton stammered out. Then, as the two EMTs loaded Ned Grady onto a gurney, asked, "What happened to him?"

"Mr. Grady was on the receiving end of a knockout punch," Tidwell said. He seemed strangely pleased at the way everything had turned out.

Drayton took a step back as he noticed the horse. "Sweet dreams, Theodosia, you bought a horse?"

"Not exactly," Theodosia said. She cupped a hand under the horse's chin, felt his stubbly whiskers, and rubbed gently. The horse lowered his head and nickered softly. "But I might. You never know."

"So what *happened*?" Drayton said to Theodosia. "After you abandoned us, you practically missed the entire second half of *Aida*. In fact, it's almost over."

Bright lights suddenly flashed on, lighting up the landscape, and a tremendous burst of applause sounded from out front.

"It *is* over," Drayton said. "You hear that applause?"

"For a fine opera," Tidwell said.

"And a clever amateur detective," Riley said, his eyes twinkling as he gazed at Theodosia. Then he turned to Drayton and said, "Theodosia solved two homicides plus a money laundering scheme."

"Gracious!" Drayton exclaimed. "So Emily Bates really was laundering money?"

"For the illegal dog racing people," Riley said.

"Oh my," Drayton said. Then his eyes got even bigger as the EMTs finally hauled a moaning Grady past them on a gurney. "And Ned Grady turned out to be the killer?"

"Quite correct," Tidwell said.

"How did you untangle all this?" Drayton asked Theodosia. "How are you going to explain it all? I mean, people will never believe all the twists and turns!"

"Don't worry, Drayton," Theodosia said. "There's a chance I might have it covered." She was thinking about Charlie Skipstead's podcast. After the subpoenas, warrants, and arrests were done, Charlie's podcast might be the perfect place to talk about the excitement of being an amateur sleuth—and solving a couple of murders, to boot.

Drayton cleared his throat. "Um, just one more question concerning Ned Grady. Who's going to break the bad news to Delaine?"

There were constrained smiles, but no volunteers.

FAVORITE RECIPES FROM
The Indigo Tea Shop

Drayton's Peach Tea Smash

1 tsp. loose white tea (Darjeeling or silver needle)
8 oz. hot water
½ peach, sliced
Juice from ¼ lemon
Ice cubes
1 tsp. simple syrup
4 oz. bourbon

BREW tea for 3 minutes. Strain out tea leaves and refrigerate tea until chilled. Take 2 tall glasses and add peach slices and lemon juice. Muddle slightly. Add chilled tea, ice cubes, simple syrup, and bourbon. Stir well and enjoy. Yields: 2 cocktails.

SIMPLE SYRUP
1 cup water
1 cup sugar

COMBINE in saucepan and bring to a boil. Simmer for 5 minutes, then remove from heat and allow to cool. Refrigerate in covered glass container for up to 1 month. Yields: 1 cup.

Indigo Tea Shop Lemon Curd

½ cup fresh lemon juice
Grated rind of 4 lemons
2 eggs
2 egg yolks
1 cup sugar
4 Tbsp. butter, room temp

IN medium saucepan, beat together lemon juice, lemon rind, whole eggs, egg yolks, and sugar. Cook over low heat for 5 to 8 minutes, stirring constantly until mixture thickens and becomes translucent. Remove from heat and strain into bowl to remove lemon rind and any bits of cooked egg. Stir in the butter until it melts. Cover and refrigerate for up to 1 week. Yields: 1 cup.

Haley's Bailey's Chocolate Truffles

12 oz. semisweet chocolate chips
¼ cup Baileys Irish Cream
¼ cup heavy cream
2 egg yolks
1 Tbsp. butter

Powdered sugar
Powdered cocoa

MELT chocolate chips over very low heat. Stir in Baileys and heavy cream. Beat egg yolks, then stir a small amount of chocolate mixture into the eggs. Now slowly add the eggs to the chocolate mixture. As mixture thickens, stir in butter. Refrigerate the truffle mixture for several hours or overnight. To make truffles, use 2 large spoons to scoop up dough and form small balls. Roll balls in powdered sugar, then in powdered cocoa. Refrigerate. Yields: 12 to 16 truffles.

Grilled Salmon with Honey Mustard Brown Sugar Crust

4 salmon fillets
Kosher salt
Black pepper
1½ cups dark brown sugar
½ cup honey mustard

RINSE fillets and check for bones. Pat fillets dry and rub on kosher salt and black pepper. Crumble brown sugar on a plate. Now brush honey mustard onto the salmon and dredge in brown sugar. Grill over direct heat until crusty and golden, turning once (about 5 to 6 minutes total). Let rest for a few minutes, then serve with your favorite salad or vegetable. Yields: 4 entrées.

Crab–Stuffed Mushrooms

1 pkg. (8 oz.) whole button mushrooms
4 oz. cream cheese
4 Tbsp. cheddar cheese, shredded
2 Tbsp. onion, finely chopped
2 bacon slices, cooked and crumbled
1 tsp. pepper
1 can (6 oz.) crabmeat, finely chopped

PREHEAT oven to 350 degrees. Remove mushroom stems and gills. Mix together cream cheese, cheddar cheese, onion, bacon, pepper, and crabmeat. Stuff mushrooms and place on greased cookie sheet. Bake for 25 minutes or until golden and bubbly. Yields: about 20 mushrooms.

Veggie Tea Sandwiches

1 cucumber
1 red bell pepper
6 carrot sticks
4 celery sticks
½ cup green onions, sliced
2 pkg. cream cheese (8 oz. each)
Salt and pepper
Butter
16 slices of bread

PEEL and seed cucumber. Now dice cucumber, bell pepper, carrot sticks, celery sticks, and green onions very finely. Combine in bowl with cream cheese, adding salt and pepper to taste. Butter bread, then spread veggie mixture on 8 slices. Top sandwiches with remaining 8 slices. Slice off crusts, then cut into quarters. Yields: 32 small tea sandwiches.

Decadent Bourbon Chocolate Pie

2 eggs, slightly beaten

1 cup sugar

½ cup butter, melted

4 oz. bourbon

¼ cup cornstarch

1 cup pecans, chopped

1 cup semisweet chocolate bits

1 unbaked 9-inch pie shell

PREHEAT oven to 350 degrees. In a bowl, combine eggs, sugar, melted butter, and bourbon. Add the cornstarch to the mixture, blending slowly. Stir in the pecans and semisweet chocolate bits. Pour into a 9-inch unbaked pie shell and bake for approximately 45 minutes. Yields: about 6 slices.

Peach Cobbler

1 cup self-rising flour

¾ cup sugar (plus 2 extra Tbsp. for topping)

½ cup butter, melted and divided

Cinnamon, scant amount

1 can (29 oz.) sliced peaches in heavy syrup

PREHEAT oven to 350 degrees. In a medium-sized bowl, mix flour, ¾ cup sugar, ¼ cup melted butter, and a dash of cinnamon. Sprinkle about ⅓ of the flour mixture on the bottom of a 9-by-9-inch baking dish. Add in the peaches with their juice. Sprinkle the remaining flour mixture on top. Now sprinkle on 2 Tbsp. of sugar. Drizzle on the remaining ¼ cup of butter. Bake for 40 to 45 minutes or until the top is golden and bubbly. Let cobbler sit 5 minutes before serving. Top with ice cream or whipped cream and serve. Yields: 4 or 5 servings.

(NOTE: You can make your own self-rising flour. Here's how: Mix together 1 cup all-purpose flour with 1 tsp. baking powder, ½ tsp. salt, and ¼ tsp. baking soda. Couldn't be simpler!)

Applesauce Brownies

BROWNIES

- 1 cup butter
- 2 cups applesauce
- 1½ cups sugar
- 2 eggs
- ½ tsp. cinnamon
- 2 Tbsp. cocoa
- 2 cups flour
- 1½ tsp. baking soda
- ½ tsp. salt

TOPPING

    ½ cup walnuts, chopped

    2 Tbsp. sugar

    ¾ cup semisweet chocolate chips

PREHEAT oven to 350 degrees. Combine all ingredients for brownies and beat for 1 minute. Pour into a greased and floured 9-by-12-inch baking pan. Mix together ingredients for topping, then sprinkle over brownies. Bake for 30 minutes or until a toothpick inserted in center comes out clean. Yields: 18 brownies.

TEA TIME TIPS FROM

Laura Childs

Shanghai Tea

Decorate your table with a bright red tablecloth and as much chinoiserie as you can find. Add small Chinese teacups as well as chopsticks for your guests. Start your tea off with tangy ginger scones, then a second course of steamed pork buns. For your main entrée, consider a chicken and vegetable stir-fry. Of course, you'll want to serve a rich black Chinese tea and perhaps some Chinese pumpkin cakes for dessert.

Jane Austen Tea

Since Miss Austen lived during the Regency Era, you might adopt an old-fashioned look for your tea table. Think: lace tablecloths, floral dishes and teacups, and bouquets of flowers. Serve scones with clotted cream and jam, cucumber and cream cheese tea sandwiches, and prosciutto, apple, and Brie tea sandwiches. Jane's Garden Tea, a flavored green tea from Harney & Sons, is the perfect go-along. For dessert, go full-on Regency again and serve small cakes with butter icing.

Princess Tea

Even little girls love sitting down for a special tea—and wearing crowns and princess dresses. Start with chocolate chip scones with swirls of Devonshire cream. Serve apple juice "tea" in small teacups. Your princesses will love tea sandwiches of peanut butter and jelly, as well as chicken salad tea sandwiches with a bit of strawberry jam. Dessert can be easy-to-manage cupcakes or cake pops. You could even serve bubble tea, which really isn't a tea at all, but a delicious tapioca mixture.

Book Lovers Tea

This is the perfect tea for book clubs, reading groups, or church groups. Ask everyone to bring a book and then do a fun book exchange. Use your best dinnerware and heap your tea table with stacks of books. Serve apple-walnut scones with Devonshire cream, crab salad tea sandwiches, veggie tea sandwiches, and perhaps an entrée of mushroom quiche. Guest favors might include bookmarks or inexpensive bookbags. You could even invite a local author to do a short presentation. When it comes to tea, check out Simpson & Vail's Literary Tea Line, or the Reading Nook Blend from Plum Deluxe.

Mad Hatter Tea

Take a cue from *Alice in Wonderland* and make this an over-the-top fun tea party. Decorate your tea table with Cheshire cats, white rabbits, clocks, and maybe even a few dog-eared copies of

Alice in Wonderland. Is there a Red Queen? Then give her a crown to wear. Serve cherry-almond scones with Devonshire cream, BLT tea sandwiches, and mashed avocado with onion tea sandwiches. Serve a spicy black chai tea and consider creating a four- or five-layer tippy-looking cake.

Great Scot Tea

Get out your tartan-plaid tablecloth or napkins, put down your best pottery dinnerware, and add a few candlesticks. If the weather is chilly, ask your guests to wear sweaters and long plaid skirts, much like the ladies do who live in drafty manor homes. Kick off your tea with cranberry scones or old-fashioned griddle cakes, served with Adagio's Scottish Breakfast Tea. Your next course might be smoked salmon tartlets with dill and crème fraiche wrapped in filo pastry and baked for ten minutes. Scotch eggs or potato chowder served with hearty bread is the perfect entrée. For dessert, serve shortbread cookies.

TEA RESOURCES

TEA MAGAZINES AND PUBLICATIONS

TeaTime—A luscious magazine profiling tea and tea lore. Filled with glossy photos and wonderful recipes. (teatimemagazine.com)

Southern Lady—From the publishers of *TeaTime* with a focus on people and places in the South, as well as wonderful tea time recipes. (southernladymagazine.com)

The Tea House Times—Go to theteahousetimes.com for subscription information and dozens of links to tea shops, purveyors of tea, gift shops, and tea events.

Victoria—Articles and pictorials on homes, home design, gardens, and tea. (victoriamag.com)

Fresh Cup—For tea and coffee professionals. (freshcup.com)

Tea & Coffee Trade Journal—For the tea and coffee industry. (teaandcoffee.net)

Bruce Richardson—This author has written several definitive books on tea. (elmwoodinn.com/collections/books)

Jane Pettigrew—This author has written thirteen books on the varied aspects of tea and its history and culture. (janepettigrew.com/books)

A Tea Reader—By Katrina Ávila Munichiello, an anthology of tea stories and reflections.

Tea Poetry—Traditional and new tea poetry compiled by Pearl Dexter.

AMERICAN TEA PLANTATIONS

Charleston Tea Garden—The oldest and largest tea plantation in the United States. Order their fine black tea or schedule a visit at charlestonteagarden.com.

Table Rock Tea Company—This Pickens, South Carolina, plantation grows premium whole leaf tea. (tablerocktea.com)

The Great Mississippi Tea Company—Up-and-coming Mississippi tea farm, now in production. (greatmsteacompany.com)

Sakuma Brothers Farm—This tea garden just outside Burlington, Washington, has been growing white and green tea for over twenty years. (sakumabros.com)

Big Island Tea—Organic artisan tea from Hawaii. (bigislandtea.com)

Mauna Kea Tea—Organic green and oolong tea from Hawaii's Big Island. (maunakeatea.com)

Ono Tea—Nine-acre tea estate near Hilo, Hawaii. (onotea.com)

Minto Island Tea Growers—Hand-picked, small-batch crafted teas grown in Oregon. (mintogrowers.com)

Virginia First Tea Farm—Matcha tea and natural tea soaps and cleansers. (virginiafirstteafarm.com)

Blue Dreams USA—Located near Frederick, Maryland, this farm grows tea, roses, and lavender. (bluedreamsusa.com)

Finger Lakes Tea Company—Tea producer located in Waterloo, New York. (fingerlakestea.com)

Camellia Forest Tea Gardens—This North Carolina company collects, grows, and sells tea plants. They also produce their own tea. (teaflowergardens.com)

TEA WEBSITES AND INTERESTING BLOGS

Destinationtea.com—State-by-state directory of afternoon tea venues.

Teamap.com—Directory of hundreds of tea shops in the US and Canada.

Afternoontea.co.uk—Guide to tea rooms in the UK.

Cozyupwithkathy.blogspot.com—Cozy mystery reviews.

Thedailytea.com—Formerly *Tea Magazine,* this online publication is filled with tea news, recipes, inspiration, and tea travel.

Allteapots.com—Teapots from around the world.

Teasquared.blogspot.com—Fun, well-written blog about tea, tea shops, and tea musings.

Relevantealeaf.blogspot.com—All about tea.

Stephcupoftea.blogspot.com—Blog on tea, food, and inspiration.

Teawithfriends.blogspot.com—Lovely blog on tea, friendship, and tea accoutrements.

Bellaonline.com/site/tea—Features and forums on tea.

Napkinfoldingguide.com—Photo illustrations of twenty-seven different (and sometimes elaborate) napkin folds.

Worldteaexpo.com—This premier business-to-business trade show features more than three hundred tea suppliers, vendors, and tea innovators.

Fatcatscones.com—Frozen, ready-to-bake scones.

Kingarthurflour.com—One of the best flours for baking. This is what many professional pastry chefs use.

Californiateahouse.com—Order Machu's Blend, a special herbal tea for dogs that promotes healthy skin, lowers stress, and aids digestion.

Vintageteaworks.com—This company offers six unique wine-flavored tea blends that celebrate wine and respect the tea.

Downtonabbeycooks.com—A *Downton Abbey* blog with news and recipes.

Auntannie.com—Crafting site that will teach you how to make your own petal envelopes, pillow boxes, gift bags, etc.

Victorianhousescones.com—Scone, biscuit, and cookie mixes for both retail and wholesale orders. Plus, baking and scone-making tips.

Englishteastore.com—Buy a jar of English Double Devon Cream here, as well as British foods and candies.

Stickyfingersbakeries.com—Delicious just-add-water scone mixes.

Teasipperssociety.com—Join this international community of tea sippers, growers, and educators. A terrific newsletter!

Melhattie.com—Adventures of a traveling tea sommelier.

Bullsbaysaltworks.com—Local South Carolina sea salt, crafted by hand.

PURVEYORS OF FINE TEA

Plumdeluxe.com
Adagio.com
Elmwoodinn.com
Capitalteas.com
Newbyteas.com/us
Harney.com
Stashtea.com
Serendipitea.com
Marktwendell.com
Republicoftea.com
Teazaanti.com
Bigelowtea.com

Celestialseasonings.com
Goldenmoontea.com
Uptontea.com
Svtea.com (Simpson & Vail)
Gracetea.com
Davidstea.com

VISITING CHARLESTON

Charleston.com—Travel and hotel guide.

Charlestoncvb.com—The official Charleston convention and visitor bureau.

Charlestontour.wordpress.com—Private tours of homes and gardens, some including lunch or tea.

Charlestonplace.com—Charleston Place Hotel serves an excellent afternoon tea, Thursday through Saturday, 1:00 to 3:00 PM.

Poogansporch.com—This restored Victorian house serves traditional low-country cuisine. Be sure to ask about Poogan!

Preservationsociety.org—Hosts Charleston's annual Fall Candlelight Tour.

Palmettocarriage.com—Horse-drawn carriage rides.

Charlestonharbortours.com—Boat tours and harbor cruises.

Ghostwalk.net—Stroll into Charleston's haunted history. Ask them about the "original" Theodosia!

Follybeach.com—Official guide to Folly Beach activities, hotels, rentals, restaurants, and events.

Gibbesmuseum.org—Art exhibits, programs, and events.

Boonehallplantation.com—Visit one of America's oldest working plantations.

Charlestonlibrarysociety.org—A rich collection of books, historic manuscripts, maps, and correspondence. Music and guest speaker events.

Earlybirddiner.com—Visit this local gem at 1644 Savannah Highway for zesty fried chicken, corn cakes, waffles, and more.

Highcottoncharleston.com—Low-country cuisine that includes she-crab soup, buttermilk fried oysters, Geechie Boy grits, and much more.

ACKNOWLEDGMENTS

An abundance of thank-yous to Sam, Tom, Dru Ann, Elisha, Kaila, Lori, M.J., Bob, Pearl, Jennie, Dan, and all the wonderful people at Berkley Prime Crime and Penguin Random House who handle editing, design (so many fabulous covers!), publicity (amazing!), copywriting, social media, bookstore sales, gift sales, production, and shipping. Heartfelt thanks as well to all the tea lovers, tea shop owners, book clubs, booksellers, librarians, reviewers, magazine editors and writers, websites, broadcasters, and bloggers who have enjoyed the Tea Shop Mysteries and helped spread the word. You are all so kind to help make this possible!

And I am overwhelmed with gratitude for all my special readers and tea lovers who've so thoroughly embraced Theodosia, Drayton, Haley, Earl Grey, and the rest of the tea shop gang. Thank you so much and I promise many more Tea Shop Mysteries to come!

KEEP READING FOR AN EXCERPT
FROM LAURA CHILDS'S NEXT
TEA SHOP MYSTERY . . .

High Tea and Misdemeanors

The killer in the camo shirt, black tactical pants, and blade sunglasses crept ever so carefully between a row of orange chrysanthemums and a row of Chinese silver grass. All around, late summer flowers and native grasses blazed crimson and gold while fuzzy yellow bees bumbled from blossom to stem. The killer didn't pay much attention to this bucolic autumnal display but was strictly focused on the mission at hand. Slowly, pressing forward, crawling on hands and knees, the killer's eyes finally locked on to the back wall of the greenhouse that was now a tantalizing ten feet away. Then, head lifted like a wolf sniffing the wind, the killer scuttled the remaining distance through late-blooming dahlias, hunched over and moving fast. Collapsing in the loamy soil, shoulders and back pressed hard against the greenhouse, the killer enjoyed a moment of blessed relaxation. Almost there. Breathing back to normal now, the killer peered carefully around the side of the greenhouse. There were six cars and a Jeep, but all were parked a good fifty yards away, clustered near a series of small white cottages. Looking right, the killer saw the wedding arch, resplendent with twisted ivy and woven with white pampas grass, sunflowers, and red bittersweet. Four dozen white folding chairs were set up neatly in front of it. No invited guests had arrived yet, probably wouldn't for an hour or so. So all was good.

Now for the slightly tricky part. Standing upright, the killer dodged around the greenhouse and sprinted the length of it, pant legs brushing tall stalks of foxtail grass, club moss squishing underfoot. Spinning around the front of the building, the killer grabbed the door, yanked it open, and darted inside. Just for a second, the killer had caught a glimpse of one person, an older man, silver haired and wearing a tweed jacket. But, luckily, the man hadn't glanced this way.

Standing inside the greenhouse, heart thump-thumping, the killer felt a swell of anticipation. Hundreds of lush, green plants and ferns along with six dozen cymbidium orchids had been draped from the ceiling like some fantastical verdant curtain. Below the flora and fauna, a long dining table was set with white linen, crystal goblets, fancy china, and silver flatware. Everything perfect for the wedding reception.

The killer's mouth pulled into a sneer. Like *that* was going to happen.

Five seconds later, this most dangerous uninvited guest climbed onto a chair swagged in white tulle and hopped onto the long table, footprints making muddy imprints on the Belgian linen. Grabbing a wrench from a hip pocket, the killer reached up and carefully loosened four bolts in the mechanism that controlled the greenhouse's overhead windows. Then, tromping down the middle of the table, kicking a teacup out of the way and feeling a perverse pleasure in doing so, the killer reached the second mechanism. Twist, twist, and then that was done, too. What was the old saying? Tighty righty, lefty loosey?

Well, the hinges were loose alright. Loose as a goose that was about to get its neck wrung. Now to set the mechanism on a hair trigger . . .

And there it was. All the anger and planning and revenge fantasies had been distilled down to this. To the bride and groom rushing through the doorway, flushed with excitement on their wedding day, only to find . . . well, their world would come crashing down on them soon enough.

In the gingerbread cottage that served as the event center for Foxfire Flower Farm, it was an entirely different story. Tea maven Theodosia Browning, who'd been tapped to cater Bettina and Jamie's wedding reception, was busy stacking rainbow-hued macrons on a silver four-tiered tray. Drayton Conneley, her tea sommelier at the Indigo Tea Shop, was double-checking his stash of Harney & Sons Wedding Tea and his proprietary Happily Ever After Tea, a blend of jasmine, lemongrass, and rose petals.

And then there was Delaine Dish, the bride's high-strung aunt, wearing a pink Chanel suit and four-inch stilettos, running around like a chicken with its head chopped off.

"It's Bettina's wedding," Theodosia said with a wry smile. "But you're the one with pre-wedding jitters."

"Because everything has to be *perfect*!" Delaine cried.

"Henry James once said, 'Excellence does not require perfection,'" Drayton said in measured tones. Delaine's hysteria and theatrics were starting to annoy him.

"Well, Henry James isn't invited to this wedding so I'm going to keep working my eyeballs off," Delaine said. She frowned, looked around, and muttered, "Where did I put the bouquets and boutonnieres?"

"The cooler in your car?" Theodosia said.

"Right," Delaine said as she rushed out the door.

"She's driving me berserk," Drayton said once Delaine had gone.

"Have faith, it will all be over soon," Theodosia told him. She was in a playful mood this morning because she was looking forward to the fantasy and romance of this autumn outdoor wedding. She and Drayton had driven out early this morning with baskets of scones, freshly made tea sandwiches, and sliced cheeses. The crab claw and shrimp platters would be coming along shortly—along with a bartender and four waitpersons.

Wiping her hands on her apron, Theodosia touched a hand to one of her sapphire blue earrings, which matched her eyes to perfection. As luck (and genetics) would have it, Theodosia had been born with vivid blue eyes, masses of auburn hair, a fair English complexion, and a wit and sense of humor that was undoubtedly inherited from Irish ancestors on her mother's side. She was clever, accomplished, and, as owner of the Indigo Tea Shop on Charleston's famed Church Street, an entrepreneur in her own right.

Drayton was sixty-something, cultured, droll in his manner of speech, and always impeccably dressed. He'd lived in China, worked at the tea auctions in Amsterdam, and once taught courses at the Culinary Institute of Charleston. Now he was a professional tea sommelier and proper fixture at the Indigo Tea Shop.

"Do you think . . . ," Drayton began, then was interrupted by a clatter at the front door. Delaine, her heel caught in the doormat, struggled as she balanced an armload of flowers.

"I've got to keep these cool for another forty minutes," Delaine announced as she finally shook herself free and lurched in.

"Lots of room in the cooler," Drayton said. He reached out and opened the door for her.

"Thank you, thank you," said an agitated Delaine. She stuffed the flowers into the cooler, stepped back, and touched a shaking hand to her heart.

"Take a breath and try to relax," Theodosia urged. "Everything's practically done and your guests should be arriving soon. Don't burn yourself out when you've got a beautiful day ahead of you."

"I don't want any screw-ups," Delaine said. "Which is one of the reasons I've strictly forbidden *anyone* from entering that greenhouse. After all our hard work, I want the flowers and decor to be a fabulous surprise for Bettina and Jamie."

As Theodosia fixed a bow on her basket of scones, she happened to glance out the window. "Then somebody better remind Celeste there's no peeking because I see her tiptoeing toward the greenhouse."

"Celeste? Bettina's maid of honor?" Delaine screeched. "That little snoop. I was afraid something like this would . . ." Her words trailed off in an angry mumble as she burst out the door again. She saw Jamie Wilkes, the groom, lounging in front of a live oak, smoking lord knows what with his best man, Reggie. "Jamie!" Delaine shouted, "Don't let Celeste go snooping in that greenhouse!" She pointed and gestured frantically as a small, blond figure in a gauzy cream-colored dress headed straight for the door.

Jamie, his lanky figure turned out in a black Zegna suit, lifted a hand to Delaine and jogged over to try and intercept the ever-curious Celeste.

Delaine, who was still watching the goings-on like a hawk, said, "He's not going to catch that little ninny."

"What can it hurt if she looks inside?" Drayton offered. "It's not that big a deal since . . ."

His words were interrupted by a strange metallic ratcheting sound that clattered and clashed, then rose in pitch as if steel wheels were grinding hard against rusty rails. Seconds later there was a cataclysmic crash and the thunder of falling glass.

"No," Delaine said, frozen in place like a statue, a look of disbelief on her face.

Drayton's head shot up. "What just happened?"

"Don't know," Theodosia said. "It sounded like metal and glass and . . . oh dear Lord . . . did something happen in the greenhouse?"

Theodosia pushed her way past a stunned Delaine, leaped down two steps, and flew across the grassy yard to the greenhouse. Or what was left of it. Because it looked as if the entire front wall had collapsed and an enormous slice of glass roof had imploded.

"No, no, no," Theodosia shouted as, without hesitation, she waded into an enormous pile of plants, ferns, orchids, and shattered glass to try and rescue Jamie and Celeste. Part of the dining table had collapsed on top of them so Theodosia prayed that it had shielded them from falling glass. Grabbing two linen napkins, Theodosia wrapped them around her hands and started digging through the debris. She grabbed a bundle of orchids and tossed them aside, kicked away a pile of ferns, and uncovered the lower half of a twitching and moaning Jamie.

Okay, there's Jamie. Gotta get him out, then find Celeste.

Theodosia grabbed a corner of the table and tried to lift it. No way, it was an impossible task. As she started digging again she was suddenly aware that Drayton was right beside her.

"Grab Jamie's legs and try to pull him out from under," Theodosia said. Water dripped down from above, making everything a soggy mess.

Drayton bent and grabbed two black loafers. But as hard as he tugged, Jamie wouldn't come free.

"Help me," Drayton said.

Theodosia grabbed one leg while Drayton took the other, and together they pulled, straining hard, like a team of horses, but finally making progress. Moments later, they'd freed a battered and bleeding Jamie from the wreckage.

"Now we've got to find Celeste," Theodosia said.

Which was easier said than done. Theodosia had to get down on hands and knees, crawl under the collapsed table, and feel around in the muck. Finally, she located a thin bare ankle.

"Got her, I think," Theodosia said, "But I've got to work carefully. There's so much glass on top of her." *And blood . . . so much blood.*

Grim-faced and determined, they gently scooped and shoved and pulled and tugged until Celeste was dragged free from the wreckage. But unlike Jamie, Celeste was glassy-eyed and still with a jagged hunk of glass protruding from her neck.

She looks as if she's been drugged, Theodosia thought. *Or . . . is she dead?*

She couldn't dwell on that now. Time was of the essence and they needed to get help.

"Did you find them?" Delaine shrieked. "Are they okay?" She'd been joined by Haley Parker, Theodosia's chef and baker, Bettina and Jamie, and Martha and Zach Hempel, owners of Foxfire Flower Farm.

"Stay back!" Theodosia ordered everyone in no uncertain terms. She didn't want any major freak-outs. Cooler heads had to prevail and render aid to the two people who'd been practically buried alive.

"Drayton, call 911," Theodosia yelped. "Get an ambulance out here. Get *two* ambulances." In the back of her mind she worried that Jamie needed an ambulance while Celeste might not.

Drayton grabbed the phone from a stunned Delaine's hand and immediately punched in 911.

Theodosia took a moment to glance up at the greenhouse, where gears and chains and motors dangled freely. And the one thought that ran through her mind like chase lights on a theater marquee was, *This was no accident, this was intentional. Someone tampered with those gears.*

Dipping a hand into her apron pocket, Theodosia pulled out her phone and started dialing as well.

"Who are *you* calling?" Drayton asked. He was already on the line and talking to the dispatch operator.

"I'm calling Riley." Riley, Pete Riley, was Theodosia's significant other and a detective D-2 in the Charleston Police Department.

Back in Charleston, Riley's phone rang once, twice, then he picked up with a lazy, "Hello there."

"You have to get out here!" Theodosia cried, fear and urgency coloring her voice. "Like, now!"

"Sweetheart, I don't even have my tux on yet," Riley said.

"Forget the tux," Theodosia snapped. "There's been a murder."

FIND OUT MORE ABOUT THE AUTHOR
AND READ EXCERPTS FROM HER MYSTERIES
AT LAURACHILDS.COM,
OR BECOME A FACEBOOK FRIEND
AT LAURA CHILDS AUTHOR.